"Caldwell' ... key to the unmasking ... ggling of personal and professional roles should win her more fans."
—*Publishers Weekly*

Red, White & Dead
"A sizzling roller coaster ride
through the streets of Chicago, filled with murder,
mystery, sex and heartbreak. These page-turners
will have you breathless and panting for more."
—*Shore Magazine*

"Chock full of suspense, *Red, White & Dead* is a
riveting mystery of crime, love, and adventure at its best."
—*New York Times* bestselling author Gayle Lynds

Red Blooded Murder
"*Red Blooded Murder* aims for the sweet spot
between tough and tender, between thrills and thought—
and hits the bull's-eye. A terrific novel."
—#1 *New York Times* bestselling author Lee Child

"Izzy is the whole package: feminine and sexy, but also
smart, tough and resourceful. She's no damsel-in-distress
from a tawdry bodice ripper; she's more than a fitting
match for any bad guys foolish enough to take her on."
—*Chicago Sun-Times*

Red Hot Lies
"Told mainly from the heroine's first-person point of view,
this beautifully crafted and tightly written story
is a fabulous read. It's very difficult to put down—
and the ending is terrific."
—*RT Book Reviews*

"Former trial lawyer Caldwell launches a mystery series
that weaves the emotional appeal of her chick-lit titles
with the blinding speed of her thrillers...
Readers will be left looking forward to another
heart-pounding ride on Izzy's silver Vespa."
—*Publishers Weekly*

Also by Laura Caldwell

IZZY McNEIL NOVELS

CLAIM OF INNOCENCE
RED, WHITE & DEAD
RED BLOODED MURDER
RED HOT LIES

OTHER BOOKS BY LAURA CALDWELL

THE GOOD LIAR
THE ROME AFFAIR
LOOK CLOSELY
THE NIGHT I GOT LUCKY
THE YEAR OF LIVING FAMOUSLY
A CLEAN SLATE
BURNING THE MAP
LONG WAY HOME: A YOUNG MAN
LOST IN THE SYSTEM
AND THE TWO WOMEN WHO FOUND HIM

Look for Laura Caldwell's next novel
ART OF THE MATTER
available September 2012

LAURA CALDWELL

QUESTION OF TRUST

MIRA®

MIRA®

Recycling programs for this product may not exist in your area.

ISBN-13: 978-0-7783-1321-2

QUESTION OF TRUST

Copyright © 2012 by Story Avenue, LLC

For questions and comments about the quality of this book please contact us at Customer_eCare@Harlequin.ca.

www.Harlequin.com

Printed in U.S.A.

For AMB, who believes.

Prologue

I didn't know Kim Parkway very well. Sure, she moved into the condo below me. And yes, she reached out to me on a day when I really needed it. She even borrowed something a few days later because she hadn't completely unpacked yet.

What I knew of Kim, I liked. I think she enjoyed me, too. But ultimately, she would have been one of those friends—an acquaintance, really—who fades from your life, remembered once in a while, and even then somewhat foggily.

But now I know that Kim Parkway will be in my life forever. I'll never forget her. Because on a Monday night in November, I found her dead.

1

"We've got a boatload of cocaine. Literally."

I looked at my friend Maggie, barely five feet tall, standing in the doorway of my office. (Technically it was her office, since I was employed by Maggie and her grandfather, Martin Bristol, at Bristol & Associates.)

"You know," I said, "when I met you in law school, I never thought I would hear you say things like that."

Maggie frowned for a second, pushing her blond, wavy hair out of her eyes. "It's the Cortaderos."

"Oh." I leaned my elbows on the desk, interested. I'd been hearing about the Cortaderos for a long time. They were clients of Maggie and Martin's. They were a Mexican drug cartel family (*allegedly* a cartel family, I should say), but I hadn't been privy to the details of any cases.

She sighed and waved a hand. "They're always getting into trouble." This was not said without fondness. Maggie had a soft spot for most of her wayward clients.

Q, short for Quentin, stuck his bald, black head in my office, as if he'd been lingering outside the door. "Did I just hear something about a drug bust?" Q had been my assistant when we were at the white-glove firm of Baltimore & Brown. He was the office manager now at Bristol & Associates. But more important, Q loved a juicy story, especially on an otherwise slow Monday afternoon.

Maggie slumped into a seat across from my desk, then waved Q inside. "Have you ever seen the boats parked on the river? By Lower Wacker?" she asked.

"Sure," I said. "Sam and I did a sunset cruise once. We went through the locks and out onto Lake Michigan."

"They did a post-Pride cruise one year," Q said. "Epic." He cleared his throat. "That was before I was monogamous, of course."

"Of course," Maggie and I echoed.

I nodded at her to continue.

"Right. Well, the Cortaderos own one of those boats. It was about to be taken down the Mississippi for winter, but it was seized today."

"And cocaine was found on it?"

"A lot." She sighed the way a mom would when discussing a teen who spent too much time in front of the computer. "Forty-five kilos."

"What's that worth?" Q asked.

"Millions. Many."

"Many millions?" Q said.

Maggie nodded. "They usually wouldn't have

that much in one place. Strange. I don't know what's going on with the Cortaderos." She looked out my window, lapsing into silence. There was nothing to see there except the blue-tinted high-rise across the street.

Q and I exchanged glances. Maggie had been like this lately—a little distracted, and also a little secretive, closing her mouth suddenly when she seemed about to disclose something, lapsing into long, thoughtful silences. I wondered what was going on behind the scenes at the firm.

"What were you saying, Mags?" I prompted her.

She blinked a few times as if clearing something, coming back to us. "Oh, um…" She looked at me. "Right. Right. So, I need you on this, Iz. I have a motion to suppress that's taking a lot of time."

The other thing Maggie had been doing lately was throwing a lot of casework my way. I appreciated that, since I was a civil lawyer by training now learning the oh-so-different criminal defense world. In general, I would do anything in the world for Maggie. Now that she was my boss, I'd certainly do anything she needed for one of her clients, no matter who they were. Drug lords from Mexico, though? Interesting, sure, but actually representing them? That made me nervous.

But this was my job now, I reminded myself. I had to make a living, and although I'd been on top of the world a year ago, I was far from that now. So, I was a criminal defense lawyer. When Maggie threw work my way, I would perform. Because this was my job. One of them. For better or worse.

I sat up straighter. "You need me on this in what way?" I asked Maggie.

"Well, in the short-term, I need you on the boat. Can you go now?"

2

I have known mad love. And once you have known that sort of thing, you don't forget. So you don't lightly enter into it (or what you sense could be *it*) because you know the absolute high that resides there is matched by a crushing low if it ends.

If you're fortunate enough that the rest of your life is fairly good, you might think maybe you don't need that high again. You certainly know you don't need the crush.

I thought about this as I took a cab down La-Salle Street toward the Chicago River and the boat owned by the Cortaderos. I thought about how I had started to tell my boyfriend, Theo, that I loved him when I knew he couldn't hear me—when he was asleep, when he was in the shower with the water pounding, when he worked on his laptop and the music from his earphones (some combination hip-hop, head-banging-type stuff) was so loud and screeching, it leaked into the room.

"Love you…" I'd say, my voice low, testing the feel of the words, experiencing a slight thrill and at the same time relief that Theo had no idea I was uttering them. Really, was I ready to go there?

It's such a cliché when people say they're "not ready" after getting out of a big relationship, but hell if I didn't understand that concept now. Sam, my former fiancé, and I had broken up a little over a year ago. Then we'd considered and rejected putting our relationship back together at the end of the summer. (That's making it sound easy. It wasn't. But life's struggles are always more simple in the rearview mirror.)

What I've learned is that plans only exist in the quiet space of our minds, because the fact is, the universe doesn't respect them. Or at least the gods in my universe don't. So I had taken great pains to weed the term *fiancé* from my vernacular, just like I was cleaning it of that *plan* thing. But also, if I were honest, I was unsure if Theo would return the sentiment.

A few months ago, we decided to call each other *boyfriend* and *girlfriend.* I had blurted it out unintentionally once during a fairly random discussion. Panic had flooded my brain at what Theo might think, but he just smiled that sexy smile of his and called me his girlfriend, over and over again. Never before had that word made every inch of my body tingle.

Now we were using the terms loosely—*boyfriend, girlfriend.* But I kept asking myself, what would the three words—those three little, but oh-so-big, words—do to him?

My cell phone bleated from my purse, as skyscrapers on LaSalle streaked across the cab window in a smear of white and gray.

I snatched the cell phone out of my bag, keen to get away from my musings. "Hello?"

"McNeil. I need you for a thing." Ah, Mayburn. I could always count on him to dispense with the pleasantries.

"What kind of thing?"

John Mayburn was the private detective I occasionally moonlighted for. It was sometimes fun, though often I found myself in big, big trouble and had to do a fast scramble to escape. But Mayburn had helped me way too much to not at least listen. Plus, my father worked for him now.

"Super easy," he said. "I need you to dress kinda...well, slutty and then open a checking account at a bank in the Loop tomorrow morning. Simple."

I stopped myself from rolling my eyes. Nothing was ever simple with Mayburn. A *simple* undercover retail job at a lingerie store had almost gotten me killed once. "What aren't you telling me, Mayburn?"

"Lots of stuff. But seriously, that's all we need you to do. Christopher and I have the rest covered."

Christopher. *My dad* and Mayburn had the rest covered. My world was so weird.

"All right," I said. "Text me the info."

A year ago, I almost married Sam. Shortly after, I'd been accused of a friend's death. Then the father

I thought was gone had returned. It had been a hell of a year.

But really, my life was returning to normal now. I was a full-time lawyer again. I had a wonderfully hot boyfriend. And the first holiday of the season, Thanksgiving, was just two and a half weeks away. What harm could a little P.I. work do?

3

By the time I reached the dock at murky Lower Wacker Avenue in the shadows of the Merchandise Mart, any contents of the riverboat were gone, removed, wiped out.

I headed toward a government evidence tech who was wearing gloves and a mask. I tried to put an officious jaunt to my walk, a concerned look on my face. "I'm here on behalf of the Cortaderos."

"Better you than me."

I asked him a couple of questions. He claimed not to know anything or have any information.

I climbed back over the ramp to the dock and called Maggie.

I waited for quick directives, sharp orders—that was the way Maggie usually worked. But this time she only said, "Umm..." Then nothing.

"Mags, I need some help here."

She sighed. "Okay, ask for the warrant," she said. "Be indignant."

Back over the boat ramp, and I did as ordered.

No luck from the tech. His boss had the warrant, he said, but his boss was nowhere to be found.

I called Maggie again.

"Order them off the boat," she said.

"Can I do that?"

"Yep."

"Really?"

"Yep." Maggie mentioned a couple of federal statutes having to do with evidence collection, warrants and search-and-seizure that the government techs were clearly running afoul of.

"Sounds fun," I said, and I meant it. I stood a second, thinking how much my career had altered. Instead of representing refined, elegant media moguls, I was now representing a Mexican drug cartel family. Instead of going into TV stations to negotiate contracts, I was going into a big, ol' boat that had just recently held a big, ol' pile of drugs. And I was about to throw some figurative muscle around.

I clapped my hands like a player in a huddle. "Break," I said under my breath.

Once again, I was back on the boat, and this time, I raised my voice. I rattled off the statutes, hoping I was getting them right. Maggie must have nailed it because the evidence tech stopped and glared. He knew I was right. But still he didn't move.

I was about to say, *Don't make me call the authorities.* But I wasn't exactly sure who I'd call. The Chicago police? That wasn't right, because a drug case like this was federal. The Feds, then. But then, what did that even mean—*the Feds?*

Luckily, the evidence tech groaned. He then turned, gathered his people and left me alone on a cold, creaking riverboat that smelled strongly of chemicals.

"The smell is probably the stuff someone used to cut the coke," Maggie said when I called her again. "We're gonna put up a knowledge defense," she continued. "We'll argue that although the Cortaderos had some ownership in the riverboat, they possessed no information that the thing was about to be used for any packaging or transport of drugs."

It was wild how much Maggie knew about the big, bad world of hard-core drug running and Mexican drug lords.

I made a couple of rounds through the creaking, freezing-cold boat, looking for anything I might have missed. Maggie and I discussed a few more details of our proposed defense, then said our goodbyes. I took pictures of various parts of the boat with my cell phone, but there was little to capture other than a ballroom with a wood bar, the stairwells, the decks and the captains' lair.

As shadows fell across the city, they bathed the empty boat with a sinister icy feeling. I left and walked toward the Merchandise Mart. Climbing the stairs to the "L" train, I shivered in the late-afternoon gray mist that had rolled in around the river.

I got on the Brown Line and headed north

toward my place. As I leaned my head against the window, I watched vaguely as the train left the Loop and passed over Chicago Avenue. I wasn't really seeing anything, though. The more I thought about it, the more the Cortadero case made me uncomfortable. Did I really want to represent a large Mexican family who potentially—allegedly—had been storing millions worth of drugs on a boat?

But I had to remind myself that I was no longer the rainmaker I used to be. Maggie and Martin worked hard to pull in cases, and as their associate I had to focus on whatever case they wanted.

There was solace in being a soldier, too. In my former job at Baltimore & Brown, I was responsible for shepherding nearly all the legal work of a large media conglomerate, and after a while the responsibility had overwhelmed me.

My phone buzzed. It was Theo. "Can you go house-hunting with me tonight?" he asked.

I felt a warm flush of flattery. Theo's lease was up, and he had decided it was time to buy a house and leave behind the rented apartment he'd occupied since quitting college. But so far, he'd been doing this mostly on his own.

"I'd love to."

"Meet me in Bucktown in an hour?" He named an address in a neighborhood that had been gentrified in years of late but still kept its youthful edge. It sounded perfect. Theo, after all, was a big, gorgeous and decidedly edgy young man with ribbons of tattoos that snaked up his arms and seemed to brush at the tips of his hair, which hung to his shoulders.

"I'll be there."

The Bucktown condo was huge—four bedrooms with a modern kitchen stocked with top-of-the-line appliances, three balconies, two fireplaces and a tub in the master bath that could fit a family of five. But Theo kept pursing his lips as we followed the real-estate agent around the place, narrowing his eyes in the way that he did when he was thinking hard about something.

"It's not right," he said.

At the next home, I thought we had it. The floors were wide-planked, the feel was casual but cool. It had a game room, which Theo and his friends would love. I could see Theo's shoes in the hallway, his jeans on the bedroom floor.

But then we saw the "outside space," which was a metal balcony overlooking the Kennedy Expressway. "Nope," he said.

The next place, near the Museum of Contemporary Art, had a striking view of Lake Michigan, its perimeter newly frozen like white crust. Theo shook his head again. "It's just not right for us."

I blinked a few times. *Us?* The word was thrilling. "It doesn't matter if it's right for me. What matters is if it feels good to you."

He turned to me. His hand brushed my collarbone, my curls, then briefly touched my cheek. "It has to be good for you, too."

Theo was discouraged going into the fourth stop, a three-bedroom condo near the Green Door Tavern that had once been a warehouse. But then we walked through the door and saw the raw, wood floors just like Theo wanted. Then we moved farther inside, gasping at the two-story vaulted ceiling, growing more and more excited. The bedrooms were spacious. The bathroom, with its intricately tiled circle tub, made me sigh. The real-estate agent excused herself, ostensibly to take a phone call, but I knew she'd seen our enthusiasm. She was giving us time to stroll some more, to think, to discuss.

I want you to fall in love with me.
I want you to fall in love with me.
I want you to fall in love with me.

That was my internal chant, my mantra, that night. I couldn't believe I'd found myself here—in love again. It's not that I didn't think it would ever happen. I just thought (and I mean I really thought I *knew*) that my heart needed a while before it could bear weight again. Before it could hold someone there. But now, I wanted Theo. I wanted him there.

And I was scared. He'd said things, lots of things, like, *Everyone who knows us tells me we should date for a long time.... You're like my best friend.... You're one of the most wonderful people I know....* And he would kiss me with that lush, greedy mouth. After some time, he would slow, then pull back to look into my eyes and it felt, in those moments, like he could see into every cell of me, into everything thought, hidden or not. He had me in those moments. He owned me.

I want you to fall in love with me.

We went into the kitchen, which bore taupe-and-white granite that gleamed, and brand-new appliances. I sat on the kitchen counter. "What do you think?" I asked Theo.

He walked over to me, nudged my legs apart and placed himself between them, his face close to mine. "I think this is it, gorgeous."

We stared at each other.

Even though I'd been muttering "love you" to him when he couldn't hear, I was only rehearsing the words. There was hesitation about getting the sentiment returned, and there was also the fact that I wasn't sure it was a correct statement. I wasn't sure I recalled what it felt like to fall in love, to be certain.

But at that moment, I remembered.

"I think it is, too," I said.

Even though I didn't say anything more, I was sure then of our place in the world. I thought that life could only keep moving one way—upward, and in the direction of good.

4

His office behind the restaurant was much nicer than the restaurant itself. Back here, in his managerial quarters, he had brocade couches and tufted leather chairs. The desk was from the 1800s and it was built to last. Just like him. That's what his father had always told him, and unlike his younger brother, Vincente, he'd always believed their *padre*. Still, it pleased him to look around, to see what he'd created, what he was entitled to.

José Ramon sat at the desk now and took in his office. With its carved pocket doors, collection of Mexican art (including one Diego Rivera), and high-tech audio and visual equipment, the luxurious room was second only to his private residences. He hoarded such places, because if one showed too much luxury, he'd learned, people started asking questions. His competition, for example. The government, certainly. The only people to whom he could show the luxury he required, and had acquired, were the few women he took home. He liked best those women who could handle it—who could step into that luxury and not be impressed by it. Or at least not show it—but who could appreciate it. That was the type of women he wanted. They were hard to find.

But he wouldn't worry about that now. Now, he was worried about the thing that would eventually get him those women. Money.

It fucking killed him that the wealth his family had amassed had been "invested" into a legitimate business—that's what it looked like anyway, a *legitimate* business—and now, what the fuck was happening? Where the fuck was the return on that money? And if there was no return—the way he'd been promised—where the fuck was all the money that was supposed to be in that goddamned business?

José slammed his hand on the table and squeezed his eyes shut. But it didn't help. He could still envision Vincente as a little boy who had always wanted to be like his brother. Except that "Vince," as he called himself now, was smarter. That's why he had eventually gotten his MBA after his father sent the boys to the U.S. from Mexico. And that was *supposed* to be why they could trust Vincente to find legitimate investments when they needed them. But Vincente had fucked it up. That was becoming clear.

He slammed his hand again, right as the door opened. "I told you never to just walk in," he barked at the new restaurant general manager.

The man didn't respond. Instead, he left, closed the door, knocked and then reentered.

"What?" José said in a demanding bark.

"The eggs that were delivered are spoiled. We'll need more to get through the week," the manager said with urgency.

He glared. This restaurant was not his identity. It was a front, like so many others the family had. He crooked his finger at the man, who came closer. Then he did it once more, slowly bending and extending and bending his finger in a methodical way. When the manager was close to the desk, he spoke in a low tone, threateningly. "If you can't handle these issues, someone else will," he said simply. "Do you get that?"

The manager had the audacity to return the glare before he backed out of the room.

As the door closed, he slammed his hand flat on the desk once more. It disgusted him that he continued to have such discussions with his underlings. But a "discussion" was not required with the people running that business, a business that was running off with his family's money. No, something much, much more than discussion was necessary.

5

"Ms. Granger? Mr. Reynolds will see you now."

I slid carefully out of my seat and smoothed the front of my pencil skirt. I undid one more button of my shirt to allow ample cleavage to show and made sure the tiny camera in my necklace was still pointing forward. After one last check in the mirror, I strutted my stuff across the bank lobby.

All right, Izzy, I thought to myself. *Let's do this.*

Mayburn did a lot of work for banks. Sometimes the cases he worked were huge and complex—big-scale bank fraud and money laundering and such—requiring me to do something dangerous like invade someone's home computer to download information. (Naturally, Mayburn always undersold such jobs, letting me figure out for myself—usually right when I was about to get caught—how much bigger and potentially threatening the situation was than I'd thought.)

Tatum Reynolds's office was about as typical as they came. One Plexiglas wall looked onto the bank. The rest of the walls were gray, the carpet blue, the desk and bookshelves black metal. Mayburn had told me the bank hired him to prove Reynolds was hoarding enrollment incentives that were supposed to be given to all new clients. When a number of his clients complained they never saw the money they were promised, the bank suspected that Tatum was depositing the money into his own bank account. However, the transactions couldn't be proven, and after watching him, Mayburn and the bank came to believe that he might be taking the money and then giving large sums to "special" clients. All the "special" clients were pretty women with almost no money to deposit into their new account. That's where I came in. I was supposed to open an account with fifty bucks. If he failed to give me the hundred-dollar incentive, we had him. If he tried to offer me more, we had him. For once, Mayburn might have been right. This was going to be easy.

"Ms. Granger, welcome to Chicagoland Bank and Trust," Reynolds said. "I understand you want to open an account?"

He was thin and pale and much younger than I anticipated. His voice had a squeak to it. If I didn't know better, I'd say this guy was a teenager, not a late-twenties, thieving bank manager. He had a bowl cut, for goodness' sake.

"Yeah, I want a checking account. One of those online ones," I answered, affecting a nasally voice. Was the fake voice a part of the undercover assignment? No. But I couldn't help myself.

"We can certainly help you with that." He gave me a crooked smile.

For the next twenty minutes, I listened to Reynolds give me options on checking accounts, savings accounts, credit cards and investments, but no mention of the cash incentive. I did my best to play my part and noted with pleasure that he glanced down my blouse, where the necklace hung, quite a few times. He even blushed a little when I laughed at one of his jokes. I handed him the ID that Mayburn had given me and started signing the paperwork.

"You know," he mumbled, "our bank offers an incentive program."

I lowered the pen slowly. "Really? What's that mean?"

"Well…" He cleared his throat. "There's this really nice restaurant around the corner. It's a French place called Tru."

Tru was one of the most touted and expensive restaurants in Chicago. Where was this going?

"We could…ah…go there," he stammered, his eyes firmly planted on his left cuff link.

I blinked at him. Did he just ask me out on a date?

"You see," he continued, "our bank offers you two hundred dollars toward a dinner at Tru for opening an account with us. It's impossible to get a reservation, but I know a guy who lets me in whenever I want."

I know a guy. Such a Chicago thing to say. The city had a strange but wonderful pride that involved being able to help others. Sometimes this was meant to make the helper feel better about himself. Sometimes it was more altruistic. But almost always the phrase *I got a guy* (or some variation thereof) came into play as the person offered a connection to make it all better—a plumber who would show up in an hour and stop your basement from flooding; the cop who would arrive in minutes, assess the situation and then leave if you didn't want to go through the hassle of a police report; a doctor who normally had a three-month waiting list, but who would get you in as a special favor to the one who said *I got a guy.*

"So if you wanted the incentive," Tatum said, "I could get you in."

Wow. Tatum was using the incentive money not just to impress women, but also to pay for a date? At Tru? Thank God the necklace cam was getting all of this or no one would believe me. (And thankfully Mayburn and my dad would be paying the tab on this job if they wanted to keep it going, because two hundred dollars wouldn't buy much at Tru.)

Reynolds was staring at me with something akin to blind fear in his eyes, and for a second I felt sorry for him. But then I remembered I had a job to do.

"I'd love to, Tatum."

At the sound of his name, his entire face exploded into an ear-to-ear smile. "Great! I'll get the paperwork going."

* * *

After saying goodbye to Tatum Reynolds, I made my way to the café across the street. Mayburn and my father had set up shop there so they could watch the feed from my necklace camera on a laptop. I weaved through the tables and to the back booth.

My father gave me a curt nod in greeting and Mayburn mumbled what was barely discernable as a salutation. It might have been my imagination, or the lighting in the coffee shop, but Mayburn looked a little red.

"Did you get all that?" I asked, trying to get a read on the situation between the two of them.

"Yeah, we got it," Mayburn answered. "He offered you the money…to take you…out on a date…." Then he burst out laughing. His face turned more apple-red, his breathing came in gasps and tears sprung from his eyes. Even my father chuckled a little.

My father rarely laughed and Mayburn didn't, either, not since he'd fallen in love and then broken up with a woman named Lucy DeSanto. I tapped my foot and waited. When the guffawing finally died down, Mayburn was completely out of breath, and I couldn't help but smile a little.

"You did good, McNeil," he finally managed to say.

"Poor kid," my father said. "Tatum Reynolds might go to prison because he wanted a girlfriend."

"The reason doesn't concern us, Christopher. I

just need to figure out how to tell the bank owners without cracking a smile." Mayburn bit his lower lip then launched into another fit of hysterics.

"All right, gentlemen," I said as I took off the necklace camera and set it on the table. "I've got to go."

"Later, McNeil," Mayburn said, finally managing to compose himself.

"'Bye, Boo," my dad said, using his nickname for me. When I stood, he stood with me. "Everything all right?"

"Yeah, sure. You?"

He nodded but looked at my face with a concerned expression. "You can tell me if you ever want help. If anything isn't all right."

"Okay... Thanks." I tried to think whether the cryptic remark meant anything. But my dad was new to Chicago, new to our family again. I figured he was just trying to get his sea legs, so to speak.

I looked at my father and allowed a small smile. It was good that he was working with Mayburn. It was good that he was loosening up a little. And I had to admit, it was good that he was in my life again.

6

"I don't understand," I heard Theo say, his voice pained. "Why would that be?"

Something was wrong. And on the day we were moving in together—well, not exactly *moving in*—Theo had decided to buy the place by the Green Door (offering nearly the entire asking price just so he could "avoid all bullshit"), and we figured that Theo might as well stay with me in the short-term since his apartment lease was up.

And so, a few uneventful days after my meeting with Tatum Reynolds, I left Bristol & Associates a little early and climbed the stairs to the "L" platform, heading home so I could help Theo situate his stuff in my condo. (I was also attempting to make sure he did not situate any of said stuff in places I didn't want it.) Also, I needed the time to think; to process the fact that someone was moving in with me. I adored Theo, craved him, couldn't believe how in tune he was with me when we were together, so dialed in, in a way that Sam hadn't been.

It was thrilling. It was scary. But I loved him, I reminded myself. *Yeah, but you don't know if he returns the sentiment.*

The "L" train rumbled around the corner at Lake and Wabash, and I moved over for someone to sit next to me.

No reason for too much analysis, Izzy. I reminded myself that Theo and I moving in together was a temporary thing.

It was a chilly, sunny November day. As I rode the "L," listening to its wheels screech awkwardly at stops, I let my mind meander into other things. I thought about how I missed my Vespa scooter, which I'd had to retire for the winter. I thought about Thanksgiving coming up in two weeks. I planned to go to my mom and Spence's place, as I always did. For some reason, Theo and I hadn't talked about what he was doing. Should I invite him to join? The fact that we were temporarily moving in together already seemed momentous enough.

When I got home, a nearly empty moving van was out front.

The numbered keypad outside the front door of the three-flat complex had been disabled by someone with the code; I could tell just by glancing at the display because I had overseen the installation of the keyless entry systems on the front door as well as the door to my condo on the third floor. (Okay, Mayburn had done the overseeing for me while I watched him watch the locksmith.) When it was first installed, we guarded the front-door code like the sphinx. But changing the code frequently quickly got cumbersome. First, my ground-floor neighbor sold his place, requiring visits of about fifty real-estate agents a week. Then my second-floor neighbor decided to rent his condo, and that allowed hordes of apartment hunters to roam the place. And now that Theo was moving in, with his buddies helping him and his moving vans, someone had given up the fight and disabled the keypad altogether. I really couldn't blame them.

I made my way up the three flights of stairs—the only downside to my condo. When I'd reached the third floor, the door to the apartment was blocked with boxes. I'd managed to stick my head in the door when I heard Theo speak in a strained voice, a voice I'd never heard before. *"I don't understand,"* he said.

A pause, as Theo listened to whomever he was talking to. "But why?" He sounded distressed. "Why would it be that low?" he continued. "I told you last night, I've never bought property before. All I've had are two credit cards." Another pause. "Yeah, well, I guess that could be it but…"

As his voice died away, some kind of trepidation said hello to my psyche.

"The business has some kind of trust account," he said. "Could we use that to get credit or cash?" A pause. "No, it's a foreign trust. I don't know much about it, but I could…" An exhale. Another moment of silence. "Oh, okay, so then…" Quiet. "Really?"

I heard him say. He sounded now not so much distressed, but like a young man surprised at terrible news.

I hated to hear it. I nudged the door to shove aside the boxes and stepped inside.

Theo stood at the bar of my European-style kitchen, his hair pulled back away from his face, wearing an army-green T-shirt and jeans. He turned as I came in. He threw me a polite smile, as if to say, *One minute.* Or maybe, *Everything is fine here.* Yet I could tell it wasn't.

"All right," he said. "Yeah, talk to you then."

I picked my way through boxes, across the room and gave him a hug. "Who was that?"

He held me longer than usual. His back muscles felt taut.

I looked up at him. "Everything okay?"

His brow furrowed. "That was Barb. The real-estate agent. She did a pre-application for my mortgage, and it was…" More furrowing. "It was denied."

"You're kidding?" Theo had money. A lot of it, as far as I knew. He and his partner, Eric, started their company—HeadFirst—while in college. HeadFirst's software allowed people to create their own artistically beautiful websites. The company had performed—*over*performed—beyond anything anyone expected, according to the frequent press about the company. Theo and Eric had left college and never looked back, walking into a dream life of travel, private planes and a constantly growing business.

Theo shook his head, still distracted, which was so very unlike his usual life state.

I kept my arms around his back, but I leaned away so I could see him better. "I heard you saying you really hadn't owned anything yet. Maybe your credit isn't extensive enough. Especially for the prices you're looking at." None of the houses that Theo had viewed had been less than a million dollars, and the one he'd decided upon was almost three times that. "Maybe you need to take out credit cards and then pay them off, that kind of thing?"

He shook his head. "She said there should be a high enough credit score, given my income. Also, I've had two credit cards, and I always pay them on time. I've never been delinquent on any bills."

"Well then, what is it? What did she say was bringing your score down?"

"She couldn't tell from the report. She's going to have her contact at a credit bureau look into it." The muscles in his back loosened a little, and he let me go, yet his expression remained stiff. "Right now, she said there's no way I'll be able to get a mortgage."

Who is this guy? The thought boomed in my brain without introduction, without warning. And I could feel the question in my body, too—a wariness that took up residence somewhere deep inside and crossed its arms.

We both looked around my apartment at his

stacks of books, piles of boxes, laundry baskets overflowing with jeans and shoes. We both knew that, as we stood there, a new tenant was moving into Theo's old apartment.

I realized then Theo was staying with me a little longer than I'd thought.

Tick, tick, tick went the silence. It was, I realized, an old clock my mother had given me years ago in college. I'd never noticed the sound before.

"You want to go out for a drink?" I said.

He nodded fast.

Within fifteen minutes, we were seated at the bar at Topo Gigio, an Italian place on Wells. Thirty minutes after that, we were in high spirits, the owner having sent a bottle of champagne after hearing that we'd just moved in together. Soon, we were making plans for Theo's condo, drawing game-room and bedroom designs on napkins and searching our phones for photos of furniture he could buy.

"Whenever you move to your new place," I said, "it doesn't matter."

"*We* are what matters, right?" Theo said, leaning toward me, moving his bar stool over.

"Exactly." I stared into those eyes, nearly breathless in his presence, the whole of him. Any irrational slices of fear were no longer cutting me.

An excited look took over Theo's face. "I just remembered," he said. "I have a folder of pictures from magazines that I've been ripping out. You know, from home magazines?"

"You've been reading home magazines?" I adored him even more, suddenly.

"Yeah, well, my mom bought me a bunch of them. And I just remembered. I've got pictures of beds, and oh, these kick-ass chairs for a TV room." He looked so excited then. "Let me run back and get them."

"No, let's just go," I said, but right then, the bartender delivered the three plates of appetizers we'd ordered.

"It's a few blocks," Theo said. He pointed at the appetizers. "You start on these, and I'll be right back."

I watched him walk from the room, watched everyone else stare at him as they always did. As always, he didn't notice.

"I love you," I whispered. I was sure about it then, sure that he would return the sentiment. "I love you," I said, trying the words again. And it was then I decided I would tell him as soon as he came back.

But a few minutes later, he was calling my phone.

"Hey," I said softly, without having to say another word. Because I felt like every word I would say to Theo now would carry those three words in it.

"We had a break-in," he said.

My mouth opened and closed. In front of me, the bartender told an apparently hilarious story, because the two people listening threw their heads back, their mouths open. But I couldn't hear anything.

"Back the truck up," I said into the phone, still trying to meet the anti-swearing campaign goals I'd set last year, despite the situation. "What did you say?"

"You need to come home," Theo said. "Someone broke into your place."

7

When I got home, the downstairs door was closed, the keypad still enabled since we'd turned it on before we left for Topo Gigio and Theo had obviously used the code to get in. So then how had someone broken into my place?

I took the stairs fast to the third floor, then stopped when I reached my door. Immediately, my eyes drew down to the keypad. The cover of that panel had been pried off, exposing the wires inside.

I felt something like fear sweep a cold brush over my body. I stopped and thought about the entry system. Many people knew the password to the keypad downstairs. But the keypad to my own condo was known to only a few. Theo was one of the few people who knew it, along with my mom and Q. Apparently whoever broke in didn't have the code. Or wanted to make it look like they didn't.

I pushed open the door and stepped into the living room. My eyes moved over the fireplace, looked at the coffee table, where mounds of Theo's belongings were stacked. I let my gaze scan the

couch, the yellow-and-white chair that was my favorite piece of furniture in the house. I looked into
the kitchen. The bar counter with the two stools in
front appeared the same as when we left it—piled
with towels and sheets of Theo's.

"Izzy?" I heard a voice that sounded like Theo
but also a little like someone else.

I jumped, flinching in spite of myself.

Theo stepped into the room. "Iz. Hey. I came
home and saw the door panel all fucked up."

"Are you okay? Was anyone here?"

He shook his head.

"Was anything taken?"

"I was just going through the place, and it
doesn't look like it, but it's hard to tell, you know?
Since I just moved in." He waved his hand behind
him toward the hallway, which was filled with
boxes. "And I wouldn't really know if anything of
yours was taken." It seemed, then, we knew so little
of each other.

"You must have been scared," I said.

He shrugged.

I went to him. "Are you okay?"

He wrapped me in those arms, and I smelled that
Theo smell—*there it was.*

"Did you call the cops?" His shirt, made of a
soft fabric that could almost make me think nothing was wrong, muffled my words.

The answer came in a rap on the door. Then another rap. "Chicago police."

The responding officers listened to our tale
while their radios squawked.

"You're a lawyer, Ms. McNeil?" Officer Potowski asked me.

I nodded. "Yes. Criminal law. With Bristol & Associates."

"That's a good firm. High profile. You guys get a lot of publicity."

I nodded again. Since Q had arrived at Bristol & Associates, we had gotten even more. Q loved a good press release.

"Since nothing is missing," the officer said, "this is technically just a B and E. A misdemeanor at best. There are no prints on the doors or number locks, either. We'll file the report, but we can file it closed if you want. And we'll just check in with you in a little bit—tomorrow or the next day—to make sure everything's okay. What do you think?"

I almost told them to close the case. I had explained to the cops that I'd been the subject of intense scrutiny from the media before, a place I distinctly did *not* want to go again. A closed case would be one of the best ways to keep the media's nose out of our business.

But then a lick of fear swept over me again. Of what? It had something to do with a feeling that this—whatever *this* was—was not done yet. I looked at Theo. Strange that this had happened tonight, when he moved in.

"Leave the case open, please," I said to the officer. "And yes. Please check in on us."

8

Twin Anchors was known for its ribs, but neither person who sat at the middle of the bar was hungry. The restaurant was also known for its love of Frank Sinatra and the fact that Old Blue Eyes had been in that very joint on more than one occasion.

A guy who called himself Freddie (he'd all but forgotten his real name) ordered a glass of Scotch.

His partner asked the bartender if he knew how to make something called a Michelada.

The bartender not only looked stumped, but he also said, "Huh," then again, "huh." He looked behind him, as if for backup. "I just took bartending school. I don't remember that."

"Don't worry about it." A Tecate beer was ordered instead.

They took a few sips, companionably sitting next to each other, not needing to speak right away.

The bartender returned. Apparently, someone at bartending school must have told him that chatting with the customers, whether they wanted to or not, would bring hundreds in tips. The guy pointed at some photos and articles pasted and shellacked behind the bar. "Those are all about Sinatra," he said. "And the guy from Chicago who wrote a book about him."

"So fucking what?" Freddie said, taking a sip of his Scotch. The guy had no idea that in Freddie's past, he had waited in alleys and cut people for reasons much less serious than bugging the fuck out of him.

"It's true," his partner said, who was apparently smart enough to sense his menace. "The Chairman of the Board used to hang out here. On occasion. We all know that. Thanks."

Freddie made a single motion with his hand, shooing away the bartender.

The bartender gulped and had the sense to turn around and start rearranging a wine refrigerator.

A moment passed. "So you think they're freaked out?"

"Hope so," Freddie said.

"Do you think they'll get it?"

"Yeah, I think they'll get it. Left the downstairs entry system enabled. Let 'em know it's not so hard to find out their little code." That was true, for him; he'd worked for the National Fire Alarm & Burglar Association and the Electronic Security Association just to learn how to master every kind of alarm. "Then messed up the panel by her door. Tells 'em we can get in, easy. They'll get that. They're smart. She's a lawyer, and he handles his own company."

"The company that can't get itself together."

"Yeah. But even with all those moving boxes, they're gonna know someone was in that house. And even though we didn't find anything pointing our way, it's a little message that says 'be careful.' Really fucking careful." Freddie had taken another sip of his Scotch, when the dipshit bartender returned, nodding at the pictures of Sinatra.

"Man, I wanna hang out with Sinatra," the bartender said. "Or at least just have him at the bar here."

"He's *dead*," Freddie said. *And you will be, too.*

"Hey, I'm just saying, somebody like him."

Freddie pushed his glass away. "There is *no one* like the Chairman of the Board."

"I know, but I'm saying someone—"

"There *is* no one. That's the point." He looked at his partner. "I gotta get the fuck out of here before I hurt him." There was no way he was going back to Stateville prison. He was hanging on, hoping to keep his natural violent flair pushed down inside. He was hanging on. Just barely.

9

"Hello?"

"I heard you had a break-in." The voice sounded familiar, but I couldn't quite place it.

"Who is this?" I asked.

A laugh. "I guess I should be glad you're over it. You're clearly not traumatized by me any longer."

Recognition grew in my head as the man spoke—the slightly snarly way of talking, the sense that a cruel laugh was right behind his words ready to be shot in your direction.

"Vaughn," I said.

Across the bedroom, I saw Theo's eyebrows shoot to his forehead. "Whoa," he said.

He'd been pulling on a pair of jeans—we were heading out to meet his mother for Sunday brunch. After the break-in and then Saturday—one gray November day sliding into the next, barely a change in light—I'd jumped at the opportunity to get us out of the house, to maybe get back to that "us" that we'd apparently left sitting at the bar at Topo Gigio, along with our good humor and ease.

"You remember me," Vaughn said in a jokey tone.

I said nothing. Detective Damon Vaughn had made my life a living hell twice in the past year—first when Sam disappeared, and second, when Vaughn suspected me of killing my friend Jane. The fact that I'd beaten up Vaughn on cross-examination in a trial a few months ago had helped. But I wasn't close to getting over it.

"So I heard you had a break-in," he said again.

"You *heard*?"

"Yeah, I heard from someone around here." His words sounded false.

"'Around here,'" I said. "What does that mean? You're acting like you work at a small-town police station, where the guys all sit with their feet on the desks and talk about their 'beat,'" I scoffed. "I think I know better than that."

"Oh, that's right, 'cuz you're a *criminal* lawyer now," he said with scorn.

"That's right," I said, sharp on the heels of his words. "I *am* a criminal lawyer now. And next time I get you on the stand, I'm going to take you down. Again." I stopped myself short of saying, *How ya like me NOW?*

For a moment I let myself bask in the glory of that moment when I had Vaughn on the witness stand. I had executed what felt like one of the best crosses of my career.

Vaughn interrupted my little reverie. "Jesus Christ, you're a ballbuster! I take back that apology I gave you after court that day."

"Too bad," I said quickly. Then in a nicer, calmer tone, "I already accepted it."

A pause. Then two or three.

"So," I said, pleasant tone still intact, "you were calling because…?"

"Look, cops know what cases other cops worked. And so when you hear something about something—or someone—in one of those cases that someone else has—"

"Then you tell your buddy, the other cop," I said, answering for him. "Yeah, I get that."

"Good. I just wanted to remind you what I told you after court that day." His voice was nearing pleasant now, too, but I didn't fill in the blanks this time.

"If you needed a favor or anything, I'm your guy," Vaughn said simply.

Something about his statement—the matter-of-factness, the authoritative assurance—made me feel okay suddenly. Safe. For a moment, the whirl of anxieties in my head stopped.

All morning those anxieties had been like shrieking bats flying around under a bridge, yelling one thing after another in my head. *Your house has been broken into. Again! But what's worse is that you have a pretty strong feeling this break-in has to do with Theo. Because he's the one who just moved in.*

But maybe it's as simple as that? Maybe someone got in the condo building during the move and somehow hid.

But that doesn't make sense because there is no-where to hide on the two flights of stairs.

And hey, so what if it has to do with Theo?

It was always at this point in the shrieking con-versation (in voices that all sounded like mine) that a really angry version of Izzy McNeil entered the scene. *"So what?" you ask? You're in love with him. Do you get that?*

And quietly, I would answer internally. *I get that.*

And then the voices would round around. *Your house has been broken into. Again!*

But although his words had momentarily halted the cacophony in my mind, I didn't entirely trust Vaughn. Not yet. Not after what he'd put me through, and not after what I'd learned about Chi-cago cops over the past few months—most of them are good, most have pure motives, but they don't see evil the same way as everyone else. And when they believe something, they make things happen—practically appear out of nowhere—just to bolster their beliefs.

The truth was, I wasn't too sure what Vaughn really believed. To say he was hard to read was an understatement.

"I'm not looking for a favor," I said.

"Hey, I feel bad about how everything went down. I told you that. And I want to do what I can to make that up to you."

I could almost hear Maggie yelling, *Yes! Great! We can always use a cop on our side.* Even if a police officer wasn't involved with the particular case you were working, they could be excellent sources of information. And maybe it was time to truly forgive Vaughn. Clearly, my anger wasn't hurting him very much, only me, making me cranky when I thought of it, making me see red.

"Yeah, well…" I said. "You're right. I had a break-in." I told him that no belongings had been disturbed. Or the front-door panel. Just the keypad on my own door.

He asked me about the front-door system, then added, "Who has the code for your own door?"

"Just a few family members. My friends Maggie and Q. And two cleaning ladies. And…" I trailed off, realizing more people than I'd thought had that code. "But it wasn't used. The panel was ripped off."

"You have an alarm?"

"Yeah, but it wasn't turned on that night. We were just running out for something to eat."

"Sounds like a warning," Vaughn said.

That made me feel cold again. "What do you mean?"

"Someone was either looking for something and didn't find it, or they wanted to fuck up your head, let you know they could get to you. Or both."

Theo had put on his clothes and left the bedroom. I felt very alone, Vaughn's casually spoken words reverberating in my head.

"Who?" I said, taking a seat on the bed. "Who would do that?"

"You piss anyone off lately?"

"No! I never piss people off."

He laughed.

"Shut it," I said, using Mayburn's favorite expression. "I seemed to have pissed you off last year. But that's a rare thing. People usually like me." I suppose that wasn't entirely true. There were people at my old law firm who weren't big fans of mine, but that was because I pulled in more work than any other associate. And there was that Italian mobster whose plans I might have thwarted. Not to mention the underwear drug dealers I sent away. Okay. Maybe there were a few people I'd pissed off.

"What about your boyfriend, Theodore?" Vaughn asked.

Vaughn had met Theo after Jane died, but he had no reason to know we were still together.

"How did you know he was my boyfriend?" I asked.

"The responding officers told me."

"Oh. Well, he doesn't piss anyone off," I said. I thought of his silences lately, his refusal to talk about the mortgage and what was going on. "I don't think so."

"Could be random. That's the case a lot of times. Someone who noticed the front door unlocked and was looking to see if you had anything good in there."

I had the feeling Vaughn was trying to make me feel better, but now I was feeling worse, unsafe. I sighed. "Thanks for calling."

"Yeah, no problem. I'll watch the case."

I didn't know what that meant. Didn't ask, either. I just said thanks again and hung up.

10

Toward the end of brunch with Theo's mom, his phone rang. He pulled it out of his jeans' pocket, looked at the display. "It's Eric," he said. "Sorry, guys, I have to take this."

"Do what you have to do," Anna Jameson said, giving her son a good-natured wave of her hand. "We'll be more than fine."

It was the first time I'd met Theo's mom. She was beautiful—tall and lean, with a willowy, lightly muscled, yoga-type body. Her hair was brown but sun-kissed, natural-looking. Her skin was luminous, her big eyes alive.

When we'd first sat down with Anna at the Walnut Room, Theo had introduced me, then reached out a tattooed arm and squeezed my shoulder. Now, as he stood to take the call, he put his hand lightly on the back of my head, holding it there for a moment. That hand had the tenderness of a kiss.

His mom saw it. Anna smiled at me as he walked away. "Thank you for letting him stay with you until he gets in his own place."

"Sure." I searched her face for a sign of whether Theo had told her about the break-in or getting turned down for a mortgage. She looked unperturbed, which I took to mean he hadn't.

"I've never seen Theo like this," Anna continued.

"Like what?"

She shrugged. "Like he is with you."

This was said without irritation or territorialism. I knew that my friend Grady's mom always seemed to take it personally when Grady dated someone, as if it were a slight to her. But Anna didn't appear to be that type of person.

She glanced around the Walnut Room. "I can't believe it's the holidays."

"But it's not yet. It's not even Thanksgiving. I've always thought they get the decorations up too early." The place was bedecked in holiday regalia— ruby ribbons and forest-green bows, glittering red lights and a massive Christmas tree in the center of the room that, this year at least, had a woodsy theme with a plethora of faux birds and forest animals covering its branches.

"I like when Christmas lights are up *way* before Christmas," Anna said. "It's one of the things that make me happiest." A smile spread across her face. "Theo is one of those things, too."

"He said you two are close."

She gave a short laugh. "Yes. Well, his father and I got pregnant when we were college sophomores. Brad never wanted a baby. I guess I didn't, either, not in theory. But once Theo was here, it was clear he was always supposed to be here. He was just the light that always shone. Brad and I stayed together until Theo was out of school. Then Brad wanted to move on, to be somebody different. I couldn't totally blame him."

"That's big of you."

She gave a shrug. "You can only do what you can do. My parents considered themselves hippies, and they always used to say that. You know, 'live and let live.' And I have to say, that kind of attitude applies to nearly every situation. I had breast cancer a few years ago, and that really helped me through that." She sighed. "So many challenges."

"Wow. That must have been tough. Were you and Brad still together then?"

"No. No. We'd just broken up, and we only saw each other like we do now—at events for Theo. We were together so long that we're more like brother and sister." She gave a rueful chuckle, shaking her head. "I ran into him the other day when I was with a girlfriend at Tavern on Rush. We sat down outside, and I looked over, and there was Brad with a woman who was Theo's age, maybe younger."

Was that a stab at the age difference Theo and I had?

But Anna just shrugged again. "Brad is like that. He's a big boy in the business world, but he doesn't want to grow up personally. It no longer affects me."

"I haven't met Brad yet," I said. "We've been trying to meet up with him but it keeps getting rescheduled."

A rueful smile. "By Brad, I'm sure, not Theo."

"Sounds like it."

She sighed. "Theo wants so badly to have a relationship with him. When he was eighteen or nineteen, he really turned to Brad and it was hard for me to watch him struggle when his father still wasn't the fathering type." She looked toward the restrooms. Theo was heading back our way. "I used to worry that Theo would emulate him, but I think it's caused him to go the other way. He's more grown-up."

Theo reached our table. Another squeeze on my shoulder as he took his seat. He looked back and forth between us, as if trying to read the dynamics. I realized then that despite the call from Eric, he might have left to give Anna and me some time alone. "How are we doing?" he asked.

"Great," I said.

"Great," she echoed.

Theo looked down at his phone as if waiting for another call. Or maybe thinking of the one he just took. His forehead creased with what appeared to be deep concern. His mom was right. Theo was grown-up. And that grown-up person was worried about something. *Was it his talk with Eric? Or was he not as happy with me as his mom thought?* His silences and moodiness over the past few days seemed directly related to the mortgage situation and the break-in, but I couldn't help worrying it was something else. Something having to do with us.

His phone dinged, the tone telling him he had a text. He read it, frowned. "I have to get to work."

"On a Sunday? Anything wrong?" his mom asked. But she asked in the way people do when they're sure the answer is no.

Theo cleared his throat. "Just some things I want to deal with."

My phone chimed, too, and I looked down. *Christopher McNeil,* the display said. My dad. I noticed he'd called a few times. Since he didn't text much, I was waiting for an open time to call him back and have a real chat with him. For now, I hit the ignore button.

We stood from the table. "Izzy," his mom said, giving me a hug, "I'd love to meet up for coffee or tea sometime."

"I'd love that, too."

We smiled at each other. Although she was much more carefree and casual than my mom, they had a similar elegance.

We said goodbye to Anna outside the restaurant in the midst of a colorless, snowy day.

When she was gone, I turned to Theo. He wore a navy blue wool coat with a mandarin collar, a masculine design with a subtle flair.

"What's going on with Eric?" I asked.

"He told me something that has me worried."

"What's that?"

"He said the company's books are messed up."

"Messed up how?"

"Look, Iz, I don't know, okay?" His voice held more of a bite than I'd ever heard. He moved back as a bus lumbered down State Street. "I don't know *anything,* all right?" he said, his voice loud, which I suppose was to compensate for the bus, but it jarred me a little.

I tried not to feel hurt. "All right."

I started to turn away, but his voice, kinder now, stopped me.

"Wait," he said. I turned back to him. He sighed, looked down as if gathering his thoughts. "What he knows is that we defaulted on a loan. A big commercial loan."

"Whoa," I said.

"Yeah, I know."

"How did that happen?"

He shook his head. "Eric's trying to analyze the situation. He keeps the books, right? So he should know. But I'm sure that's why I didn't get the mortgage. It was a loan we applied for when we first started the company, and we personally guaranteed it."

"Oh, no, that's not good." Immediately, I regretted my words. "What can I do to help?" I asked quickly.

"Nothing." He was shutting down. I could see it, even though I'd never witnessed such a thing before. I could see him distance himself from me. "I'll figure it out by myself," he said as if confirming my suspicion.

He kissed me and hailed a cab, its yellow sides spattered gray with slush. I watched it drive away, then I turned away and began to walk west down Washington. Mentally, I ran through the events of the past few days—from the mortgage denial, the break-in, now the troubles at HeadFirst. I thought the world of Theo. But I had serious doubts that he could figure it out alone. Maybe he would turn to his dad? Or his mom, with whom he clearly had a strong bond.

Later, I would think how it was the last time Theo's mom saw him before everything started to truly crumble.

11

His cell phone vibrated again. Then again.

"Hold on a sec." José Ramon shifted the woman who sat astride him and grabbed his cell phone. The woman, Lucia, was dressed. But just barely. And not for much longer. He would turn off the damn phone.

But then his eyes grazed the text messages appearing on his screen. Saw those messages were about Theodore Jameson. He scanned them. The last one read, He just left lunch.

"Give me a minute, baby."

A woman like Lucia didn't pout. It was beneath her. She simply stood, her lavender panties, sown through with tiny black ribbons, stretching across her hipbones as she did so. With a few elegant movements, she'd adjusted her breasts back inside the matching bra, and she strode quietly, confidently, from the room.

He almost moaned, watching the way the muscles in her ass moved, the purple thong tucked between her tanned cheeks.

He made himself look back at his cell phone, and he typed, What restaurant?

Walnut Room. He's heading to work.

Why do you think he's going to work on a Sunday? Don't assume anything. Even though he was only typing, not speaking, he knew his underling would hear the snarl in his tone. How many times had he told his people not to assume? Never assume.

I assume nothing, the next text read. I got close enough to hear them.

Them?

T and his GF and his mom.

He let out a grudging exhale, impressed at the level of skill. The kid was good. Had proven that time and again.

He kept his people—the ones outside the legit businesses, like the restaurant—working in solitude. That way no one could collude with another. A coup would be hard, if not impossible, to stage. But often, forcing people into a lone-wolf situation made them paranoid, especially the type of people he had on the hook.

Yet every so often, someone like this went above and beyond. Sometimes the ones he'd strong-armed recognized the uselessness of resistance, had the sense and intelligence to not only join him, but also to stand up and be a soldier in his army. Incrementally, they assumed more responsibility. Slowly, without pissing him off, they thought outside the box. And this kid was one of them.

The girlfriend is the lawyer? he wrote.

Yeah.

We need to find out more about her. His face began to curl in a snarl again, but then he got the next text.

Way ahead of you, it read.

He gave a short laugh. The only kind of laugh he knew. Good work, he typed into his phone. He didn't say such things often.

He was a little surprised at the slight gap in time it took to get a reply. But then, Thank you. I appreciate it.

He put his phone back on the nightstand and thought for a moment. Yes, suddenly he could imagine allowing this one into the next level of his business, might be told why they were keeping an eye on Theo Jameson.

Lucia was back. In the doorway. Her dark hair, turned copper on top from the sun—she had just been on a friend's yacht in the Caribbean, she'd said—fell over her shoulders in rivulets, covering her breasts, which were bare now.

She locked his eyes in with hers. Then she hooked one finger through one of the black ribbons that ran through her panties. Then the other hand on the ribbons on the other side. Slowly, rhythmically, she undulated her hips, letting ribbons untie, then smoothly unfurl themselves until the flap of purple silk covering her in the front fell away. Nothing remained except two scraps of silk around the tops of each thigh. Nothing in between. Except heaven for José.

She strolled toward him. Slow, slow, almost predatory. Although she was a scientist, had a PhD and gave speeches at conferences around the world, she said nothing now.

When she reached him, she straddled him, not letting his eyes go anywhere but hers, and then, without warning, like he liked it, she moved herself over him.

Oh! Some primal exclamation had escaped him as he felt the tightness, the wetness and the scraps of silk on either side.

As she slipped him farther inside herself, Theodore and his girlfriend slipped away from his mind, knowing he could let them go. But not for long.

12

I heard my name being called. *"Izzy?"* There was definitely a question mark in the way it was said, but not as if the person were unsure whether they'd seen me, but rather they sounded surprised I was there.

I turned around. *"Sam?"* There was decidedly a question mark at the end of that, as well. And a touch of panic.

What in the hell was Sam doing at the River North nightclub Underground? Granted, Underground, with its military hideout vibe and revolving door of visiting celebrities, was a hot club, one that had survived when others opened and closed in six months. But it was still a nightclub. And Sam, my former fiancé, was not a nightclub guy. At least as far as I knew.

Then again, I also hadn't realized that Brad, Theo's father, was a regular at the city's late-night, bass-thumping, the-stalls-in-the-bathroom-go-all-the-way-to-the-floor kind of places.

Theo had called his dad earlier that evening from

home and, about ten minutes later, he'd come out of the office. "Want to meet my dad? Turns out he can swing it tonight."

The air in the condo had been tense since Theo returned from HeadFirst not wanting to talk. So even though it was a Sunday night, and I felt the pull of my bed, I immediately said yes. We took a cab to the club. The wooden door was marked only with a triangular sign out front. But when the door was opened, even a crack, we heard the hard pumps of bass.

"Swanky," I said after we'd walked through the place and stopped in a relatively quiet spot to look around.

"My dad has a thing for these kinds of clubs," Theo said. "Ever since he and my mom got divorced. For a while, he said he had to be out at places like this for business, but…" Theo raised his shoulders in a distracted shrug, and his words died out as if he couldn't be bothered to continue the sentence.

"What does he do?"

"He's a venture capitalist. Sort of. He takes small companies and grows them."

We got jostled by people packing the dance floor as the DJ began pounding on bongos. Theo looked around the club again. "Yep, this is my dad's kind of place." He peered. "There he is." He pointed to a man in a taupe leather booth, tucked in a corner beneath a stone wall. Another guy—the friend of his father's?—sat at the other end, while a few young women packed the rest of the booth, all boasting impressive cleavage. Theo's dad was clearly telling some story, and the women leaned in, listening, then threw back their heads, laughing at the same time. In the center of the table was an ice bucket, highball glasses, bottles of whiskey and vodka, some mixers.

Theo didn't move right away.

"You know what this place reminds me of?" I said to Theo. Or rather I shouted due to the rising volume of the music.

"What?" he said.

"When I met you. The club on Damen."

When Theo and I had been introduced by my friend Jane, she'd practically shoved us together on a leather booth.

"That's where it all started," I reminded him, nudging my hip into his thigh. It was a small gesture that no one else would see but had become one of our habits, a thing we did, just the two of us, a signal that indicated so many things but mainly lust and love (or something like it) in equal servings.

Theo grinned, but it wasn't one of those looks he usually gave me—one I knew was created just for me, that made me feel as if we were at the center of the universe. (A universe that was kind. And fair. And safe.)

No, it wasn't that type of look. But unfortunately, I couldn't read the expression. His mouth, normally so lush, was stretched straight across to show teeth. His eyes were lifeless. *Where did you go, Theo?*

"Is your dad going to remind me of you?" I asked to pull him back to the present.

"Nah." He pointed at his dad, who wore a black blazer, clearly expensive, and a large watch. He pointed at the women. "And they are not like you."

"Who are they?"

"Who knows? They change all the time." He laughed then. "My dad will never change."

"Sometimes that's not a bad thing." I thought about the changes I'd gone through—the ones my family had gone through—over the past year. Sometimes it felt as if we were hurtling through life at light speed. And many times that was hard to get used to.

We made our way to the booth. When we reached it, the syrupy smiles of the women dropped. All eyes shot to Theo. They all sucked him in with their gazes, shot each other glances that said, *Who is THIS?* I didn't blame them one bit.

"Theo!" His father stood and grasped Theo's hand, throwing his arm around him and thumping him on the back. When we spied him across the bar, Brad Jameson had looked like a player with all the women around him, but now, with Theo, he only looked like a happy, proud parent.

"Hey, Brad." Theo had told me he called his father by his first name. Always had. I thought it was strange, but I also had one of the strangest father-child relationships around, so I wasn't one to talk. Theo grasped my elbow gently and pulled me toward him. "This is Izzy."

"Izzy." Brad Jameson shook my hand. "I've heard wonderful things about you." He gave me a genuine smile. As with Theo's mom, I'd wondered if he might have some misgivings about the eight-year age difference between Theo and me, but based on the women at the table, he clearly was a supporter of dating the youth.

We spent an hour talking to Brad and his friend Kent and sometimes talking to the women—LaBree, Jenni ("with an i") and Erin. (Or Karen? It was some variation on that theme.) LaBree was a cool girl—gorgeous and smart. The other two, though, weren't much interested in conversation unless one of the men was giving them attention.

When I had the chance, I studied Brad. I couldn't quite figure him out. I could see that Brad had given Theo his straight, strong jawline, the piercing eyes, the full lips. But those physical traits on Brad couldn't help him in the crowd of injection-perfected twentysomethings. To me, he appeared like an older, somewhat shrunken version of Theo.

But he was pleasant enough and appeared to be a smart guy. Every so often, when LaBree went to the restroom, he and I had the chance to talk, just the two of us. The topics flowed from the Chicago political climate to a trip he'd taken years ago to hike in Machu Picchu, something he wanted to do again.

At one point in our conversation, I'd asked him

the question at the top of my mind. "Theo told you he was turned down…"

Before I could even finish, or decide whether I should finish, he answered, "…For a mortgage?"

"Yeah. Why do you think that happened?"

Brad nodded right away. "It's killing me. Theo has worked so hard. I don't know what's going on. HeadFirst just has to figure out their situation here and overseas. But hopefully, it'll…"

LaBree returned then, and Theo, whose mood seemed to have lifted a little, began telling a story about a surf trip to Mexico. I watched Brad, and it was evident he adored his son, nodding enthusiastically, looking around as if to make sure everyone was noticing how wonderful Theo was. And since I thought Theo was wonderful, too (even with his absent nature the past few days), that made me like Brad Jameson a lot.

And then that voice coming from my right—
"Izzy?"

My ex and I now blinked at each other, the *thump-chucka-thump-chucka-thump* of music reverberating around us.

In all the time since we'd broken up, we had never simply run into each other.

Sam's blond hair had grown a bit long, darkened a little in the months since I'd seen him. His skin, too, was more fair than usual, but all this only made his green eyes more intense, like emeralds dropped in the snow.

Seeing Sam someplace random was something I'd feared for a while. What if we bumped into each other and he was with new/old girlfriend Alyssa? It would be so awkward, so…sad.

But thankfully my fears never materialized, and, in fact, I had stopped fearing it all together. And yet, here we were—Sam with his green, green eyes, and me in a booth with Theo, his father, his father's friend and some very, very hot, young girls.

Sam looked at our little group, blinking. I glanced past him, fearing the sight of Alyssa, but only saw R.T., Sam's musician friend, who wore a small smile that he was clearly trying to stop from spreading across his face at this amusing turn of events. I waved at R.T., and he waved back, then pointed toward the back, gesturing that he'd return in a minute.

I climbed over LaBree and Brad, careful not to flash anyone. For a moment, I regretted my dress and high-heeled boots. But when I saw Sam's eyes drag up and down my body, revealing what I knew to be pure lust, I was grateful.

I took a step toward Sam and we embraced—a kind of brisk, pat-pat hug that was more like something you'd share with a cousin.

Theo stood from the booth, too, and I felt his presence next to me. I gestured between the two men. "Theo, this is Sam. Sam, Theo." I almost giggled inappropriately, the moment was so weird.

Theo knew who Sam was and said, "Oh, hey, man. Great to meet you."

He stepped forward and shook Sam's hand, pumping it congenially, if a little forcefully.

Sam had heard about Theo this past summer

when I was in Italy and Theo had come over to visit me. He knew I'd been dating someone, but I'd never used Theo's name when we'd briefly discussed it. In fact, Sam had seemed uninterested, as if he preferred to not know the details. But now the details were right in front of him.

Sam's eyes squinted for a moment, as if trying to figure out or remember who Theo was. Recognition broke across his face and he seemed to take in all of Theo then, all his gorgeousness. He shot me a look that I actually couldn't read, then turned back to Theo. "Hi. Nice to meet you, too."

"So what're you doing here?" I asked.

"R.T. is the sound guy for some band that's playing in the back room. Some party." He said nothing further, asked nothing of me, and so we stared uncomfortably, my mind scrambling for conversation and finding none.

"What about you guys?" Sam said finally, the phrase *you guys* ringing like a self-conscious bell.

"We're just hanging with my dad," Theo said.

Brad disentangled from LaBree and slid out of the booth so Theo could introduce them. Sam reached out to shake hands when Erin/Karen barreled through from the dance floor with Kent in tow. She clamored into the booth, apparently not caring whether *she* flashed anyone her underwear (which matched her dress—what little there was of it). Kent dove in after her, grabbing her ass on his way. Karen/Erin giggled and reached for a bottle. Sam seemed to be waiting for an explanation of their presence as I tried to force my face into an expression less appalled and embarrassed.

"Brad Jameson," Theo's dad said, his voice loud in order to be heard over the music, offering Sam his hand.

Sam responded by shaking Brad's hand, smiling gamely. "Nice to meet you. So you guys—"

But Sam was cut off by LaBree, who scooted between them, then reached up and planted a wet kiss on Brad's neck, her hand sliding down his back. She whispered something into his ear and walked off toward the dance floor.

Brad stared appreciatively at LaBree's body.

"Very nice to meet you," he said to Sam earnestly. But then his gaze drifted. "Excuse me for a moment," he said without looking at any of us, then headed off after LaBree.

Suddenly, I found myself alone between Sam and Theo again. I looked from one to the other. Strange, strange, strange. I liked both of them so much. They were two of my favorite people in the world. I felt like saying to Theo, *Isn't he great? Isn't he cool?* To Sam, I wanted to say, *Okay, how hot is this guy? And isn't he so sweet and smart?*

I knew that wasn't the way to go, however, and so, uncharacteristically, I once again found myself mute. A long awkward moment ticked by.

Theo was the one who finally spoke. He gestured at the table. "Can I get you something to drink?"

"No, I'm cool. Thanks." Sam looked at me. "I should find R.T."

"Right. Yeah."

Theo looked between the two of us, giving me an expression I couldn't read, then excused himself and left.

Sam and I just smiled at each other. "So how's…" I stopped. I couldn't say it. *How's Alyssa?*

But Sam, apparently, could still read me. "I'm not sure."

"You're not…?" I glanced down at his left hand. No ring.

"Alyssa and I broke up. After we…" He pointed between himself and me.

After we almost got back together this past summer.

I felt bad at how happy I was that he wasn't with Alyssa anymore—perfect, tiny, blonde Alyssa, his high school sweetheart, who seemed to love Sam even more than I had.

Sam glanced behind him. "I should see if R.T. needs any help."

"Sure. I'll come back there later and say hi."

But when I did, there was no sign of Sam.

13

When Theo and I got home from the club, Theo turned on his Xbox to play Madden NFL Football. He played against people around the country and won a lot. Still, it was almost one in the morning.

"You're playing *now?*" I asked him.

"Yeah, I just need to blow off a little steam." Theo scrolled through the Xbox menu, trying to find an opponent at his level.

I sat in my favorite yellow-and-white chair, yet it failed to comfort me as it often did. "Did you have fun with your dad?"

After Sam had left, I'd spent an hour trying to listen to LaBree and Brad, who were talking about the patent LaBree was working on and that Brad was helping her with—some kind of invention to hold bra straps in random places. The product actually sounded rather smart, but I couldn't focus. Kept replaying over and over my run-in with Sam. Then Theo and his dad began having what looked like a serious discussion, and soon after that he had been ready to leave.

"*Fun* probably isn't the word for it," Theo said now.

"Right," I said. Then, "What is the word for it?"

He didn't reply, just clicked a button to enter a game.

I put my head against the back of the chair for a minute. Then I lifted it again. "Hey, have you ever given anyone the code for the door?" I asked him. "Talking to Vaughn yesterday made me think about it."

"I haven't given it to anyone." Theo mashed a few buttons. "If you think about it, anyone from the street could watch and see us using the code, then use it to get in when we're not around."

"But why not steal something if you're going to all that trouble?"

Theo stayed silent, his jawline set.

"What about people you're with when you come in the front door?" I asked.

"Like who?"

"Well, didn't you meet Eric here before that show at the Congress the other night?"

"Yeah, that's true."

"Did you come here from work together?"

Theo nodded, tucked a lank of light brown hair behind his ear.

"So he could have seen you entering the code downstairs."

"What about people who've been here with you?" Theo said leaning toward the TV.

"Spence was with me a few months ago. Other than that…" I gave a one-shouldered shrug. "My mom was with me once, too, but she already has the code."

"What about Sam?" There was a little something bristly in Theo's tone.

"What about him?"

"Does he have the code?"

"No, I'm sure I changed it since we broke up. But wait... There was that time that we hung out." I shook my head. "But no, that wasn't here."

"What do you mean, you hung out?"

My stomach clenched, as if I had something to hide. And I guess I did. "Last summer. We met up. He'd gotten engaged..."

"And he said he'd get back together with you if you wanted."

"Yeah."

He focused on his game.

"What?" I said to his back. "What's wrong?"

He kept playing for a moment or two, then paused the Xbox. He turned around from his seat on the ottoman, and now we faced each other. "There's something between you guys," he said.

"Oh, is there?" I started thinking about it. He was right. Even though we'd hugged like fishing buddies, I'd seen the way Sam looked at me. "I mean, there will always be something, right? We were sorta family, you know? Almost sorta married." It sounded sorta brainless and deranged.

"When's the last time you saw each other?" Theo asked. "Before tonight."

"Hmm." I thought to myself. "Maybe at the

hotel? No, no, it was after that. In court." I focused back in on Theo. "Yeah, in court during Valerie's trial."

"What hotel are you talking about?"

"Oh, you know. What's it called? The one right off of Michigan Avenue? The Peninsula, that's what it is!" I sounded way too enthusiastic, and I was talking faster than normal.

"So you guys went to the bar at the hotel, right?"

"Yes," I said with assuredness. So far I hadn't lied. I just hoped he didn't ask any more questions.

"And then did you go upstairs?" The hope got shot out of the sky. "Like, did you get a room?"

Oh, this was not good. Not good. Not good. "Here's the thing…" How to explain this?

Theo crossed his arms and looked at me with something approaching disappointment on his face.

"Here's the thing…" I tried again. "We did get a room, but we didn't use it, if you know what I mean. We didn't sleep together."

We had, in fact, made out in a major way, and there was some nudity, but no sex.

"You never told me that," Theo said, the disappointment apparent.

"There was nothing to tell. We wanted to see if there was anything left between us to rekindle. There wasn't. We weren't right for each other."

Silence.

"We aren't," I said, liking the present tense of that word better. "We aren't right for each other."

"Whatever." Theo turned and picked up the game controller.

"Are you mad?"

Nothing.

"Jealous?" I was oddly flattered at the thought, but I didn't want him to feel bad. I stepped behind him and began to rub his shoulders. He shrugged me off.

"Look," Theo said without stopping his game, "we're not married. You can do what you want.... And so can I." He started mashing the buttons harder and harder until he growled in frustration and tossed the controller to the floor. "Damn it," he blurted as *Game Over* flashed across the screen.

"I'm going to bed," he mumbled with a gruffness I wasn't ready for. Then he strode purposefully to the bedroom and slammed the door.

14

If I thought that once I joined Bristol & Associates my life would be one big, rollicking murder trial after another, I was wrong.

"Your Honor," I said, "the defense requests supervision on this matter. As you know, Mr. Hemphill—" I gestured to the fourteen-year-old kid on my right "—does have one other obscene-conduct offense involving public urination. However—"

I heard a little snort. I glanced at Johnny Hemphill, Maggie's cousin's kid, who tried to conceal a laugh. He'd told me when we first met that he couldn't help it. He found the term *public urination* funny. It hadn't helped when Johnny's father, sitting next to him, also guffawed.

Johnny shot me an apology shrug.

I tried to muster a glare, but these kinds of cases didn't inspire me enough to do so.

Since we'd started working together, Maggie insisted that handling criminal defense matters that were small and mundane was good for me. She said I had to learn the ropes of Chicago's criminal legal world, and the only way to do that was to start from the ground floor. So when her neighbor's brother's boss got a speeding ticket or Maggie's grandfather's dry cleaner was accused of stealing a pearl button from someone's coat, Maggie assigned me as the go-to girl. Maggie said that criminal defense warriors like her had to take a lot of these little cases because your brilliant handling of them put you on people's speed dial. Then the dry cleaner would call you from jail after a hit-and-run accident and the boss might give you a quick jingle when he was arrested for sexual harassment or when some other large-ticket, moneymaking, cunning-intelligence-required case emerged.

I understood the marketing aspect. And I also knew lawyers had to be available for their clients on matters both great and gratuitous. Even more, I needed busy-ness to distract me from thinking about Theo—Theo and HeadFirst, and more important, Theo and me.

Now, I scrounged up a stern look for Johnny Hemphill, then squared my shoulders back to the judge. Raising my right index finger, I made my impassioned plea for one more round of supervision for this kid who simply thought it was funny to pee behind the movie theater on Roosevelt Avenue.

Thankfully, I won. *This is the last time,* the judge had intoned, looking at me and not Mr. Hemphill.

I thanked him, did a geisha-esque bow and hustled out of the courtroom before he could change his mind, leaving Johnny with his guffawing father.

I took the elevator to the first floor of the courthouse at 26th and California Avenue and ran to the big bulletin board that hung on the wall. There, sheets of paper in rows were tacked, each listing a courtroom and the cases to be called that day. Next to each case number was a description—armed robbery, murder, assault, drug trafficking, etc.—the sight of which made me remember I was far, far away from the civil courthouse where I used to spend all my professional time.

I elbowed and jostled my way toward the front of the small crowd huddled there, everyone craning their necks. Maggie had assigned me four cases to handle that morning, but I'd forgotten to find out what courtrooms they were in. Frantically, I searched the multitude of papers. *The 26th Street Shuffle,* I'd heard other criminal lawyers call days like this.

As I ran toward the elevator, I paused for a brief second, as I always did, in the old vestibule of the courthouse. And maybe it was that pause that allowed me to feel the faint vibration from my shoulder bag. I glanced at my watch. I had more time than I thought—at least five minutes until I had to be in Judge Johnson's courtroom. I pulled the phone from my bag.

My father. I hadn't been able to call him back since he called yesterday while I was at brunch. I hadn't seen my dad in almost a week, and I knew he had no one in this town. He'd been here only a few months. He'd been in our lives only a few months. And it had occurred to me that when I'd seen him at the diner last week, he had said something to me—*You can tell me if you ever want help. If anything isn't all right.* I'd been wondering if he might have been referring to himself, subconsciously or not.

On the far side of the vestibule were marble stairs, each worn sufficiently in the middle from the hundreds who had climbed them in the hopes of justice.

I sat on the first one and was about to answer the phone when a security guard started toward me. "Miss," he said, "you can't…"

I knew what he was about to say. The stairs were closed now, part of the old glory of the building, the glory that had mostly given way to ruin.

I gave the guy a pleading smile.

He raised his hand and gave me the you've-got-one-minute gesture, then respectfully turned his back.

"Hi," I said to my dad. "So sorry I haven't called you back yet, I've been running from one thing to another." *And trying to figure out what's going on with my boyfriend and worrying even more now that I confessed I'd been with Sam. And didn't exactly tell him the whole story of that night, which had come very, very close to being sex-filled.*

"Boo, I've got some bad news."

"Bad news…" My stomach clenched.

"It's about Theo."

"Oh." I hadn't expected that. My father had met Theo only once, only briefly.

My dad paused. And it was a weighty silence.

"What?" I said.

"Something's going on with him."

True. "How do you know that?"

He sighed. "Izzy…" There was a slight layer of irritation in his voice.

"I know. I should stop asking how you know these things. But it's just—" *what was the word?* "—off-putting." My father had disappeared from our lives decades ago. But he had watched us during that time. (I suppose I would say "watched *over* us," except that would make him sound angelic, which wasn't exactly right.)

"It's not good, Izzy," my father said.

I'd gotten better over the past year at taking bad news. And things were easier, I learned, if such news was simply laid out flat.

True to form, my father gave it to me. "Theo is being investigated by the U.S. Attorney's Office."

15

Bristol & Associates was on LaSalle Street near Monroe in an old high-rise, home to a host of criminal defense firms. Like 26th and Cal, you could tell the lobby was once impressive, but now the marble was yellowed and the lighting spotty.

On the tenth floor, Bristol & Associates wasn't much better. Maggie and her grandfather made more than enough money to afford a sleek office overlooking the Chicago River, but like many criminal defense firms, they didn't care about image. They cared about the work, the clients and the cash. Q had already started a campaign to get them to move. So far, Maggie and Martin had been impervious.

I walked in and blew by the receptionist, Leslie. Usually, I stopped and talked to her, or at least waved. She called out to me. "You okay?"

"Yeah, thanks," I lied. I was still replaying the conversation with my father in my mind.

"He's *what?*" I had blurted after my dad said

those words—*Theo is being investigated by the U.S. Attorney's Office.*

I knew Theo had financial issues. Or his company did. But how did any of that rise to the level of a federal/criminal investigation? I tried to muster all I'd learned from Maggie over the past few months as I shifted from civil to criminal work, but there were too many layers of feeling and concern for me to sort through them for possible facts.

"We'd better meet," my father had said.

"Does Theo know this?" As soon as I'd asked the question, I heard its odd nature. Why was I asking my father what my boyfriend might or might not know?

"Doesn't look like it from what I can tell," he said.

"Then I have to tell him. I should—"

"No," my father said forcefully. "I didn't get this information from…uh…mainstream sources."

"Do you ever?"

"Izzy," he said with a cautionary tone like you would with a young kid. Instead of pissing me off, it reminded me of *being* a kid. When he was still around. When he was still a regular dad.

"Let me tell you what I know," he said. "Then you can decide how to handle it. I will leave it to you. Do you feel comfortable coming to my place? We'll have privacy."

The truth was I'd only been to my dad's mostly empty studio apartment a few times, and it had mostly depressed me. "I'm in court for a bunch of things," I told him. "Then I've got to get back to the office to drop off orders Maggie will be waiting for. I'll come right after that?"

"Make it one o'clock," he said. "I have a few more things to track down."

The thought had made me woozy. There was *more?*

Now, as the receptionist hit a button under her desk that unlatched the door to the inner sanctum, I wondered what that *more* meant. And I feared it. Felt like old demons were coming back to grab me, choke me, make me doubt myself and who I loved.

I tried to push the thoughts away, just as I pushed through the door and began walking the hallway toward my office.

Q popped out of his office as if he'd been waiting for me. This was fairly typical. After I'd been let go from my old law firm, Baltimore & Brown, Q could have worked for another lawyer, but he'd met his wealthy boyfriend by then. For the past year, while I tried a variety of different gigs, Q had lazed and lounged, now leaving him energized and raring to go. Since he'd accepted the manager position—Maggie had been doing it herself before—he'd gotten the law firm an incredible amount of PR and marketing. So much so, that Martin had to tell him to lay off on the press conferences. Q hadn't exactly listened.

So when I saw Q waiting for me, I wasn't surprised that he was wide-eyed and kind of clasping his hands the way a coach might when he was about to talk to a player. One of the things he'd kept from the life he'd led when he was straight (or pretending to be) was a love of football. He would be the first openly gay football coach of an NFL team if someone let him.

Q wore navy pants and a tailored gray jacket that matched his gray eyes and set off his black skin nicely. The lights in the hallway glinted off his bald head.

"I know I'm supposed to tone it down," he said when I reached him. Per our usual custom, he hadn't bothered to say hello. "But check this out— NBC needs someone to talk about what it's like to be a suspect in a case, and they want that person to *also* be a lawyer. I mean, you're perfect for this, right?"

"Local NBC?"

"*National,* girlfriend. You would discuss how horrible it is to be wrongfully accused and explain that's the reason Bristol & Associates work so hard for their clients. Maggie and Martin already gave it a green light. You know how Martin is about wrongful convictions."

I nodded. "Is Maggie here?"

"Not yet."

I wanted to tell Q what my father had said about Theo. I told Q and Maggie nearly everything. But after our discussion last night, after seeing Theo walk away, seeing the hurt on his face, I realized that I had a responsibility to him. I had to find out more and help him. And keep his confidences, what little I had of them, in the meantime.

"Maggie had a hearing in Markham," Q said. "So, about NBC—will you do it?"

I tried to focus on his question. He was right that I'd be ideal for the interview. A year ago, Vaughn suspected me of killing my friend, Jane Augustine. And as a result, my face had been splashed across TVs and newspapers. But I wasn't sure I wanted to talk about that time. And I wasn't sure I could talk about anything, given my distraction about Theo and the U.S. attorneys.

"I don't know," I said. "When would this happen?"

"They'd come here. We'll put you in the library in front of all those books so you look supersmart. It would start about one o'clock."

I shook my head. "I should leave by one." *I have to go to my father's to learn why my boyfriend is being investigated.*

And then I had to wonder—was this some kind of media trick? Could this interview have anything to do with Theo's investigation? If so, I should tell Q, *No way.* Except that wasn't the way I operated. If there was something to know, I wanted to know, and I didn't care about the source.

Q raised his hand and snapped his fingers in a Z. "Not a problem." He looked at his watch. It was eleven-thirty. "I'll have them here in a half hour, if not earlier, and they'll be gone in thirty minutes."

Q turned and, without further discussion, dodged into his office. I kept walking down the hall until I got to my own. It was an old-school office, once inhabited by a former associate of Martin's.

From him, I'd inherited a black bookshelf, towering wood file cabinets, an old, red oriental rug with a blue border and a large wooden table that served as my desk. So far, my only contribution to the place was a white leather-and-chrome office chair that Maggie let me purchase from a furniture store on Franklin Avenue.

I sank into the chair now and stared at the documents on my desk—grand jury transcripts, motions to suppress, rap sheets, mug shots.

I spun around and stood, looking out the window at LaSalle Street. I put my face toward the glass and peered south to the Board of Trade Building that sat at the foot of the street, an art deco building with a carved stone facade. Somewhere down there, Sam was working at a trading firm.

A year ago, at this time, authorities were investigating Sam.

And now Theo. *Why was this happening again?*

"What's up, sister?"

I turned around. "Mags." Relief seeped into my veins, into my body.

Maggie wore a green wool suit that looked vintage, even had a slim felt collar that would have been gauche on most. But Maggie, with her tiny frame and short, retro, gold-blond waves of hair, could get away with it. More than that.

"Cute," I said, pointing to the suit.

She looked down at herself. "Thanks. Got it at a resale shop in Bridgeport." She looked back at me. "You're doing the NBC interview."

"Yeah."

She peered at my face, gave a teasing grin. "Are you going to get the flops?"

"Shut it," I said, channeling Mayburn.

"What?" she said, all fake-innocent like. "Should we tell them to bring a makeup crew to control the sheen?"

"Mags," I said, warning her, not hiding my irritation.

The truth was, I had a little problem that Maggie and I called the flop-sweats, or, as she had recently dubbed them, the flops. This condition occurred when extreme nervousness set upon me. That first time was during a mock trial in school, the second time during a real trial. Maybe it was a redhead problem? Who knew, but when the flops struck, my insides boiled, the sweat poured and it was mortifyingly embarrassing.

"You know," I told Maggie, "Grady used to be the one who gave me crap about that, not you." Grady and I had worked together at my old firm.

"I know," Maggie said. "And now that you work with me, it's my duty."

I glared.

"Not in the mood?" she asked.

"*Not* in the mood."

I wanted so badly to tell her about what my dad had said, but I held my tongue. It didn't matter anyway, because Maggie smiled. And it was a shy kind of smile, one I wasn't used to from her.

"Okay," she said, "well, I'll talk about something else, then. I have news. He's moving here."

"Bernard?" I didn't even ask who she was talking about. She was always talking about her long-distance, French-horn-playing boyfriend, Bernard. Had all but papered her office and home with pictures of him—a huge Filipino guy who towered over everyone, especially her. "Is that why you've been mysterious lately?" I asked.

The smile went away. "I've been mysterious?"

"Yeah, I mentioned it to you."

"Did you?" She was back to her distracted state.

"Anyway, tell me the details! Bernard is moving in with you?"

"No, no," she said, "he's not moving in. That would be too much."

"Yeah," I said sarcastically, "and moving to an entirely new city after knowing someone for six months isn't too much at all."

She beamed. "It's not. Thank God. It's fast, I know. And it's…challenging. But it feels natural."

"What will he do here?"

"You know how he substituted for that French horn player last year, the one who had to take a leave from the CSO?"

I nodded.

"Well, they loved him. And then that horn player announced he had to leave the symphony altogether. And I guess it caused all sorts of uproar at the orchestra, but they called him for an audition last week, and he *got* it."

"Wow, that's a big deal."

"Yeah. It is." She looked at the ceiling.

Q popped his head in the office. "The TV peeps are here already. I guess they were right down the street." An exaggerated shrug. "Anyway, they want to hustle," he said. "Let's go." He scrutinized my face in the same way Maggie had. "You're not going to—"

"No, I'm not going to sweat!" I stood and grabbed my bag. "But I will spackle on the powder, I promise."

A minute later, I walked into the firm's library to find a cameraman settling his equipment and a woman in a blue dress speaking into a cell phone.

She clicked the phone off when she saw me, and came toward me, hand out. "Izzy, hey," she said. "Maggie Cullerton from NBC." She looked closely at me, and I knew she was remembering when I'd been a favorite suspect of the Chicago Police Department. Even if she hadn't covered the story, even if she wasn't here to ask me what that time had been like for me, she would have recalled it. Everyone in the media did, since I'd been on-air when a reporter had interrupted the broadcast and commenced to break the news.

"Nice to meet you," I said.

There was a lull, but then like any good reporter she began to chat to loosen me up. "So I hear you've got another Maggie in the office," she said.

"Yeah, Maggie Bristol, one of the partners here."

She nodded. "Great, great. And what kind of legal work are you doing now?"

I dredged up my normally friendly demeanor and soon she had me feeling more at ease.

The cameraman directed me to a chair in front of an imposing, colorful array of legal volumes. He handed me the lavalier microphone, and I threaded it through my blouse, attaching it to my collar, the once-familiar movement returning to me. He flicked on the lights over the camera.

A minute later, we were rolling. As the reporter interviewed me, I felt the skills I'd learned at *Trial TV* coming back. My confidence grew. I remembered that this was something I did reasonably well. And since Q seemed like he wouldn't be easily deterred from the marketing aspect of Bristol & Associates, I might as well get used to it as part of my new job. I could even thrive. Maybe I'd be the firm's spokesperson.

But then Maggie stepped into the library.

At first, we all kept going, figuring she was just there to watch. But as soon as I'd answered another question, she stepped in front of the camera and looked at me.

"Mags," I said, making a move-it gesture.

"I'm sorry, folks," she said to the news crew with her forehead creased. "We're going to have to do this another time."

The reporter shot a glance at her cameraman. "Is everything all right?"

"Yes, yes," my best friend lied. "Just some emergency firm business that Izzy needs to be a part of." She apologized for having to cut the interview short, but asked the cameraman to pack up and then ushered them out of the library. "Thank you so much for coming. Please talk to Q in the lobby. He'll set up a time to reschedule."

Once they were out the door, Maggie closed it and took a deep breath.

"Mags, what is going on?" I asked, trying to keep my voice low. Was there more to her mysteriousness other than Bernard moving to Chicago?

"Theo is on the phone," she said, surprising me.

"Oh. Theo." Upon saying his name, I felt a stir—a stir of longing that I couldn't help, a Pavlovian response that immediately declared itself whenever his name arose. But then I remembered—*Theo is being investigated by the U.S. Attorney's Office.*

I looked up at Maggie. She bit her bottom lip.

"What?" I said.

She took a breath. She leaned in and put her hand on my shoulder. "He's in lockup."

"Lockup?" I said, loud, surprised. "Lockup like he's been—"

Her eyes locked in to mine. "He's been arrested."

16

The Metropolitan Correctional Center is something of an anomaly. A jail, yes, but its appearance is that of an ugly, triangular hotel tower. The MCC, as they call it, is perched on the edge of the lively Chicago Loop at Clark Street and Van Buren.

I'd never given the MCC much attention before because it housed federal prisoners, and most of the clients I'd been associated with through Bristol & Associates were in state court. I'd minimally (very minimally) gotten used to the 26th-and-Cal bull pens—the underground prison cells where county defendants waited to appear in court. The bull pens were pits of despair and trepidation, filled mostly with men who all fell quiet when you walked in, staring at you, staring for more than one purpose, you knew, not the least of which was that you were a lawyer, and therefore, their possible savior.

But now Maggie and I were off to see my boyfriend in the MCC. I had no idea what to expect.

We walked, both of us holding the collars of our coats close to our faces to protect from the Chicago wind that barreled down the street. "What if they rough him up?" I ask.

She shook her head quickly. "The Feds aren't as into that as the county people can sometimes be." She paused. "Plus, they know Theo is a businessman, so they know he's smart. They know he can call a press conference with a minute's notice."

Maggie's phone rang. She flipped it open, listened and said, "Great, thanks." She took my arm and began steering me east. "He's going before a magistrate to set bail."

My phone rang. I had been gripping it inside my pocket. I pulled it out and my eyes shot to it. My dad. I'd been calling him since we left the office, leaving the NBC crew a little annoyed. I heard the reporter bugging Q for leads on what was happening.

"Where have you been?" I asked my father now, not bothering with pleasantries. I hadn't often used an irritated tone of voice with him, and strangely it made me feel as if we knew each other better than we did.

"Looking into something," he said unapologetically.

"Something to do with Theo?"

"No." He said nothing else. Of course.

I told him that Theo had been arrested.

"Merda," he said, speaking in Italian. Then translating. "Shit."

"He's apparently going before a magistrate shortly. We're heading there now. But I need to know why, Dad. Why was he arrested?"

"Damn. I wanted to be able to tell you in person, to explain everything in a little detail. I had no indication they were moving this fast." A pause. "Basically, they say he's been bilking money ever since he started his company. They said he's like Bernie Madoff. But smarter."

"They're alleging he's stealing from the company? Or from the customers?" None of this sounded like the Theo I knew.

"Both."

I was about to say that was impossible. Because Theo was the most honest person. Sometimes to a fault. He simply didn't know how to lie, to deceive. But then I stopped the thoughts in my head. Because although Theo didn't seem devious, not when I'd met him, not even as of late, there had been those other recent traits—vagueness, evasiveness, irritation.

But still. They were logical emotions given the mortgage problem and moving and a break-in. That was a lot to deal with. (Not to mention the fact that I'd added to his woes last night by admitting— okay, half-admitting—to an indiscretion of sorts with my ex.)

"This has got to be wrong," I said.

"I hope so," my father said. But his tone was bleak.

17

I looked at Theo, and I hoped he couldn't see what I was thinking. No, I guess what I really meant was I hoped he couldn't sense what I was feeling— like I was a little scared of him, like I wasn't sure I believed him when he told me and Maggie that he hadn't done anything wrong. *Why? Why the mistrust?*

When Maggie turned away to speak to a law clerk who had come into the courtroom, I faced him. I closed my eyes for a second and took a breath. And I cleared out my prejudices as best I could. *Because isn't that what Maggie and I were forever asking the cops and the prosecutors to do? To keep an open mind? Couldn't I do it at the very least for my boyfriend?*

When I opened my eyes, I looked him up and down, taking in his jail uniform, determined to be honest and forthright, to say the first thing that came into the foggy depths of my head. "You look good in neon-orange."

I shook my head. Theo. He made me think, *sex, sex, sex,* no matter what the circumstance.

I heard Maggie issue orders to her clerk while we waited for the judge. Some attorneys came into the room and put their pleadings on their table. Maggie made a beeline for them.

Not much time. Had to get the sex off the brain, and get back to basics. "So," I said, "what are they going to say?"

"I don't know. I—"

"Yes, you do." I realized we had to cut to the chase. The criminal courts, I had learned, do not allow for taking time to hold your clients' hands. I adjusted the collar of my blue suit, sitting straighter. "I'm putting on my lawyer hat. And we don't have time for bull-spit, okay?"

Theo's face scrunched at my swearword replacement. Not one of my best, granted. Theo nodded, then looked grateful. And right then I felt good that I could contribute, that I could be Theo's lawyer. When Sam had disappeared, I'd been so helpless until Mayburn let me work for him and let me contribute to the solution.

"Okay. Great," I said. I gave him a stern face. "So, I don't have time to draw this out of you anymore. You have to tell me—right now—what you know and what you don't. No more secrets, Theo. I'm not just your girlfriend anymore." I noticed, vaguely, that I'd directed the comment about "secrets" at him, not exactly including myself in the statement.

He nodded. Then, as if something occurred to him, he said, "Can you do that? Represent me, even though we're…"

"We're boyfriend-girlfriend?" I answered for him. "We're living together?" God, it felt good to be taking over.

"Yeah."

"I've heard of people being represented by their spouse, so we should have no issues there. Plus, you have Maggie."

"You've always said she was one of the best attorneys in the city."

"In the country."

"Then I'm glad to have her." He reached out and touched my knee. "But, Iz, thank you. I see what you're doing, too. I see you."

I've always disdained the expression about arrows piercing someone's heart. But I got it, then.

"Okay," he said. "Okay. I'll tell you what I know. They say they're charging me with wire fraud and money laundering. But I don't even know what that means."

"They're saying you were stealing from the company and from investors."

"You already talked to the government?"

I shook my head. "My dad was looking into this situation."

"Since when?"

"I'm not sure."

"You asked him to?" He sounded disappointed.

"No. He decided to, on his own." I sighed.

"That's kind of how he is." I reminded myself that if I wanted honesty I had to return it, as well. "But once I knew he was investigating you, I didn't stop him."

Theo shook his hair away from his face. It seemed to irritate him suddenly. He raised his hands and tucked his hair behind his ears. "I didn't steal from anyone."

I took a breath, but I didn't have a chance to say anything.

"Don't you think," Theo said, "that if I had stolen a bunch of money I could have bought that house I wanted? With cash?"

"I don't know, I—"

"Wouldn't I have a lot of money? Wouldn't—"

"All rise." Judge Diana Sharpe stepped up to the bench. Her eyes zoomed to Theo, silencing him.

A tall black woman who was said to have been a college hoops player stood above us for a moment, waiting for all eyes in the court to turn to her. Then she gave a regal nod and took a seat. A court reporter, clerk and her security detail—two U.S. Marshals in their thirties wearing cargo pants and blue shirts with gold stars embroidered on them—took positions around her.

Maggie scurried back to the table, giving Theo a confident smile and a squeeze on his forearm.

The U.S. Attorneys rattled off the charges against Theo and then everyone—Maggie, the U.S. Attorneys, the judge—spoke in shorthand. Soon they were talking about bail.

"We would oppose bail, Your Honor," the lead U.S. Attorney said. He was Indian—Anish, his name was—and he was a lean and stylish guy. "Mr. Jameson owns a share of a corporate plane. He travels frequently to remote locations."

"The travel that counsel mentions," Maggie said, "is for things like skiing and surfing."

I liked how confidently she said the statement, which could only have been dredged up from my ramblings about Theo when I first met him.

"Mr. Jameson does not have any family or personal connections overseas," she continued, "nor does he have dual citizenship."

"The corporate plane is equipped for travel to other countries," the U.S. Attorney said. "Mr. Jameson could easily head to Midway Airport in the middle of the night and be gone before anyone is the wiser."

"Mr. Jameson will forfeit his share in the jet until the charges are dropped," Maggie said.

Now I liked how she talked as if the dropping of the charges were about to happen. I really, really hoped she was right, but the troubles Theo was having felt as if they were picking up steam.

Theo felt further away, too. He was scared. I could see that. If I were really honest, I'd tell him that I was, too.

The U.S. Attorney refused to give up. He continued his argument about why Theo shouldn't be allowed out on bail. Every sentence seemed to make Theo itch to punch the guy. He was like a live wire.

Maggie argued that, in addition to the other factors she'd mentioned, this was "the first time Mr. Jameson has been arrested, much less charged, with anything at all."

"Bail is granted," the judge said finally. She then started asking questions about what Theo owned—a house, car, other property.

Maggie shot me a questioning glance, and I shook my head.

"Nothing, Your Honor," Maggie said. "Mr. Jameson does not own any such property. We would request a cash bond."

"Bond is set at fifty thousand dollars."

Judge Sharpe stepped off the bench, and the U.S. Attorneys peeled out of the courtroom.

"Okay," Maggie said, leaning in to talk to us. "So, Theo, we just need fifty thousand to get you out—"

"No, no," I said, interrupting. "Five thousand, right? Because that's ten percent of the bond?"

"Not in federal court," Maggie said. "You have to pay the total amount. You guys figure that out, and, Iz, call me when you're done."

"Okay," I said.

Maggie left. I felt a little relief. We would get Theo out of here, out of that orange jumpsuit, no matter how much he was rocking it, and we'd start to slow down.

But then Theo said, "Iz. I don't have fifty thousand dollars."

18

I sat in the chair of my home office, swirling back and forth and back again. My mind felt fuzzed out, overloaded. Synapses seemed to have slowed. Nothing was processing well. So far, I decided, this had been the longest Monday of my life. And it wasn't even five yet.

Since I'd had to leave Theo at the MCC, had to watch him being led away by the marshals, I couldn't seem to complete a full thought. I'd called Theo's partner, Eric, twice and hadn't heard from him. I'd emailed Eric twice, as well. I debated calling Theo's mom or dad, but I didn't have their numbers, and I was hoping to get a better handle on things before I made either of those calls.

I soon realized the swirling of the chair was making me dizzy and ramping up my frustration. I hated how black outside it was already. It felt as if it were nine at night. I looked down and saw I still wore my coat and my lavender-colored scarf. I took them off and threw them over one of Theo's moving boxes.

After the hearing was over, I had asked Theo so many questions about HeadFirst. But either he knew little or he was closing himself off from me. If the former were the case, I couldn't blame him. When I have big news or issues lingering in my psyche, *I'm* my first line of defense. I have to figure out at least few things before I can try and introduce anyone to the jagged shores of my mind.

If he were closing himself off from me, then... That's where I kept going around in circles in my mind—thinking mostly about Theo and me and what that meant, and if he was okay, and if I was okay, and if he would be okay, and if he wasn't okay, what did that mean, and how would he fare, and would we ever be okay?

I blinked a few times to try and clear away the endless questions. And my eyes landed on Theo's moving boxes.

If you had asked me a few weeks ago what I would have felt upon seeing those boxes—in my house—I would have told you that, stacked one on top of another like that, they would make a sweet tableau, a physical reminder that Theo and I had entered a new time and were in a new state of our relationship. A good one.

But those boxes now felt hulking to me, taking up too much space in my office, when I didn't know what was in them, what they could be hiding. I stood and took a tentative step toward them. Then another. I *wasn't* a snooper—was completely opposed to it—and yet, although I hadn't been tempted to look in the boxes before, they seemed to call to me now.

I should, I thought as I talked myself into it, check the boxes to see if they were empty after the break-in; see whether anything had been taken from them. You could never be too careful. And as Theo's lawyer, I should see if there was anything in there that could be used in his defense. Anything that could explain the very puzzling development that Theo had no money that was liquid. He hadn't been able to say more than that before the sheriffs had to take him away.

I took another step toward the boxes. Then another. The pulse in my ears seemed to get loud.

I blinked to try and scare away the odd feeling of dread that had fallen over me.

My feet moved another step. I stared at the words Theo had written on the sides in thick black marker—*BOOKS, LACROSSE EQUIP, FOOTBALL EQUIP, TECH, PLATES/BOWLS,* and so on. And I dove in.

An hour later, and I felt like a fool. There'd been nothing untoward in Theo's boxes. To the contrary, everything pointed to exactly what he had told me about himself—his sports background, his '70s baseball card collection, a book by Irving Stone about Van Gogh that he'd marked up and dog-eared extensively. It was his favorite book, he'd told me.

And what else had I really expected to find? Any business documents relating to HeadFirst would be at the office.

I was about to close the last box I'd rummaged through in a fugue state when I came upon a photo of Theo with his mom and dad. The image was of him as an early teenager who lacked the hormones and confidence of the Theo I knew. I peered at the picture, suddenly fascinated with the thought of the younger Theo, the not-so-developed Theo.

I looked at my watch. Eric hadn't called back. Maggie's checks into whether he had been arrested as well were answered in the negative. But she'd also said that they could have someone in custody "for freaking ever."

But certainly there must be something tangible I could do for Theo right now, some skill I must have learned over the years? *C'mon, Izzy, think.*

I reminded myself that during my thirty years, I'd been a law student, a law clerk, a lawyer, a private eye, an investigative reporter and, hey, even an underwear saleswoman. I had, I realized, accumulated some excellent skills in research (in addition to panty-folding). I should perform some research, that's what I should do. I would figure out a way to help Theo, or at least to understand the basics of the problem. Because right now, he wasn't getting out. He didn't have any liquid cash. Maggie was calling various bondsmen, but she warned we might not hear anything until the next morning.

Where to start?

I slid into my chair and scooted toward the computer.

I did searches for loan defaults, focusing primarily on business loans. I didn't know if HeadFirst's problems with defaulting on such a loan had led to the allegations against Theo or whether it was a simple product of it, so I just studied general information. I learned that defaulting on a business loan could mean serious consequences for a business. If they did default, and if property or funds had been used to secure the loan, those could be confiscated.

I decided to back up a little. Instead of trying to jump into the middle of this situation, I should start at the beginning. With Theo himself.

I put Theo's name into a search engine. When I saw how much was there, I decided to print out different articles or mentions about Theo or HeadFirst and study them. I approached them the way I did when preparing for a deposition or trial. I analyzed the documents for inaccuracies or irregularities or patterns. I studied the quotes. Nothing incongruous there. Everything showed Theo was a wunderkind of sorts, who'd graduated from high school, spent a year at Stanford and left to start HeadFirst, a web design software company, with his friend, and now business partner, Eric.

I clicked on "images." And there he was—my boyfriend at some black-tie event with a T-shirt and tuxedo jacket, his arms around a well-known philanthropist; my boyfriend on his Facebook page, a photo from years ago showing him with his arms around two very gorgeous girls; my boyfriend being handed an award, the banner behind him reading, Young Technology Award. He had a life before me, I realized for the first time. He had seemed so young to me—twenty-one when we met last spring—he had seemed so fresh and new that I hadn't imagined there could be much behind the gorgeous-guy front, but I was wrong. Theo had definitely lived a life before we met. And that's what worried me.

19

I decided to take a quick walk to refresh my brain. I threw a big sweatshirt of Theo's over my head and pulled a knit Bears hat over my curls and left the condo. But since I'd been in my office, the hallway on the second floor had become filled with moving boxes. It was like Theo moving in all over again. *What the...?*

A woman stuck her head out of the second-floor condo. She had shiny, dark brown hair that hung to her chin and a friendly smile. "Hey," she said. "Sorry about all this. I'll have it cleaned up soon. I'm Kim. I'm moving in."

"Oh, hi." My neighbor Steve had been trying to sublet his condo since he'd moved to the West Coast to be with a new girlfriend. "Welcome," I said, taking a few steps toward her. We shook hands. I wished I could give her a real smile, but my expression felt false as I parted my dry lips and tried to grin. "Did Steve tell you everything you need to know around here?" I asked, determined to be friendly.

She laughed. "Not really. He seemed so relieved to rent the place that he agreed to my first offer and arranged for the keys to be hand-delivered."

"Yeah, he's been trying for a while."

"Anything I *need* to know?"

"Just the garage situation and the back stairs. Oh, and the garbage. I can show you. Tomorrow, or…" I drifted off. *What would tomorrow be like? Or the day after that?*

Kim peered at me. "Are you okay?"

"Sure. Yeah. So the garbage situation…" But again I faltered.

She reached out a hand, lightly put it on my forearm.

And that kind gesture made my bottom lip tremble a little. "I'm sorry," I said, getting my composure together, right on the edge of crying. "It's been a bad day."

"Oh, I'm sorry, too." She rubbed my arm a little. "I know how those can be." She gave a laugh. "Do I ever."

"Yeah?"

"Oh, yeah."

Why did it feel ever so slightly better to be reminded that the God of Bad Times occasionally visited other folks?

She smiled at me and I smiled, too, feeling the little lift that comes with the hint of a possibility—that of a new friend.

"Hey, could I ask you about the heat in here?"

She pointed inside Steve's condo. "I can't seem to get it to work right."

"Sure." I had the feeling she was just asking to be nice, to get my mind off of my bad day. And I appreciated it.

Inside, I recognized Steve's furniture from the few times I'd been there, but all his personal effects were gone. A few suitcases and boxes covered most of the living room floor.

I showed her how to deal with our tricky thermostat controls. She offered a cup of coffee, which I didn't normally drink. Which I didn't normally like. "It's decaf," she said. "It won't keep you up."

"Sounds great," I said. Kim seemed so nice. I could pretend to like one cup of coffee.

She handed me a steaming cup that smelled amazing. It was coffee, sure, but it had the aroma of almonds and a hint of chocolate. I blew on my cup and took a small sip. Coffee, to me, was always bitter and harsh and sometimes sour. She'd clearly put some milk in my mug, and it was smooth and creamy as it filled my mouth and decadently rich as the smell filled my nose. For the first time, I kinda understood the whole coffee thing.

That little lift in my spirits kept moving higher as we sat on Steve's stools sipping coffee and talking as if we'd known each other awhile.

Kim filled me in on her recent breakup with a local doctor, causing her to move out of his place.

"What kind of doc is he?" I asked.

"Plastic surgeon." She smiled ruefully and pointed at her chest. "Can't you tell?"

Her breasts *were* rather large, now that I looked.

"Yeah, I've had just about everything done." Kim started listing the other products and procedures her ex had only been too happy to provide—Botox, Restylane, an eye lift, tummy tuck, butt lift. As she talked, I wondered how old she was. She had that vague, hard-to-tell-age quality that could range from twenty-seven to forty-seven. "But," she concluded with a sigh, "it didn't seem to matter ultimately. Once he was done fixing me, he was bored."

"And you? How were you?"

She looked at me, blinked her brown eyes a few times. "I loved him. I really did. I would have done anything."

There was the first lull in our conversation, and I heard the ticking of a clock that hung from Steve's kitchen wall.

"I'm sorry." I suddenly realized that even though we felt like friends already, I really didn't know what would help to make her feel better.

She shrugged. "What about you?"

I told her I used to be engaged to a guy named Sam. *Why are you leading with Sam?*

I told her about Theo. "You'll see him around the building," I said, then my words stopped abruptly. When would that be true? When would Theo get out of the MCC?

"So you're lucky in love," Kim said. "You had

that Sam guy, and now you have this young hottie who you really like." She peered at my face like she had earlier, with inquisitiveness, with empathy. "Who you maybe love."

"Huh. Lucky in love. I never thought about it like that," I admitted.

A phone rang. Kim moved her tall, perfect body from the stool and picked up a cell phone off the counter. She answered and listened. "Yeah, of course. Stop by." She looked at her watch. "Yes, I'll have it. I'll see you tonight."

She turned back to me. "Some friends are stopping over to wish me well on my new place. Just a casual thing for an hour or two. Want to join?"

I started to ask for details. I started to think about what Theo would want to do that night. But then I stopped all that. Theo wouldn't be home.

Still.

"I can't," I said. "I've had a hell of a day and a lot to do tomorrow." *Find funding to get my boyfriend out of jail. Start telling his friends and family.*

"Why don't you stop by for five minutes?" Kim asked. She reached out and touched my arm again. "Seems like you need a little break."

I looked at Kim and felt again that warm glow of a new friend. "I'll try," I said.

My phone rang. *Eric.*

"Kim, I've got to take this. I'll try to stop by later."

20

"Eric, are you in custody?" I said, scrambling to put my lawyer hat on, and scrambling up the stairs to my condo.

I probably couldn't represent Eric, I figured, since Maggie and I were already representing Theo. But I could help find someone.

"No," he answered quickly.

"You know about Theo being arrested?" I asked.

"Yeah, I got your messages."

I used the keypad to open my condo door, looking around now, instinctively asking, *Has anyone been here?* when I'd only been downstairs for thirty minutes.

"So have you heard anything from the Feds?" I asked Eric. As equal partners, if Theo were accused of fraud, wouldn't Eric be in some kind of trouble, as well?

"Yeah, I have." He said nothing else.

"Eric, what's going on? Do you need to talk about this with a lawyer? I could find—"

"I have someone," he said.

I walked through my silent condo, feeling a creeping sense of…*bad.* I tried to find a reasonable thing to say, despite my warring emotions. "That's good. Who did you get to represent you?"

He paused as if not sure what to reveal. He mentioned the name of a law firm—Heller & Heller—that I'd never heard of. He began telling me how he'd gotten their name from a family friend.

As he was talking, I hurried into my office, leaned over the computer and typed in the name of the firm and found it quickly. *Heller & Heller,* the home page said, *has earned a reputation for providing high quality, aggressive legal representation in Chicago and around the United States. We provide our clients with the highest standards of diligence, knowledge and professional advice and steadfastly protect our clients' constitutional rights.* It went on to list the various types of cases the firm could handle—*Mail Fraud, Wire Fraud, Bank Fraud, Hobbs Act Extortion, Possession and Delivery of Controlled Substances, Conspiracy and RICO Violations, Bank Robbery, Tax Offenses, Public Corruption, Embezzlement, Money Laundering.*

Eric had, I realized, gone quiet again. I debated what to say. Technically, if someone had a lawyer, I couldn't speak to them about the case if I was representing another litigant. But I could ask the question I'd called about to start.

"Eric," I said, "do you think you could help Theo post bond?"

A long inhale and exhale of breath. Still he said nothing.

I slid into the desk chair. "It's fifty thousand," I said.

At that Eric seemed to wince audibly. "We can't afford that."

"We?"

"The company."

"I know." I paused. He didn't offer any response. "Or I guess what I know is that something is going on with you guys. Theo got turned down for that mortgage. He was turned down because of an unpaid debt at HeadFirst, and now he's been arrested for some kind of fraud dealing with the company. And he said that you told him the books were messed up. Or something to that effect."

"Right."

"What's going on, Eric?"

A groan. "I'm not entirely sure."

"Well, then—"

"The attorney I hired said I shouldn't say anything. To anybody."

"You lawyered up pretty quick, didn't you?" I half noticed that I was speaking criminal-legal terminology without so much as blinking.

"Yeah. Don't you think I had to?" His voice sounded pained.

"I guess." I didn't know what to say. Although I'd been getting better at talking to clients (paying clients) about their criminal situation (*alleged* criminal situation), it was entirely different than talking with your boyfriend's business partner about something that had landed him in jail.

I decided to round back to the original topic. "Can you help us? Theo, I mean? Could *you* come up with the bond money?"

Nothing.

"Or part of it?" I said.

"I'm not sure, Izzy. I've lost a lot already."

"What do you mean?"

"I've got to go," Eric said. "I'm really sorry I can't help Theo anymore."

"Can't help Theo anymore? What does that mean?"

Eric didn't explain. "Sorry," he said, his voice a whisper, before he hung up.

21

"Did you know that she's had problems before?"

As José Ramon walked down Clark Street, he pulled the phone away from his ear, pushing his lips together to suppress his irritation. Then he spoke. "What the fuck are you talking about?"

He liked the phone calls from the kid with the random information, little things above and beyond what he had asked, but these calls with the open-ended questions, calls with no introduction as if the two of them were equals, rather than him being the boss, were grating his nerves.

"Izzy McNeil. She's been in trouble before."

He didn't know that Izzy McNeil was in trouble now except for the fact that she apparently had shitty taste in men, but his irritation waned. "Tell me."

José's steps slowed. With the sun long gone, it was really freaking cold out, not that it mattered. Despite where he had grown up, the Chicago weather didn't bother him. This indifference toward the conditions that he possessed was something he prided himself on. *Everyone* in Chicago said the weather didn't bother them—they had to in order to live here—but when it got to be a bleary November day, like today, the sky spitting little bits of hail, everyone's mood tanked and people showed their real colors. But not him. He could accept anything. Including the shitty fucking weather. He had been hurrying from a meeting back to the restaurant only because he knew there would be more bad news, more to manage. But maybe, maybe, the kid was about to help them, give them some kind of good news.

"You didn't know this before? It's easy to find on Google."

"Know *what?*" Now he was pissed off again. He increased his pace once more, passing an Irish bar that was blinged-out in more Christmas lights than should be legal.

"She was suspected in a murder not even a year ago."

His eyebrows rose toward his forehead. "You're fucking kidding me."

"I'm serious. Do you remember that broadcaster who died in the spring? Strangled."

"Hell yeah." He remembered Jane Augustine not just because she'd been ridiculously hot, and not just because she'd been in his restaurant a bunch of times, and not because she always brought people who spent money, and not even because she'd been murdered, which registered with him about as much as a mugging. He remembered her because after she died it had been revealed that she was a freak show in bed in a really good way, and he regretted not trying to tap that.

"Well, Izzy McNeil found her dead. And then the cops thought maybe she did it."

"Is that right?" He began to mull this over, but when he reached the door of the restaurant, he decided to throw it back at the kid. "What are you thinking?"

"I think we could use it. Or at least find out as much as we can and then keep it in our back pockets. Just in case. You want me to make some calls? I know some people in the CPD because—" The kid halted, likely recalling that he knew *exactly* why this knowledge of the Chicago Police Department existed and was none too happy about it.

"Yeah, handle it. And do not fuck it up." He paused. "Do. Not." He let the threat hang there, didn't have to make it known exactly what kind of trouble could follow a mess-up, didn't have to remind the kid that some already existing fuck-ups was why a debt was owed to him.

He hung up then, pleased that the kid had raised the bar and that if the bar wasn't met, then the kid knew exactly what could be expected.

22

I like to consider myself the Life of the Party. At least once in a while. But that night, Kim Parkway had a much better shot at the title than I did.

From the moment I walked back into Steve's place (now Kim's place, I reminded myself) around eight o'clock that night, she was grabbed in fierce hugs by entering friends. Most of them were male, quickly introducing themselves and their partners to everyone there, and then kissing Kim on her cheeks and hugging her some more. She was asked constantly, *How are you doing?* And it was usually followed with things like *He's such a jerk. He doesn't know what he's lost.* Everyone wanted to talk to her, it seemed. She was pulled into conversations in other rooms, only to return to the kitchen and living room, where others were waiting to talk to her.

The guests were garrulous and fun, too. At one point, a couple named Danny and Jeff and two of their friends, Jean Paul and Rudy, began a guessing game with me—*What kind of guy would Izzy date?*

"Someone ripped, absolutely ripped," Rudy suggested.

"No, no," Danny countered. *"Someone athletic sure, but more Man of Business. Except that he'd be hot, too."*

"Yeah, but he'd have some flaws," Jean Paul added. "Because he's human, too. He's real."

They looked at me for my reaction. I had to laugh. "You are on the mark. Precisely."

I told them about Theo. *I'll ignore the part about him being in jail. For now.*

"And that's it?" Jeff asked. "No one else?" Disappointment lingered in his tone.

"Well, I did run into my ex-fiancé recently at a nightclub."

That drew much more interest. "Tell, tell," Danny said.

And so I told them.

When I was done, Danny took the opportunity to give me a healthy pat on my ass, the way a football coach would a player. "A girl like you, with that body and that hair and that mind... Oh, you should have your pick of those two."

"You should get more than one pick," Jean Paul said.

"What is it with straight people and monogamy?" added Rudy.

That was the stumper question apparently, which drew everyone into slow shakes of the head, trying to ponder the heterosexual population and our continued and often failed attempts at faithfulness.

Kim came back into the room again. She had a

big smile on her face, her eyes wide. Seeing friends, apparently, was just what she needed. In fact, everyone seemed happier now that she was here.

My phone rang. Brad Jameson.

Earlier, after talking with Eric, I'd found Brad's number on the internet, but he hadn't answered when I called. I didn't know the number for Anna. And my attempts to reach Theo in the jail were patently unsuccessful.

"Did you think you could just phone him up?" Maggie said when I called her.

"He's my boyfriend," I reminded her.

"Right. Well. He's in a federal prison."

"It's not a prison," I said, bristling. "It's a jail. A holding cell. I thought *you* would remember that." I stopped. "Sorry. This whole thing is making me cranky."

"Who can blame you?" I heard Maggie moving around, then saying, "No, put that in the closet, will you?"

"Who are you talking to?"

"Bernard." She cleared her throat.

"Oh, tell him hi."

She did. Then fell silent.

"What's going on?"

"Ah…" More clanking in the background. Still more silence. She was like this so often lately.

"What. Is. Going. On?" I said. "C'mon, Mags."

"So you know how Bernard was moving here, but he wasn't going to move in?"

"Yeah."

"He's moving in."

"Wow." I laughed.

Maggie laughed a little, too. "We decided to throw caution to the wind." She sighed whimsically. "I guess I'm taking a chance."

"Wow, Mags. I'm excited for you."

"Thanks," she said. "Thanks a lot."

"Weird that we've both had guys move in recently."

"Yeah, that is weird."

Neither of us pointed out the obvious difference—the guy who'd moved in with me was in jail.

I had no idea what to make of Maggie's relationship with Bernard. They had professed their love almost immediately upon meeting in Italy and it almost seemed (although I'd seen them together only a few times) like they were already married. Like they were committed. Like they'd just been traveling the planet solo until they met one another.

But now Brad was calling me. I dodged out Kim's front door and into the hallway. "Brad, thanks for calling."

Thump-chucka-thump-chucka was all I could hear through the phone.

"Brad," I said, half-yelling. "Are you in a club?"

"Izzy?" Brad was almost shouting, too. "Is Theo with you? I can't find him. I wanted to invite the two of you to Deluxa."

I sighed heavily. The guy went to the clubs even on Monday nights? "No, Theo isn't with me." When I'd called Brad before, I hadn't wanted to leave him a message about Theo's arrest. I wanted to tell him in person, or at least in person on the phone.

"What's that?" he shouted. "Come out to Deluxa!" I heard the squeal of a woman in the background, more thumping music, someone ordering a bottle of Jack Daniel's.

"Brad, I need to talk to you."

"Sounds great. Talk to you when you get here!" I heard him laughing, telling someone Theo and Izzy were on their way.

I called him back but no answer.

Kim came out in the hallway. She was wearing platform boots, which made her at least five inches taller than me now. She threw an arm around my shoulder. "I'm so glad you came over."

"Me, too." I squeezed her around the waist. "But I've gotta take off."

"Putting yourself to bed? I should be doing that, too."

"No. I'm going out to Deluxa."

23

Deluxa was hopping, moving. Lights and music and waitresses swirled. I searched through the crowd for Brad and found him with LaBree in a booth similar to the one we'd been in last night. LaBree's friends were different that time. She introduced them. One was an interior designer and one was an HR person.

Green lights, emanating from the DJ booth, streaked and burst around me as I shook their hands. The lights and noise felt incongruous to what was happening outside the club.

"Brad!" My voice shot out—overly cheerful, overly loud to combat the music.

I was determined to be as gentle about this as possible. But what to say—*Hi! Just came to tell you your son is in jail. Yeah, they say he's like Madoff. But smarter. Isn't that nice?*

Maybe Brad knew of his arrest already? The thought hadn't occurred before, and it suddenly made me nervous. What kind of person would he be if that were true?

But as soon as Brad stepped from the table to talk to me, and LaBree and Company disappeared toward the restrooms, I could see Brad didn't know anything was amiss.

"Great to see you," he said with a smile. "Where's Theo?" He looked around again, an expectant expression.

"Theo is…" I stalled. "Could we talk somewhere else? Somewhere a bit quieter?"

Now Brad appeared concerned. "Sure, uh…" He looked around and I did, too. There was nowhere quiet in Deluxa.

We walked to the front door and stood behind the hostess stand, where the music was a tad softer. Still, I had to raise my voice and lean toward Brad's ear.

And then I just went for it. "Theo's been arrested," I half shouted in his ear.

His reaction was worse than I could have imagined. His features immediately twisted in pain and confusion. He put a hand out as if to break a fall he felt coming, but there was nothing to grab on to.

I put a hand on his shoulder. "Brad, I'm so sorry to just tell you like that." I gave him the story of the day—how it had started normally enough, with Theo off to work and me to court, but ended with Theo in jail.

"What could he be charged with?" Brad said, his voice shocked.

I explained the allegations as best I knew them.

"That's ridiculous," Brad said. "Theo would

never embezzle from anyone. Or defraud anyone. Or whatever they're saying." He shook his head back and forth.

"That's what I think. But I don't know much about HeadFirst."

Brad's head shaking stopped. "What about Eric?"

"I talked to him today. He hasn't been arrested, but he's hired lawyers."

Brad scowled. "Eric is more the leader in that company than Theo. Theo is just the creative side."

"That's what Theo has told me. He said he's been trying to learn more about the whole business," I said, "since he found out…" I stalled. Felt overwhelmed. But I took a breath and kept going. Brad and I talked again about how Theo had been turned down for a mortgage, and how maybe it was due to unpaid debt at work. Then I decided to change the topic. "I've asked my friend Maggie to handle the case. She's one of the best criminal lawyers in town. We'll both represent him."

"So he called you first," Brad said. When I nodded, he said, "He really loves you, Izzy."

The statement threw me. Was that true? "Thanks," I said. The only thing I could think to say. Then I remembered why I was there. I told him how they'd set the bond and that fifty thousand was required to get Theo out of jail.

"Fifty thousand?" Brad's eyes went big. "Wow." He nodded, thinking. "Well, maybe I can sell something, liquidate something. Let me start working on it."

"Okay, thanks."

"Yeah… Maybe…" His forehead was creased with concern. "This is horrible."

"Yes."

"Horrible."

I wondered for a second if he might cry. I considered giving him a hug, but I was afraid that if I did, I'd start crying, too.

He gestured with his head toward the booth. "I'm just going to say goodbye, and then I'll head out."

"Great. I'm glad we'll be able to get this taken care of."

He looked right at me then. "I hope we can." He paused and thought for a moment. "You said Maggie is the best. What's her opinion about the case?"

"We don't know enough yet about their allegations or their evidence. According to federal rules, they don't have to give us the evidence they have for a few months."

"A few months?" His voice sounded shocked and tormented.

"Yeah. The judge set a deadline so they can collect everything. It's making me crazy, too. Maggie is going to try and work something out." What Maggie had actually said was, *Let me see if I can back-door some information,* but I wasn't even sure what that exactly meant. No sense in getting Brad's hopes up any more than mine.

"Brad!" LaBree and another girl were squealing with laughter and headed in our direction.

Brad half glanced over his shoulder, but didn't respond. "I just hope I can get something liquidated in time. When do we need the money by?"

"Whenever we can get it. Theo will stay in the MCC until then." I felt a pang of fear and sadness. I wanted Theo back at my place—our place?—more than ever before.

"Can I see him?" Brad asked.

"I'll find out when visiting hours are."

"But can I go now?"

I shook my head.

Brad said nothing, his forehead still creased. "I can't believe this," he said, his voice sounding far away. "I'll try and find the money."

The uncertain tone of his voice scared me. Then I thought of something else. "Someone should tell Anna," I said. "Do you want me to call her?"

"Yes. If you would. I'm sure she'd rather speak with you."

I looked at my watch. It was getting late. "I'll call her in the morning."

"You really should call her now."

I nodded and took Anna's number from him.

Leaving Deluxa and stepping into the misty, cold November night made me feel alone. I hailed a cab and called Anna Jameson.

I didn't hesitate when she answered. I just laid out the story of Theo's arrest.

"What?" she said. "*What?* This can't be. Oh, God, no."

I filled her in on everything I knew, including the fact that Theo didn't have bond money, Eric didn't either (or wasn't willing to post it) and Brad had said he would try to liquidate some asset as soon as possible.

Anna made a scoffing sound. "Brad loves his son. I know that. But he can't take care of anything quickly."

"He seemed really broken up about it."

"Maybe."

"That's what he said."

"Hold on one second." I heard the phone being put down, then the click-clack of fingers on a keyboard. "Izzy, I just checked my retirement account online. I have enough. I'll get the bond money for Theo."

I started to say that she should keep the money she'd saved, that she shouldn't use it to pay bond money for her son. But if she didn't, who would?

"Thanks, Anna," I said.

24

On Tuesday morning, bleary from my never-ending Monday, I met my dad at a Greek diner on Halsted Street that opened early for breakfast. I watched as my father adjusted his copper glasses, looking at the gyro-and-feta omelet he'd ordered as if studying it like a specimen in a lab. Then he tentatively cut open the omelet, putting a delicate bite in his mouth.

"Hmm," he said, as if considering it. Then, "Mmm." He took another bite, while I watched. My father had rarely seemed interested in food. In fact, he rarely let on when he was interested in anything.

"Why did you choose this place?" I asked. When I reached out to him, he had immediately made the suggestion for our meeting place.

He took another bite. "I'm trying to learn the different parts of the city. You know. Ones I'd never paid attention to. I really only know the parts…"

His words died away and I finished for him. "You only know the parts of the city where Mom went or I went or Charlie. Because you followed us while we thought you were dead." A silent bomb seemed to detonate. "Sorry," I mumbled. "I don't know why I said it in a mean way like that. I'm a little off."

"You certainly have reason."

"No, I am sorry. And I need a break from thinking about Theo. Let's just have a normal conversation like two family members would in the morning."

"Perfetto." I liked how he spoke Italian when he wasn't censuring himself.

He looked at me. I could see from the way his eyes squinted under his glasses that he was struggling with what to say. He opened his mouth and closed it. Then opened it again and said, "That's a lovely suit you have on."

I couldn't help it. I laughed. It was my father's way of trying to bridge a gap, to try and comfort me in some small way. I looked down at the herringbone suit I wore with a purple ruffled blouse. I remembered in a burst when I'd worn the same outfit to negotiate the contract of an executive producer with a local TV news show. That was only a year or so ago, and yet the memory was hard to hold on to, so different it was from my world now.

"So what are you working on with Mayburn?" I asked, just for something to get the conversation going.

My father looked up from his plate. "This and that."

"What kind of this?"

He said nothing.

"What kind of that?" I shook my hair off my shoulders. His reticence was starting to make me hot with irritation.

"You know the attorney-client privilege?" he said.

I nodded.

"I believe there is a similar such privilege when you're working on an investigation." He said nothing else, then resumed eating. He really could be infuriating.

"But even with the attorney-client privilege," I said, raising an index finger, as if to represent that this was point one in a list of many, "I can tell you about the type of cases we're working on without revealing any specific information that my clients told me. For example, I can tell you that I'm working on a case where people loaded a whole bunch of drugs…" I stopped myself, felt the lowering of my brow. "Let me rephrase that. People had *allegedly* loaded a whole bunch of drugs onto a boat. See? I'm not telling you their names. I'm not telling you any details about these guys. I'm not telling you who they are or anything they said to me. So come on. We're trying to establish a relationship here."

Well, that caught his attention. He looked up at me, his eyes rather wide. Did I see a shot of hope or excitement? He put his fork down. "Okay. Okay. I understand what you're saying." He seemed to be pondering. I realized this was probably strange for him—sharing anything. He had lived his life mostly in Italy, working to shut down an arm of the Italian Mafia called the Camorra. And he had trained to keep everything quiet. Silent.

Then he started talking. "We're working on a case where this young woman was in France, a college student from America. And she was arrested for drug trafficking to Thailand."

"Wow," I said. "Hey, we're both working on drug cases." It wasn't the usual thing that brought glee to a family, but it was a start. "Who hired you? Generally speaking, I mean. The student?"

He hesitated, seemed to be considering whether answering that question would be revealing too much information, then he shrugged. "The parents retained us. John knows them from growing up along the Northern Shore."

"The Northern Shore?"

He blinked. "The suburbs north of the city?"

"Oh. That's the *North* Shore. And you'd say he grew up *on* the North Shore. Not *along*."

My father nodded, seemingly un-insulted by my vernacular lecture. "It's a really interesting case. It's giving me a lot of opportunity to utilize my contacts in Europe."

"That's fantastic." There was an enthusiasm in my voice, as if I were encouraging a small child into using their potential, pushing to see what they were capable of.

My father caught it. He looked at me quietly.

Then lifted his fork and cut off an end of his omelet. We sat in silence.

When he still said nothing, apparently unperturbed by the silence at our table, I was forced to realize our daddy-daughter talk was probably over. I took a breath. "So," I said, "tell me what else you know about Theo's case."

"I found out that the Feds were investigating HeadFirst."

"I know that. But how?"

He chewed more of his omelet. "I have a number of contacts who give me a heads-up if they come across something I should be interested in."

It reminded me of what Vaughn said about cops keeping an eye out for other people's cases.

"I learned," Christopher McNeil continued, "that there was possible fraud, possible embezzlement, maybe some other things, and then yesterday morning I found out they were specifically looking at Theo."

"And you heard that he was like Madoff?" I said, incredulous. "I've been up thinking about that all night. How is that true? Madoff was involved with securities. He ran an investment firm."

My father gave me a bland look. "I think it was a vague comparison, that's all. But the core of it is the same—they say people invested money in his company, and he bilked them of it."

"But even if that's all true, which I'm having a hard time believing, why wouldn't the government go after Eric, too? If HeadFirst was wreaking all this havoc, why hasn't he been arrested? From what I know, he's more the business-side guy anyway."

My dad put his fork down. "Have you spoken with Eric?"

I told him I had. And that Eric had retained legal counsel.

"When do you believe he hired them?" my dad asked.

"Probably as soon as he heard about the investigation."

"Probably." My dad pushed his omelet plate away.

"And...?" There was something more, something he was thinking but not saying.

"And when do you think that was?"

"What was?" I asked.

"When do you think Eric heard about the investigation?"

"Recently?"

My dad shrugged.

"Make your point, please," I said.

"You're right that Eric likely hired counsel when he first heard from the Feds. But what if that wasn't recently? What if it was weeks ago or months ago or even a year ago?"

A beat went by. Then another. A busboy clanged an armful of plates and coffee mugs into a plastic container. The door of the kitchen swung open and closed and opened again. I thought about what my dad was saying. I was trying to no longer become exasperated at how he liked people to figure things out for themselves. I didn't know if that trait had to do with his background working for the FBI or his covert work in Italy. Lately, I'd just accepted that my father was the person who would lead the proverbial horse to water, but he would never force the horse to swallow anything.

I decided to put on my lawyer hat and treat him as a witness on cross-examination. "You're suggesting that Eric might have heard about the investigation into HeadFirst before Theo."

"Yes."

"You don't know this for sure, but it's a strong feeling of yours."

"Correct."

"You're also suggesting that Eric didn't tell Theo about the investigation."

"Let me ask you a question. When is the earliest Theo knew about the problems with HeadFirst?"

I thought about it. "Well, last week was when he knew something was really wrong with the company. Because he was turned down for a mortgage. On Sunday, he learned that there was a commercial loan that was defaulted on, which had Eric's and Theo's individual names on it. It was obtained when the company started and they had nothing. So Theo and Eric were looking into what was going on at the company. Theo didn't mention anything about a federal investigation, though. I got the feeling he didn't know until he was arrested."

My father was silent, but I could read the question he was now asking me. *So what does that say about Eric and his involvement?*

I ran through what I'd learned about criminal investigations from working with Maggie and her grandfather. "The authorities have to get evidence, or at least indication that evidence exists, before they arrest anyone, or even before they execute a search warrant."

"Right," my dad said. "And have you seen anything to indicate a search warrant was ordered?"

"Not yet, but we haven't really seen *anything*. Maggie says they have thirty days to get the case indicted, and we'll get some information then, but they've already requested and been granted extensions. Likely, it'll be three months."

My father pulled his plate back toward him, cut off another bite of omelet. He was giving me time, it seemed, to draw some conclusion.

But I didn't need long. "No one has mentioned anything about a search warrant," I said. "Not Eric, not Theo. And not the Feds. Because there wasn't one. And the HeadFirst office isn't the kind of place anyone could just stroll in. Yesterday in court, Theo told me where an extra key card was, and he had to give me all these instructions and two sets of codes in case I needed to get into his office."

"So if they didn't get a search warrant," my father said, dabbing his mouth with a white paper napkin, "then how did they get the evidence they needed to arrest Theo?"

The answer came quick and clean. "Eric." I

smacked the tips of my fingers on the table, wishing I could slam both hands, feeling angry on behalf of Theo. "Eric was working with the Feds. And that's why he wasn't arrested."

"We don't know that for sure, but..." My father raised his fork and pointed it at me. Then he gave me a succinct nod, as if to say, *Bingo.*

25

As usual, Eric Deringer was the first to arrive at the offices of HeadFirst. He had always cherished the mornings, being able to knock things off his list, before Theo arrived with his loud, joking ways that always got the rest of the staff in a happy mood. Yet there had been no happy moods around the office lately, not from Theo's side. The staff was more subdued than usual, although they had no idea the cause.

But they would today. Because today Eric had to tell them that Theo had been arrested. He had to tell them that HeadFirst had major issues. And worst of all, he had to tell them that some of them could be let go.

Yet with the place desolate and empty, he couldn't get anything done at his personal office, so he took a pile of personnel folders, along with a laptop, into the glass-walled conference room. Maybe he could focus in there. He put the folders in rows, dividing them along the lines of which employees had been with the company the longest,

then rearranging them in the order of who the company could do without. He tried making spread-
sheets to keep track of his analysis, but he kept
changing the results, kept reshuffling and rearranging the folders, because he couldn't imagine Head-
First without any of these people.

He heard the quiet *ding* that meant a key card
had been slid through the slot next to the front door,
then heard the door open.

He stood and steeled himself. The first employee
had arrived.

Theo's arrest had not made the news, thank God.
He had no idea the reason for that, except that the
U.S. Attorneys likely wanted to keep it quiet for
now. And that made him nervous. Did it signify
that they planned on other arrests?

Feelings of futility and ignorance swarmed him.
Those feelings were becoming second nature by
now, but it didn't make them any less uncomfortable.

Eric walked toward the door of the conference
room, ready to greet whatever employee was there,
ready to simply tell them straight out what was happening. He couldn't stand the secrecy anymore.
The fact was there were still too many secrets out
there, many of which he didn't know or understand,
and that left him feeling jarred and slanted, and he
didn't like it, couldn't take it.

He pulled open the conference door. He expected
a programmer named David, who usually arrived
first, but instead of David's methodical, heavy

steps, he heard *click, click, click,* fast and sharp on the hardwood floors.

The sound came quicker, sounded angrier.

"Izzy?" he said, his voice shocked, when he saw who was there. "How did you get in?"

When Eric and Theo first built the office, consultants had told them, *Put in high security, spend more than you think you have to, because you'll always need it.* Eric thought it extreme at first, then had grown grateful for the advice as they became more successful.

Izzy held up a key card and a piece of paper with what he recognized as security code numbers. "We need to talk."

Ten minutes later and it felt like an hour had gone by. Eric had always thought Izzy was pretty— that red-orange hair, the body. Although Theo used to be the kind of guy who talked about his sexual exploits (he certainly had enough of them), he'd gone mostly silent when he started dating Izzy McNeil.

She's different was what Theo said to him often. *She's the real deal.*

Real what? Eric remembered asking him once. They were at a Cubs game, one of the first of the season. Although they could afford box seats, they preferred the bleachers, where they could squeeze in next to a pack of hot girls and soon find themselves in a party in left field. But that day, Theo wasn't interested in women. He just wanted to talk about this redheaded lawyer he'd met. He'd said how smart she was. Said it so many times, Eric had started to wonder if it was something Theo was saying to reassure himself, because it seemed apparent that Theo was trying to move from the vacuous-gorgeous types to the accomplished-gorgeous types.

Eric had met Izzy briefly here or there, and Theo was right—she seemed intelligent and authentic. Another time, when he'd been unable to fight his curiosity, he'd asked Theo how she was in bed. Theo just closed his eyes and smiled and said something like, *Unbelievable. I can't even describe...*

And so Eric had always been impressed and a little fascinated with Izzy, but he'd always been on the outside, looking in. Yet now, suddenly she was very much *in* his office and *in* his face, and she was showing no sign of backing off.

"You and Theo have known each other how long now?" she asked, demanding.

He had sat down at the conference table when she first entered, and invited her to do the same, but she remained on her feet, her black coat still on. She had her arms crossed and her face was a little red.

"We met the day the semester started," he said. "Freshmen weren't supposed to be in this mathematics class I was in, but somehow Theo had gotten permission. I knew it must mean the dude was smart. I was right. We started working together on some things that day, just for the hell of it."

"And now, here you are, owning a company to-gether."

"Yeah. Here we are."

"And you're supposed to be best friends."

"I thought we were."

"What's that supposed to mean?" Her voice was loud.

"Izzy, I told you I have a lawyer."

"And I told you I'm just here to ask some questions about you and Theo, and the loyalty I thought you had for him."

Eric felt a sear of pain somewhere in his chest, and then…oh, Jesus, he felt like he might cry.

He looked down, squeezed his eyes shut. *Stop it, stop it, stop it,* he told himself.

But when he looked up, Izzy's face was full of sympathy. "Oh, honey," she said.

And that did it. He couldn't help it. A few tears slid down his cheeks.

Izzy unbuttoned her coat and threw it on a chair. She came around the table and sat on a black leather chair next to him, scooting it next to him. She put her arm around his shoulders. "Okay," she said. "Let's just stop for a second."

He hung his head.

"C'mere," she said. She pulled his shoulder so that his chair swung to face her. And then she hugged him.

A sob escaped him, and he cried a little. Felt like he used to when he was a kid and his mom was comforting like this. Before his mom remarried and moved to Tucson. She had a new life, and she didn't need him or his brother anymore. Didn't even need his money since she'd married a wealthy doctor who'd created some kind of coronary stent that had made him way wealthier than Eric.

He cried a little more into Izzy's shoulder, felt the softness of her long, curly hair and at that moment, instead of resenting Theo, he envied him.

"Sorry," he said finally. He sat back and wiped his eyes with his hands. "Sorry," he said again, pointing at Izzy's purple shirt. There was a wet splotch on it the size of a quarter.

Izzy glanced down, didn't even react to it. "You okay?"

"I don't think so."

She waited.

"I don't know," he said.

She put her hands in her lap and clasped them, then sat up straight, composing herself. "Look, Eric. I don't know what in the hell is going on here. I'm just trying to help Theo, and I thought that's what you would be doing, too."

"I *am*. I *have* been. I've been trying to help both of us, but it's not my fault we're in this situation."

"So it's Theo's fault? Explain that to me. Please."

"My lawyers…" He heard the warnings they'd given him.

She held up a hand. "Don't tell me anything you said to your lawyers or vice versa. I don't want you to blow your attorney-client privilege. But tell me this—were you working with the Feds? Without telling Theo?"

He waited a long time, he enjoyed the way life was different now than it would be in a few seconds. Finally, he said, "I had no choice."

"Why?" Her voice was anguished. "Eric, you're the person he trusts most in this world. Loves most."

"Except for you."

She shook her head. "We're not talking about me and Theo. We're talking about the two of you. You're best friends and partners. What happened to change that? Why would you go around him on this?"

He thought about what to say. The lawyers, to whom he'd paid a thirty-five-thousand-dollar retainer—*that'll get us going,* they'd said—would want him to call them now, to tell Izzy to leave his office. And he was about to. But he felt he owed her something. Owed Theo. "I talked to them.... I helped them, I guess, because I thought Theo had caused our problems."

"Do you still think that?"

"Likely."

"Whoa. Back the truck *up.*" She sounded exasperated. "Maybe you caused the problems, Eric."

The lawyers in his head were talking now, talking louder and louder and they were telling him the same thing he had been telling himself a minute ago when he was crying—*stop it, stop it, stop it.*

He took a deep breath, stepped back into the

adult he was now—the businessman, the person who had to deal with this situation no matter what.

He stood. "Thanks for coming, Izzy. But now you have to go."

26

Maggie appeared in my office doorway, arms crossed over her chest, a stern expression on her face.

"What's that look?" I asked.

She stepped inside, her frown deepened. Unfortunately, I'd seen her wear that frown—or something like it—for a while. What was going on with her?

"I just got a call from the Cortaderos," she said.

"Is something happening with the coke-on-the-boat case?" That was Q's nickname for the Cortadero case. I felt a pinch of excitement, of something different than the confusion and sadness and fear I'd been feeling for Theo. And I guess for me. After talking with Eric that morning, I'd gone to work, constantly checking my phone and my email, waiting for word from Anna that she had posted bail.

"You know that the Cortaderos are the cartel family involved in most of our big drug cases?" Maggie said.

"Right."

She didn't say anything then, just started gnawing at the corner of her bottom lip. I knew that habit of hers. She was worried. And although she'd seemed worried (and distracted and a little off) for a while, she was really worried now. Her light pink lip gloss soon disappeared from her mouth.

"So what did they say?" I asked.

"They said they're pulling all of our work."

"What?"

"Yeah. Except for your boat case. It's too close to the arrest on that one. They think if they get another attorney now, it will signal weakness and cause the prosecutors to go after them harder."

"But other than the drug-boat case?"

"They want us off everything."

"Why?"

Maggie looked around. She didn't say anything.

"C'mon, Mags," I said. "This is getting old. Tell me what the hell is going on with you."

"Me? This is because of Theo."

I blinked. "What does Theo have to do with a cartel family?"

"I thought you could tell me. They specifically said his name and said if we're Theo's attorney, we're not going to be theirs."

My turn to be silent.

"You have no clue what Theo has to do with the Cortaderos?" Maggie said.

"No clue." Theo and a cartel family? What could be the connection there? Had he been selling drugs?

Is *that* what Eric had meant when he talked about
Theo "causing" their problems? Was that why the
Feds were involved? But there were no charges
that could lend themselves to any allegations about
drugs.

"Well, as soon as he's out of the MCC, you better
talk to your boyfriend because as long as we're representing *him,* the Cortaderos said we won't be representing them." She started chewing at the corner
of her upper lip then. I'd never seen that one.

"Why do I feel like there is more?" I asked.

"Well, I was just talking to Marty about it."
Maggie always called her grandfather by name
while at work. "If the Cortaderos pull all their
work, then…"

"Then what?"

Her expression grew stern, eyebrows drawn
closer together. She said nothing. She was killing
me with this stuff.

Still, I played out her comments in my head.
She'd called him Marty; that meant they were talking business. If they were talking business, then
what topics might arise? I had it. "Do the Cortaderos have enough cases right now that they're paying
for a lot of the firm expenses?" I asked.

Maggie nodded, solemn.

"If most of their work disappears would you still
be able to pay an associate? Like me?"

Maggie shrugged in a grand fashion.

"What about a manager like Q?"

She shook her head definitively then.

I didn't know what to say. In addition to Theo and his problems, I could lose my job again? And Q, who was so happy now that he was working here…? I felt my mouth hanging open a little.

I thought about Theo and the Cortaderos and once more I was baffled. The topic of drugs had never even come up between Theo and me. I didn't do them. And as far as I knew, he didn't, either. I tried to imagine him selling drugs. The image was grainy and in the distance.

"They didn't give you *any* reason?" I asked Maggie.

"No. Just that they can't work with a lawyer who is representing Theo. When I asked for specifics, their local attorney in Mexico reminded me about attorney-client privilege and all but threatened me not to repeat this."

"Whoa."

"Yeah." Maggie uncrossed her arms and swung them back and forth a little as if stretching them out in preparation for a fight. "I don't like anyone threatening me." She stopped the swinging. "But they're the kind of people you take very, very seriously when they do."

Maggie was wearing a black wrap dress and a large gold, cuff bracelet that I knew she'd gotten from Bernard.

I pointed at her bracelet, wanting desperately for a moment to get a break in my mind from Theo and the case. And now the Cortaderos. "Enjoying the new jewelry?" I asked.

She nodded. Then there was no more movement. Nothing, just Mags and me. I felt like it was a cross-roads, like Maggie and I were at a time when our lives were very close together. So why did it also feel like we were staring down two different divergent paths?

Maggie slipped into a chair opposite my desk. Another smile. "I love having Bernard in my house," she said, her voice low as if divulging a large secret. "He's so great."

I nodded vigorously in a show of support.

"And there's the stuff I didn't expect," she said, her mouth suddenly running. "He does so much for me. So many little things." She listed off a number of household chores. "I guess I've never had anyone before who helped me with that stuff."

"I'm glad. You deserve it."

"So do you, Iz, with Theo. I just hope…" she said, her voice dropping lower, almost to a whisper. "Iz, this is getting weird."

I felt a thin layer of fear enter my body, as if through the cells of my skin, and as soon as I could speak I did. "I know."

"Anything new?" She meant on Theo's case.

"Lots. I talked to Theo's partner this morning." I told her about my surprise meeting with Eric. "He said it was Theo's fault—actually, he said it was *likely* Theo's fault—that they were in this mess."

Maggie went into her patented lawyer mode—face tucked in around itself, as if the gathering of skin and muscle could help her figure this all out. "Did he elaborate?"

"No."

She nodded, face still tight. "Keep going."

"Also, my dad figured out that Eric was probably working with the Feds for a while."

Maggie's face cleared, like someone who'd seen a white light. "Huh. Yeah. Yeah, that's right. I can't believe I missed that. I'm so weird these days, so…"

I wanted more. "So…what? You're so weird, and so…"

She shook her head. "I'm fine. So does Eric have an attorney?"

I told her the name of the firm he'd hired.

"They're good. That'll make the case easier actually. We work well with them."

"Well, that's some good news," I said. "I guess. I just can't wait to talk to Theo. I'll go see him during visiting hours if he doesn't get out sooner. I need to find out more about what he knows."

"Even if he doesn't think he knows anything," Maggie added.

"Exactly. Here's the thing, though. I'm his attorney, right?"

Maggie gave me a brisk nod.

"So I can't necessarily push Theo, right? I mean, isn't that what you and your grandfather have been trying to teach me for a while? That you can't force your defendant to tell you if he's guilty or not? Or to give you any more information than he's willing up front? In fact, sometimes it's better to know as little as possible."

"Yeah. You're right." She shifted around, tugged at the neckline of her dress. "But now this is affecting our business."

"I know." I groaned. "This is such *Beijing.*"

She peered at me. "Another replacement word for 'bullshit'?"

I nodded.

"They're getting worse."

"Gotcha."

Q stepped into the office. "Hey, all, everyone ready for a good day?"

Since joining the firm, Q liked to give everyone daily pep talks. Like the good coach he was, he rubbed his hands together. "So, Mags," he said. "You've got a prove-up at ten, right?"

"Yeah," she said distractedly.

"You ready?"

"Mmm-hmm."

"Okay, Iz. I know we're waiting for Theo to get out, but you've got to keep busy in the meantime." God love Q. He knew how my mind worked. He knew I could spin into a fit of worry if I didn't do something other than think about Theo's case. "So don't forget you're handling the Marvin Wills case. We have to file those pleadings today."

I pushed a stack of paper at him. "They're already done. They just need attachments."

"Good work, good work. Then move to the Melanie Chambers case." Q gave a pleased smile. But then he stopped, finally seeming to catch on to our somber mood. "What's going on, ladies?"

Maggie told him about the Cortaderos. That left even Q speechless.

Then I stood. And left.

27

Awkward, that's what it was. Awkward, awkward, awkward.

Over the course of my relationship with Theo, I'd felt a lot of different emotions, but this discomfiting self-conscious awfulness had never been one of them. He appeared to be so very aware of his own physical state, of how his place in the world had changed.

He was out of jail. That was the good part. But he didn't seem to be the Theo I knew. Although he wore the same clothes they'd arrested him in, he carried his other belongings in a paper sack that seemed as flimsy as his mental state.

"Let's get out of here," I said.

"Is my mom around? I want to thank her."

Right then Anna walked into the lobby of the MCC. "Honey," she said, pulling him into a hug. She wore a peach-colored cashmere cape, and with her rosy cheeks and wind-swept hair, she looked a stark contrast to the pallid son who usually bore a carefree, sun-kissed resemblance to her.

When he tried to pull back a moment later, Anna clung to Theo. I could see that she was fighting tears, that she didn't want him to see them.

The whole scene made me want to bawl wildly.

Instead, I took a huge breath, and held up my phone, told them I was going to double-check on a few things. "I'll give you a minute."

"Thank you, Izzy."

By the time I returned a few minutes later, Anna and Theo were talking quietly, their heads inclined. For a moment, I could imagine Anna and her son, when he was younger, when there weren't such things to worry about. And it felt like a rip in the fabric of my heart. I knew my mom had worried about me at times. How did mothers do such things? Put up with so much for the sake of their kids? I wasn't sure I could ever do it.

"Go home and get settled," Anna said to Theo. "I'll call you in an hour."

He nodded and thanked her again. Then she left.

"Your mom is a trooper," I said, as Theo and I pushed through the doors, finally out onto the street.

"She is. She's been through a lot. My dad behaved like a jackass to her."

"Really?" I asked, wanting to talk about something other than his case.

"Yeah. Especially when she had cancer and no insurance, and he wouldn't help her out because he was too busy with his own world. And his collection of twentysomethings."

"Ouch."

"Yeah."

"She told me at lunch that she and Brad were like brother and sister now."

Another laugh. "Yeah, the kind that don't like each other very much." He shrugged. "I'm lucky she came through for me. With the bail."

"Amen to that."

Clark Street in the Loop only moved southbound, so we walked to LaSalle and hailed a cab, giving my address on Eugenie.

Neither of us said anything for a minute. It was freezing and Theo actually seemed to shiver, something I'd never seen him do. I leaned forward and put my face through the space in the Plexiglas toward the driver. "Can you turn on the heat, please?" I asked.

"It don't work back there," was all he said.

I gave Theo a smile that felt very false. "We'll be home soon." I liked using the word *home,* as his mother had. I hoped it would give him some kind of comfort.

But home was where the awkwardness intensified. Theo showered, taking a long time, and when he came out of the bedroom in faded jeans and an army-green sweater, he didn't look much better.

He sat down next to me at the bar in the kitchen, where I had an untouched tea in front of me. "Let's not talk about me," he said, as if sensing impending questions. "How are you?"

"We got some bad news at work." I didn't mention right away that this would, in fact, be a talk about him.

"Oh, shit. What's going on?" He looked interested, but then a wary look passed through his eyes, followed closely by—if I read it right—alarm. "Is it about my case?"

I liked that he could read me like that. "Yeah. Sort of." I explained to him the phone call Maggie had received from the Cortadero family.

"How in the hell does this Mexican family have anything to do with my case?"

"You tell me." There was a snap to my voice, one that was foreign to me.

His expression softened, and he moved closer to me. "I'm sorry," he said. "Let's go into the living room.

"I don't do drugs," he said, when we were on the couch, turned toward each other. My body felt stiff, as if I were bracing for…what? I didn't know. He kept talking. "I mean, I did shrooms once my freshman year in college, but I was a mess."

"Well, just because you don't do drugs doesn't mean you don't sell them."

His eyes narrowed. He looked pissed. "I don't *sell* drugs, either. God, Iz, I can't believe you would think that."

"I don't know what to think!" I felt hot suddenly. I put a hand under my hair and lifted it up. "What do you expect me to think when Maggie gets this call and the firm gets fired from a lot of work?"

He didn't have an answer.

"What could the reason be for why we can't work with them if we work with *you?*" I asked.

"I don't have any idea. None. What did you say their name was?"

"The Cortaderos." I spelled it for him.

"I've never even heard of them."

We were both silent for a moment.

"What about Eric?" I said.

"What about him?"

"Well, maybe it's got something to do with him. Maybe he's somehow involved with this."

I expected him to protest right away, to say something like, *Hey, Eric is a good dude.* But Theo took a moment to think about it.

"I've never known him to do drugs," he said finally. "Or to sell drugs."

"You wouldn't necessarily know. I mean, what does a drug dealer look like? I'm sure that there are lots of people whom we would never suspect that do drugs and sell drugs."

More silence.

"I suppose that's true," he said. He looked so tired then, more exhausted than I'd ever seen him, almost defeated. I scooted toward him, placed a hand on his arm. When the defeated look deepened, I climbed onto his lap. I hugged him, and, like a child needing to be comforted, he put his face on my chest. I squeezed tight. I thought about hugging Eric that morning.

After a few moments like that, I moved back,

and then I braced myself again, because I had to tell Theo that Eric had been working with the Feds.

The heartbreak on Theo's face—that face framed by tawny brown hair, soft and thick, those lips that now seemed to have no words—nearly sunk me.

"He was working with the Feds?" Theo asked, a shocked tone. He'd asked that question twice already.

And so I told him again. "That's the reason he wasn't arrested. That's also why there was no search warrant."

"Okay, but tell me this. What did he give them? I don't know of anything there is to give. He said he was looking into the issues at HeadFirst, but he also told me he hadn't found anything."

I could only shrug.

"Does he think I'm guilty?" Theo asked, his tone even more baffled. "Does he think I did something?"

I tried to hug him again, but Theo was stiff, his body an unyielding mass now. And he was sending out waves of energy, an anxiety that was almost palpable.

"Iz," he said, "I didn't do anything wrong."

I believed Theo. I did. His reaction to the Cortaderos news? He had seemed as befuddled as I was, as Maggie had been. And his response to

Eric's betrayal? It was shock, nerves. I trusted him.
I did.

But if he were telling the truth about not doing
something wrong, then who had?

28

The next day at work, I pushed aside everything on my desk, retrieved the file for the coke-on-a-boat case and tried to create a timeline of what might have happened—from the purchase of the boat to the alleged importing of cocaine, the packing of the boat, the planned trip down the Mississippi.

I stopped there. If they had been successful, if the seizure had not occured, what would have happened with the massive amount of drugs when they reached New Orleans?

I found Maggie in her office. But instead of the piles of transcripts and motions that usually covered her own desk, she had design magazines lined in rows across the desktop.

"What do you think about this look?" Maggie said, waving me in and turning a magazine around to face me as I took a seat. The glossy photo-spread showed an Asian-inspired room with red paper screens, stone floors and lots of dragonheads on the corners of the furniture.

"It looks like a temple," I said.

"A temple?" Maggie swung the magazine around and scowled at it. "I don't want to live in a temple."

"What did I miss? Why would you live in a temple?"

She sighed, looked at me. "Bernard doesn't like my apartment decor."

"Why? He doesn't like modern?" Maggie's place in a South Loop high-rise was her haven, completely different from the wood, leather and crap-laden confines of her office. Her home, instead, was white and minimal with low, Swedish-style couches and pristine glass tables.

"He likes modern, but wants something more Filipino, more Asian."

"And what do you think about that?" I crossed my arms across my chest, and settled in for what was hopefully a long and distracting chat about absolutely nothing concerning Theo or his business or his case or drug dealers. I hoped I'd learn more about what had been going on with Maggie lately.

"I think I don't like Asian," Maggie said. "I think I never have."

"So you'll compromise."

"I don't want to compromise." Maggie voice was getting a little louder. "Not about my house." She looked down at the magazines on her desk. "I can't live with dragons." She returned her gaze to mine, fear in her eyes. "What if we're doing the wrong thing?"

"Oh, c'mon, get a dragon lamp instead of a couch and you can always get rid of it."

"No! I'm talking about Bernard and me and…
What if we're making the wrong choice?"

"You're in love with him," I reminded her.

"Yeah, but will I still be next summer? And by
then I'll have…" She shook her head.

I could only blink and look at her for a moment,
surprised at the uncharacteristic show of self-doubt.
"You'll have…" I finally prompted her.

"An apartment filled with Buddhas and bam-
boo."

"Mags," I said, "you make good life decisions.
You always have."

"But what if this is the bad one? The bad one that
derails my whole career, my whole life?"

"Whoa, whoa, Mags." I reminded her of the
way she'd negotiated her life, her career, with total
aplomb.

"*Aplomb?* What does that even mean?" Maggie
scoffed. "Wyatt was a bad decision. One I made at
least twice."

Wyatt was a lying, cheating charmer Maggie had
dated on two disastrous occasions. So she had a
decent point there.

"But!" I said, suddenly striking on an idea that
felt like it had a lot of truth to it. "Being with Wyatt
made you realize exactly what you *don't* want.
That's why you were able to recognize the bril-
liance of you and Bernard, and the fact that you *do*
want him. You do want a life with him."

Her mouth opened as if to respond in protest, but then she fell back against her chair, with a breath of air escaping her. "You're right."

"I'm right," I repeated, liking the sound of it. If only I could be assured of such rightness in my own life. "So, Mags," I said, "shifting gears for a sec to work. I'm looking at the coke-in-a-boat case."

She sat up, nodded at me to continue.

"I'm wondering what they would have done with the drugs—"

"And by *they*," Maggie said, interrupting me, "you mean the people who were not Cortadero employees, who were apparently going rogue with this shipment of cocaine?"

"Uh, right."

Maggie took her clients seriously. And since our defense in this case was going to be lack of knowledge, lack of employment of the people involved, she was going to take every opportunity to talk up that defense, even around the office so she could use it, feel more and more confident about it.

"So," I continued, "what would *they* have done with the drugs when they got to New Orleans?"

"Distribute it."

"That much coke? All in one place?"

"Yeah. Well, sort of. You couldn't do that everywhere, but it's really easy in New Orleans. It's why cruise-ship employees keep getting busted for bringing heroin and everything else there. If you can get it there, it's one of the easiest places to sell drugs."

I thought about that for a second, told Maggie about my timeline. "I'm doing this to try and understand these Cortadero cases."

Maggie studied me. "So you can also understand what the Cortaderos might have to do with your boyfriend?"

"If anything."

Maggie said nothing. And I didn't like that silence very much.

"So the next thing in the timeline," I said, "would be taking the money they made from distributing the drugs and doing what with it? That's got to be a lot of money."

She nodded. "Hell yeah, millions and millions, baby. The truth is I try not to know where the money goes. The prosecutors always want to know the same thing so they can confiscate the money or property bought with drug money. It's probably in a foreign trust somewhere, but for me—"

My phone blared, making me jump. At the same time, my mind pulled at something. What was it? "Sorry," I said, pulling it out of my suit coat pocket. "I've had it on loud ever since Theo got arrested." I looked at the screen. "Theo."

I gave Maggie the one-minute sign, and she waved me away, picking up another design magazine with another scowl.

"What's up?" I said, taking the phone in the hall.

"Meet me for a late lunch?"

It sounded so normal. It sounded wonderful. "Yeah," I said softly.

But Theo said, "I just had to fire ten people." And that brought me back to reality.

29

The Gage, a restaurant on Michigan Avenue, was crowded when I arrived. Tourists huddled at the bar, taking a break from the cold, and office workers shared pre-happy-hour drinks. The result was festive—cheerful voices bouncing off the high tin ceilings, smiles and hugs reflected in the mirror behind the long oak bar.

Festive wasn't exactly the same mood I was in, alas.

I managed to find a couple of stools around a small high-top table. When Theo walked in, he appeared stressed. His cheekbones were more prevalent, his eyes bigger, the shadow of his beard darkening the overall effect of Theo Jameson. I was relieved to see, though, that when his eyes searched the room and found mine, he smiled—reflexively, it seemed, but also in a genuine way, as if some relief had entered him.

He hugged me when he reached our table, squeezing me harder than usual, longer than he often did.

"So you had to fire people?" I asked, as he shed his coat.

"Everyone. There was just no way around it. The company isn't liquid enough to pay them, and I still don't know why, or if, it can be remedied." He sighed, rubbed his beard. "I met with everyone personally. I wanted to give each of them a review of their work and thank them for what they'd done for the company."

"That's great, Theo. That's amazing you took the time to do that."

"They took the time to help us start HeadFirst."

I didn't know what to say to that.

"So anyway," he said, signaling the waitress and ordering a whisky, neat, something I'd never known him to drink.

"Was Eric in the office?" I asked when he said nothing else.

Theo's lips curled in disgust. "He hasn't been there since I was arrested. He's telling everyone he's depressed, and that's why he's not coming in, but I know what it is."

"What?"

Theo's face was hard to read. "*He's* the one who got us into trouble."

"How do you know that?"

"Because I know it wasn't me, and he runs the business side of the company. *He's* the one who pays the bills and deals with the money. I figure he probably cooked the books to make it *look* like it was me." He shook his head. "I didn't think he would do something like that. Ever. I trusted him."

"I'm so sorry," I said.

"Yeah. He can't even face me now," Theo said.

"Were you able to figure out what he might have given them?"

We'd talked last night about how the government didn't have to turn over their evidence yet. Which meant if we wanted to figure this out, Theo was going to have to look around and keep his eyes open.

"Yeah." The lips curled more, and his eyes narrowed in anger.

I sat forward. "What was it? What did they take?"

"I'm not exactly sure because it was mostly from Eric's office—but what seemed to be missing were documents about the venture capital stuff we did to launch the company and the original private offering of stock."

"Who bought it, the stock?"

"Me. Eric. My dad."

"Your dad?" Hmm. "I hadn't realized he was involved with the business. Does he still own stock?"

"Yeah."

"Do you all have equal parts?"

"Eric and I have a bit more."

"Just a bit?"

He narrowed his eyes further and looked at me. "What's that supposed to mean?"

I sat away from the snappy tone to his voice. "Nothing." I raised my hands in surrender.

"You think my dad caused this."

"I'm not saying that. I'm just saying it's interesting."

"My dad would never do that."

"Did you say the same thing about Eric?"

Zing. Theo winced.

"Sorry," I said. "Look, I just didn't know your dad had a stake in your business. This is exactly the kind of stuff we need to know."

"Okay, okay." He seemed to be thinking hard.

"I'd always thought you and Eric owned the predominant amount of stock," I said. "I guess I'd always just assumed that."

"We owned the controlling interest. But my dad had some and there were other investors, too."

"Who were they? I wonder if we should contact them. Get them on our side as witnesses before the Feds do."

Theo's face cleared and he pointed at me, then snapped his fingers. "Yes," he said with sudden gusto. "I like that. Let's talk to my dad and everyone who put in money, and maybe they have information on what Eric did."

If it was Eric. "Do you still have a contact list that would include those investors?"

"Yeah, I'll email it to you this afternoon."

I downed my water and stood. "Let's get at it now."

Theo smiled at me, then scooped his arms around me. "I love that you're my lawyer."

It wasn't exactly *I love you* (and I didn't make any response in return except to hug him tight) but it was something.

30

"Yeah," José Ramon said, answering the phone with one word and a flat tone. He'd been waiting for an update, but he would never let eagerness enter his voice when talking to an underling.

The kid didn't deal with any bullshit small talk, either. "They were at the Gage on Michigan. They talked about investors in his business when he first started. Anything you're interested in?"

"I'm interested."

"He said that's the thing the Feds took from his office. Well, one of the things."

"He said *what's* the thing the Feds took from his office?" Now he was irritated. Having the sense not to bullshit chat with him was one thing, but not having clarity was another. He fucking hated people who were too stupid to remember or to realize when the person they were talking to didn't know what they were talking about. Fucking *hated* it.

"The contact list. That's what they were talking about."

"*What* contact list? Jesus fucking Christ, be clear with your words."

"It includes the people who took part in the initial public offering. Of HeadFirst."

He despised the little bit of fear he felt. But just as quickly as it appeared, he banished it, slashed it, refused to go there.

"Well, then we better get that list," he said.

"That's the plan."

Now the kid was being clear, back in his good graces. "Whatever it takes," he said.

"And I take it you don't want the details about how I get it. Just get it done, right?"

He felt a little better. "That's right," he said. "That's exactly right."

31

By the time I got back to the office, Maggie was out, so I updated Q on my talk with Theo. There was one thing about the drama with Theo that was positive. Q had been listening to me talk about it, and we felt closer than we had in a long time.

He nodded and nodded as I spoke. Then said, "Check your email. See if Theo got you those contact lists yet."

I pulled out my phone. "Not yet."

"Well, you've got other cases," Q said. "Get to work."

I frowned at him, about to remind him that this was the only case that really mattered, but then I realized that wasn't true. I needed to focus on all the cases that had been assigned to me. I would be a help to the firm, not a drain on it. Especially if I wanted to keep my job. And maybe by working harder, I could somehow allow Q to keep his. Maggie had asked me not to say anything yet about the potential he might lose it.

Q watched my face, watched my expression grow determined. "Go get 'em, tiger," he said.

I went to my office and closed the door. I analyzed police records from a case where one client was accused of picking pockets on the "L" train. I wrote a motion for nolle prosequi on a marijuana possession case where there was no evidence the pot was our client's. I called the state's attorney on a DUI case and tried to negotiate a plea.

When all that was done, I felt calmer, and that I'd accomplished something.

And so it was time to work on Theo's case. To orient myself, I pulled up the federal embezzlement statute on my computer, reading it closely, looking for anything—even something tiny—that might provide a defense. Then I studied the statutes on search warrants or permitted entry. If I could prove the contents of the office were somehow obtained illegally, they wouldn't be able to use them as evidence.

I got on my email and—finally!—I saw one from Theo with an attachment. "Let's get at it," I muttered to my computer, trying to channel Q and his coachlike motivation.

I opened the attachment and found lists of buyers for the initial offering of HeadFirst stock. Theo was mentioned, then Eric, then Brad Jameson. The rest of the names were unfamiliar to me. I searched the internet for them, and found a few were partners of hedge funds and venture capital firms that routinely put money into new businesses. A few other names I could find nothing on.

I sat back for a second and thought about what I knew. According to Theo, some documentation about HeadFirst's initial public offering seemed to be missing, and so we assumed the Feds could be interested in who was involved in that initial stock offering. But whether their case was based on who bought the stock, I had no idea.

Stymied, I printed out the contact list, then picked up the coke-on-a-boat file again, thinking I would tackle it once more. But my brain felt as soft as mush.

I would, I decided, take the records home and read them in the morning when, hopefully, a more optimistic frame of mind and a well-firing brain would help me.

My phone vibrated as I slipped on my coat. A text from Theo. I'm going to stay at the office a little later.

I felt disappointment. I'd hoped we could spend time together, time that didn't involve his case, but I understood.

Take your time, I texted back.

When I got home, Kim Parkway stepped out of the second-floor condo as I climbed the stairs.

"Oh, I'm so glad to see you!" she said. She was wearing a black sweater-dress under a black shearling coat and a light blue scarf that sparkled at the ends. "Hey, I'm on my way to meet Danny and Jeff for dinner. Do you by any chance have a black bag I could borrow? I still haven't quite finished unpacking my stuff."

"Sure. C'mon up."

I walked the stairs, Kim following me.

Inside, Kim looked around. "Your place is great."

"Thanks."

She gestured at the door we'd just walked through. "Why doesn't everyone have the same locks on their doors?"

"I put mine in last year after I had a break-in. That's when I asked the building management to put the keypad on the front-door lock, too."

Kim's face was concerned. "So there was a break-in right before I moved in?"

I tried not to grimace. "Yes. I'm sorry, Kim. This place is safe. I swear. I've just had some strange things happen over the last year. I'll tell you the whole story when you've got time."

"Was anyone else's place broken into last year?"

"No, just mine. My fiancé had disappeared." As if that explained everything.

Kim stood there, looking like she was trying to process it all. "And Theo…" she said. "The person who owns the condo on the first floor told me…" Her voice died away, but I could hear the rest of that sentence.

"Yes, Theo was arrested. He's out already. He's at work actually."

Thankfully, Kim only laughed. "Sounds like we need to have that talk over a bottle of wine."

I laughed with her. "Exactly." I gave her the choice of a few handbags and she left with one. As I watched her trailing back down the stairs, I found myself looking forward to sharing that wine with Kim.

32

"Kill her," the guy said. He was huge, tattooed, his face covered in a beard, his bangs long and in his face. He looked around the room, then back at me.

Tentatively, I shook the hand he offered. "I'm Izzy," I said.

"David. Your place is killer. Love it."

"Oh, *killer*. I thought I heard you say something else. Well, thanks." I glanced around. The condo did look pretty good tonight—candlelit, Theo's stuff stashed in various closets, about forty people mingling.

It was the end of a long, tumultuous week. Our studying of the contact list had revealed little, and the past few days had crawled by. I wanted to help Theo feel better in some way, so I'd suggested that we have a small party. I knew from experience that taking part in social activities, trying to be as normal as possible, helped to get over the slivers of shame and paranoia that could creep in after traumatic events. And I wanted Theo to feel like the condo was truly his place now. When he suggested he invite all the people from HeadFirst whom he'd had to let go, it made me like him even more. When I heard that most of those employees had quickly accepted the invitation, it made me proud of him, knowing that those people wanted to support him.

"Yeah, I heard a lot about you from Theo," the big guy, David, was saying now.

"You did?"

He nodded. "He talked about you a lot at work."

I smiled. "What did you do at HeadFirst?"

"I'm a SAGB." He said it like *sag-ba.* When I squinted in confusion, he said, "Systems analysis gigabyte detailer."

I squinted some more.

He laughed. "It's kinda specialized."

"And how did you like it at HeadFirst?"

He paused, and I wondered if he would reveal (or if I could get him drunk enough to talk about) anything he might know about what was going on at the company. Maybe if I understood Theo's work more, I would understand his world. Then I could help him more. Be a better lawyer on his case.

David's face filled with a little bit of wonderment. "HeadFirst was a kick-ass place to work. I loved it. Everyone I know loved it."

"Huh. I'm a lawyer. I don't often hear anyone say that about their job."

He laughed. Then his face turned sad. "We believed in Theo and Eric," he said. "Still do." He gestured with an arm around the room, where people were talking in groups, and Theo was showing some women how to play Madden on his Xbox. "We're all moving on, but we'll be there when they need us back."

I thanked David for his loyalty and showed him toward the bar we'd arranged on the kitchen counter.

When I turned around, Mayburn was there, frowning at me. "You set up my girlfriend?" he said indignantly, no other greeting acting as a buffer.

On one case that Mayburn and I had worked together, he met Lucy DeSanto, a Lincoln Park mom with a husband she didn't know was a bad guy. The bad guy was now in prison, he and Lucy were getting divorced, and Mayburn was in love with her.

I looked around and saw sweet, blonde Lucy talking to one of the other guests. "She's not your girlfriend, is she?" I asked him. "Last I checked, she didn't want to move on to another relationship and you two were hanging out as friends."

I'd always thought of Mayburn as being average height and weight, but last year, when he thought he might lose Lucy forever, he couldn't eat. He lost weight, and despite efforts to the contrary, had kept it off. So now, the cheekbones in his face were distinct, his skin pale. His brown hair looked spiky somehow. The whole thing made Mayburn appear sharper and a little dangerous, in a good way.

He glowered at me now.

I told him what I was thinking.

"Dangerous in a good way?" He mulled that over. "Thanks."

"So anyway, I didn't set Lucy up exactly," I said. "She came out with Theo and me at the end of the summer and she met someone."

"Well, you should have stopped her."

"Excuse me? The two of you were broken up, and she's an adult."

"But you're my friend. You should have had my back."

"I don't know how to tell you this, but you sound like a seventh grader. A seventh-grade *girl.*"

Mayburn's brown eyes searched the room, searched the faces of Theo's friends. He leaned toward me. "His name is C.R., right? How freaking stupid is that name? Which one is he?"

I debated whether answering his question could cause trouble. Mayburn was a low-key guy— except, it seemed, when it came to Lucy. "You're not going to get all caveman and hit him or anything, are you?"

A pause. "Of course not."

I looked across the room toward my fireplace, where Theo was now helping C.R. shove in some logs. Neither of them looked like they knew what they were doing. I was about to point out C.R. when I thought of something Mayburn could do to him, something worse than jacking C.R. in the face. "They're not going out anymore, you know that, right? You're not going to dig up info on him and mess with him."

As one of the best private investigators in the

city, Mayburn had tools in his arsenal that were more powerful than a fist.

"Shut it, McNeil," he said.

"You're very pleasant this evening."

He gave me a glance that said his patience was thin.

I jutted my chin toward the fireplace. "He's the one with Theo."

Mayburn stared, glared. C.R. was probably the hottest guy in the room besides Theo. He had eyes like dark blue denim. He wasn't the smartest guy, and he wasn't particularly charming, but he sure was pretty.

I heard the door opening behind me. Then I heard Mayburn say, "Whoa."

I turned around quick and saw a man towering in the doorway. Got a flash of panic. But then I recognized him. "Bernard!" I said as I walked over and gave him a hug.

"Hey, man!" I heard Theo say as he crossed the room and patted Bernard on the back. The two had met during the summer when Maggie and I were in Italy, the same trip where Maggie met Bernard.

Bernard was a massive Filipino man with thick black hair that always seemed to stand up. He wore his typical off-duty uniform—a pair of baggy jeans and a solid color shirt.

"Where's Maggie?" I asked.

"She's looking for parking. I told her I would do it. But she doesn't trust me."

"You have to know how to park in this city," Theo said.

"That's what she said, but I'm from Asia, man."

I laughed. Maggie thought that everything in the city of Chicago required inside knowledge.

A few minutes later Maggie was there, and she and Bernard were talking with Mayburn. And next to them, Theo was planning to see a band with my brother, Charlie. Next to them, Charlie's friend Zim was talking to Spence and my mom.

I stopped for a moment and smiled. This was the kind of scene Sam and I had envisioned when we planned our future, when we'd decided to get married, to live in Old Town, to keep our friends close and each other closer. We had envisioned occasions just like this—when all of our friends would be around, friends from different places and different stages in our life. Times like these were a human scrapbook of sorts—a place to see all those people and family members in one place. Now here they were, and Sam was noticeably absent.

I heard a knock on the door, but by the time I'd reached it, Q had opened it up and was greeting people as he shed his coat.

I hugged him and his boyfriend, Shane. "How are you guys?"

"We are lovely," Shane said. "But how are *you?*"

Shane was a short guy, shorter than me with the high boots I wore. "I'm fine."

"You are?" He peered at me. "Call us if you're not good. Or even if you are good but you just want some fun. Or anytime. You and I go back a long time."

"That's true. Thanks."

"And hey, we met your cool neighbor," Q said.

"Kim?" I'd invited her but she already had plans.

"Yeah, she was on her way out and we said hi."

"But I swear we met her before," Shane said.

"We did," Q said, adjusting the gray velvet blazer he wore over a black shirt and pants. "I'll remember it eventually. My aging brain needs a little time." He looked over my shoulder. "Or maybe a little champagne."

Q led Shane toward the bar and I was about to close the door when I heard someone coming up the stairs.

I waited, but then the sound stopped. "Hello," I called down the stairs.

No answer.

"C'mon up," I called.

Still nothing. Had I misheard the footsteps due to the sounds of the party?

But right then, I heard someone take a few more steps. For some reason, I held my breath, felt like slamming the door closed. What if the person who had broken in was trotting back into my building now? What if by having a party, I had invited them right back in?

Two more steps. They were almost on the landing now, where I would see them. I took a breath, got pissed off all over again about the break-in and took a step outside, crossing my arms and looking down. Hell if I was going to be scared in my own house.

And then I saw who it was. "Eric."

Theo's partner had fair skin and dark hair that was cut close to his head. His hairline was inching back—he'd be one of those guys who lost his hair early—but he had keen green eyes and a chiseled-looking face with a straight jaw and prominent cheekbones. He would be handsome for a long time. Except that now, his face looked more ravaged than when I'd seen him earlier in the week, his skin dry and delicate.

I'd first been introduced to Eric the same night Lucy and C.R. had met. I understood then how he and Theo had been successful partners. Both were talented programmers and designers, but Theo had the charisma, the ability to explain and to sell. Eric was the more contemplative one who thought long-term about their business and their employees and the day-to-day intricacies of starting and running a company. But was Theo right? Had that contemplativeness turned toward ways to bilk the company of money for his own gain?

"Hi, Izzy," he said. "How are you?"

He took a few more steps and kissed me on the cheek, which struck me as an odd gesture, one you'd expect from someone much older. But then again, Theo said Eric had always been mature.

"What are you doing here, Eric?" I asked softly.

He raised his eyebrows, as if asking himself the same thing. Then the expression drifted away, land-

ing again at a seen-too-much look. "I heard everyone was here, and—"

"And you just thought you could walk in and
we'd all be happy to see you?" The voice behind
me sounded hurt. And pissed off. Theo.

I stepped aside to let him next to me.

"You just left me out there to dry," Theo said.

Eric's mouth opened, then closed.

"You worked with the *government*." Theo's voice
was loud now, incredulous.

"Only because you made me," Eric said.

"I *made* you?" He was shouting now, and I heard
conversations behind him start to wane. "What the
fuck does that mean?"

"You got us into this," Eric said.

Silence behind us now. I heard only the sound
of a song from my iPod—Bob Schneider singing,
I've got a long way to get before I get back home.

Theo took a step closer, and for some reason,
as if moved by a deep, deep instinct, I took a step
back.

Thwack!

I heard the sound before I saw Eric's head swivel
on his neck, before I realized Theo had punched
him. Hard.

33

With one arm still supporting him over me, Theo put the palm of his other hand lightly on my chest. Then his hand was on my collarbone. He stared into my eyes. His hand moved to my neck. He tightened it minimally. His gaze intensified.

And right then, I knew what we were both thinking.

"Can we talk about this?" I asked.

It was what I had asked him earlier, although on a different topic.

Eric had left quickly after Theo punched him. And so did everyone else, all the goodwill from HeadFirst employees flowing away. When they were gone, my friends stuck around, asking if there was anything they could do. But with Theo in the bedroom with the door closed and the majority of the guests gone, it was clear the party was over.

I cleaned up, giving Theo time to calm down. When I went in the bedroom, he was staring at the ceiling, lying flat on his back.

"We should talk about this," I said.

"No," he responded simply.

"Theo, we have to."

"Okay," he said, sitting up. "But let's talk first about Sam and you at that hotel."

I hadn't seen that coming. Since Theo's arrest, the topic had occurred to me once or twice, but I'd thought it had lost any meaning given the rest of what was going on. Apparently, I was wrong about that.

"Don't want to talk about it?" Theo asked, his voice hard.

"Not really. But I think—"

"Well, I don't want to talk about this. The same way you don't want to talk about that."

I paused. Waited. Theo and I stared at each other, and his expression softened, seemed to say, *Please.*

"Okay," I said.

I got ready for bed and when I climbed in, Theo wrapped his warm self around my back, around my whole body. And he held me, just held me for the longest while. Then one hand moved between my legs and nudged them slightly apart.

"Yes?" he said.

"Yes, yes."

He waited.

"Yes," I said.

Then he was inside me, without warning. It was...exquisite.

He turned me over so he could see me. From that moment, his gaze never left mine while I sucked in the sight of him lit by a bedside lamp—that hair, those lips, those eyes. The red ribbon on his arm seemed to undulate as we moved. I stared at it, mesmerized, but then I shifted my gaze back to his eyes, always those eyes. He moved faster, watching my reaction, subtly changing to reach me deeper, slowing and halting when he thought I was drifting away on bliss.

But then that hand on my neck. Squeezing. And then I said, "Can we talk about this?"

He took his hand away, leaned down and nuzzled my neck, breathing me in. Then he slid out of me and lay at my side, his hand on my belly.

After her death, it was learned that Jane, the *Trial TV* anchorwoman who'd introduced me to Theo, had a predilection for infidelity and for occasional autoerotic asphyxiation. Also exposed was the fact that Theo had been one of the men she was unfaithful with.

Now, here Theo was with his hand on my neck, and I was not so much shocked as nervous, even oddly titillated. And yet I felt the need for some discussion, some definition.

"How often did you two do that kind of thing?" I asked him.

"Not often."

"Is it good?"

He raised his eyebrows and nodded his head as if to say, *Really good.*

He started kissing me again, moving his body right next to mine, so we were pressed against each other. He twirled my hair, pulling it around his face. Soon we seemed like one person. Soon he was inside of me again.

One hand moved to my neck, again a little squeeze. "We could do it," he said, his words lighting my insides. "But only if you want."

I got a burst of excitement in my mind, quickly followed by a flicker of fear. Of what, exactly? I wasn't sure.

"Not now," I said. "Not yet." I had spoken quickly, as if I wanted the discussion over fast.

Theo nodded. "No worries, no worries."

But the moment was dead.

34

And somehow the next morning it got worse.

"No" was the first word I heard Theo say that morning. I could tell he was in the next room. Then, *"No."*

I mumbled, turned over in bed. Strangely, I had gotten a full night of deep and desperately needed sleep.

But now this voice. I raised my head. The bedroom door was slightly open, but I couldn't see outside it.

"No," Theo said again. There was something about his voice that sounded very off, almost in pain.

"What?" I heard him say. Loud. He was rarely loud. "I don't understand," he said again. He sounded like that night he'd heard he was turned down for the mortgage, but now anguish laced his voice.

I got up and wrapped a blanket around myself, took a few steps toward the door.

"How?" he said. There was a pause, then a strangled sound.

I hurried through the door and into the living room. He was crouched on the hardwood floor, one hand holding his cell phone to his ear, the other hand in his hair as if he'd been running his fingers through it and they had stuck there. His whole body was frozen like a sculpture, low to the ground. He vaguely reminded me of Rodin's *The Thinker*.

He didn't look up at me. He kept listening, then he shook his head back and forth, back and forth, holding tight to the phone. The rest of his body didn't move.

I heard a moan from low in his chest. "Okay," he said. "Okay, I'll do that, but…Mrs. Deringer…I don't understand."

He stood then and turned to me, his eyes wide, shocked. "It'll be okay," he said into the phone in an unconvincing way. His face seemed to contort then, as if he couldn't stand what he was listening to. "It'll be okay, Mrs. Deringer." He didn't sound as if he believed his words. He closed his eyes, listening again as if in pain.

A minute later when he was off the phone, I took a few steps toward him. "Mrs. Deringer?" I said. "Was that Eric's mom?"

He nodded. "Eric tried to kill himself."

We stood there in my living room, staring at each other, Theo's face contorted again in pain. It seemed so long we remained like that. Days.

Finally, as if in a delayed response, I felt myself flinch. "Suicide?"

Theo nodded. "That's what she said. But it doesn't seem right."

"How did he…how did he try?"

"They said he OD'd."

"On what?"

"I don't know. Eric doesn't do drugs. He…" He paused. "He didn't," he said, as if testing out the past tense.

The Cortaderos were a drug cartel family. Allegedly. And they wouldn't work with us if we represented Theo. But could their reasoning have anything to do with Eric?

Theo ran his hand through his hair. This time it didn't get stuck. He kept running it over his head, over and over as if he could rake the worries from his mind. "He *doesn't* do drugs."

"Well, you might not know. I mean sometimes you don't always know a person."

Why was there a trickle of a thought in my brain that said, *Like I don't always know about you?*

Theo glared at me, as if he could read my mind. "He doesn't do drugs."

"Well, then what happened?"

More shaking of his head. "His mom said she was surprised he'd been at the party, because she hadn't heard from him in days, which was strange. They almost always talk on Saturday mornings, so when he didn't call today, she sent his doorman to his apartment. He was in bed and…" He squinted, like he didn't want to picture the scene. "He was unconscious. He still is. And…there were some kind of drugs by his bedside."

"What kind of drugs?"

Again, Theo glared. "I said I don't know, Izzy."

"Well, don't get mad at me."

His face softened. "I'm not."

I took a step toward him slowly, unsure whether he wanted me near. A few more slow steps and I'd reached him. I put my arms around his waist. "I'm sorry, baby. I'm so sorry."

He fell over me then, willing, it seemed, to let me hold the weight of him.

"Oh, Jesus, did I make him do this?" he asked, his voice anguished.

"Of course not." But I was wondering the same thing. About him. And myself. I thought of how I'd told off Eric in his office earlier in the week. Thought of how after Theo punched him I hadn't been exactly comforting—just let him walk down the stairs alone.

"Oh, Jesus," Theo said again. And then, he cried. I kept holding him.

Finally he stood straight. "I'm sorry," he said, his hands to his eyes.

"Don't be."

"Eric's mom wants me to go the office and see if there's anything there."

"Like what?"

He sighed. "I don't know. I told her I had looked through Eric's office this week, but now this has happened and I think she wants to see if there are any clues that he was heading this way."

"Are the police looking into this?" I wondered if the office would be considered a crime scene. I couldn't think of how it could be. And I remembered Maggie once saying that if it wasn't a crime a scene *yet,* then it wasn't a crime scene at all.

"I'll go with you," I said.

35

Now that I wasn't at Theo's office to confront Eric, now that I was going farther than the conference room, I tried to look at it more objectively, to get my mind away from the awful fact—*he tried to kill himself.*

The office—in a building on West Fulton that had been developed into four units—had outside walls of exposed brick and inside, heavy-glassed walls surrounding eclectic offices decked out with technology, but also diverse artwork, beautiful rugs and interesting furniture.

But it was fairly small. Or smaller than what I envisioned Theo's company to be like. "Your company gets everything done from here?" I asked Theo as we walked the hallway.

He shook his head. "Just the creative and the business side of it. The manufacturing and packing is done in Malaysia. But we don't even have to do much of that anymore. Most people just pay for our software online and download it. The legal is all handled by a firm."

"Here's Eric's office," Theo said, leading me farther down a hallway and stepping past a glass wall.

The space was square, about twenty feet around. On top of a massive desk—surrounded by three different office chairs—sat five computer screens, papers, notes.

We both looked around.

"I can't believe he's in the hospital. I can't believe he tried to kill himself," Theo said. "This is just so crazy. God, why did I hit him?"

"It wasn't you." *It might have been me.*

I put my arm around him and we stood a little while longer, as if in a moment of silence for Eric.

Theo looked at his watch, sighing heavily. "I wonder where my dad is."

"Why?"

"I wonder if he's heard about Eric."

"Wouldn't you have had to tell him?"

"He's close with Eric," he said, "since my dad was like our unofficial founder."

I felt my brow furrowing a little. "What do you mean?" I asked Theo. "I mean, I know he has stock in your company, but 'unofficial founder'?"

"Since we were just college kids when we started HeadFirst, my dad raised the money and got the lawyers and helped us form a corporation and find offices and all that."

"Really?" I thought of Brad in Deluxa, clearly pained when I told him Theo had been arrested. But even though we'd discussed allegations of Theo embezzling funds—funds it now sounded like Brad should know about—he hadn't mentioned anything.

"Yeah," Theo said, but his eyes were sweeping the office. "Let's look around."

Picking through Eric's office, I felt like I was tampering with a grave, a memorial. Each item seemed to ask, *Will you throw me away if he dies?*

Theo had talked to Eric's mother again. Eric was in a coma at Northwestern Hospital, she reported. No one else was allowed to see him yet. In my imagination, Eric seemed to be floating somewhere, not sure whether he would return to this world or join some new one.

I watched Theo get on Eric's computer, scanning for who knows what, while I looked at things on his bookshelf. We were mostly silent during this process. An hour or so later, Theo started to look through Eric's desk drawers. He began to tell me what certain things were—*our first lease; the articles of incorporation for HeadFirst; Ha! Eric's ID for that first building.* He turned the ID to face me, and I smiled. In the picture, Eric's dark hairline had yet to begin its recession. His eyes looked clear and big and happy. He looked carefree.

Theo looked at the ID again, seeming to see the same difference between the Eric of then and the one we now envisioned in a hospital bed, mute, gone, at least momentarily. The smile bled from Theo's face.

He kept searching, occasionally filling me in on the title of another document. When he came to what looked to be a legal document or contract—probably thirty or so pages long—he flipped through it, then stopped for a time, seeming to study a page.

"What's that?" I asked.

"Just some legal stuff. I was thinking Eric's mom might need it."

"That's a good idea. Should we gather any info about his medical insurance?"

"Yeah," Theo said. "Or life insurance."

The words *life insurance* made both of us stop. I wondered if Theo might cry again, but he just shook his head, rolled up the document, then turned to another drawer. He began to search its contents slowly, methodically; moving the way a factory worker might at the end of a long, draining shift.

36

I called my dad for help. Eventually.

When I woke up Sunday morning, the morning after Eric tried to kill himself, I was in a very blue frame of mind.

Okay, labeling my mood a "blue frame of mind" is sort of like calling Van Gogh's predominant mental state a "bad mood," but I was unaccustomed to depression.

The fact that I had a pretty decent reason—the arrest of my boyfriend and attempted suicide of his business partner and both of our guilt that we might have contributed to his decision to do that—didn't help. I was used to looking somber moods in the face and winning that staring contest. But now the grim malaise kept creeping in, seeping around the edges of everything.

Theo had gone to work, convinced he had to do so for Eric, to keep together whatever remained of HeadFirst and figure out where they had gone wrong. I noticed he referred to he and Eric as *we* again—*We went wrong somewhere. We got a bad deal somewhere. We have to figure out what we should do.* It was hard to think of Theo alone in that office, which only a short time ago had held employees and a partner who was alive and well, but he was insistent.

As soon as he was gone, my mood plunged further.

I tried to annihilate it, I really did. I jumped when Maggie called, saying the Bristols were getting together and did I want to come over?

I adored her grandfather, who I saw as a mentor. And I loved the rest of her family, as well.

But my mood only blackened with the jocularity of the Bristols, the way they all seemed sure of themselves and their lives.

In Marty Bristol's penthouse apartment in the South Loop, I snuck away to his home office and took a seat in front of a huge plate window that overlooked the museum campus and Lake Michigan. Usually such a view of the lake raised any dark shades that had fallen over my mind, but that day the view was blocked by heavy fog, like cigarette smoke in front of a beautiful woman's face.

I said my thanks to the Bristols, left the building and went to the Macy's on State and Washington. Oftentimes the sight of that building, which used to be the old Marshall Fields, would hand me a little happiness even if the thought of shopping didn't. I loved the green clocks hanging over the street, the granite columns. Inside, the Tiffany glass ceiling and the burbling fountain always inspired me, lifted me. I stared at the green-and-red decorations, which covered everything from floor to ceiling.

I took the escalators up and began doing some holiday shopping for Spence and my mom. I even found an odd little navy blue globe on a gold stand that I thought my father might be able to tolerate in an office or on an end table.

When I got to the men's floor, I stalled. What to get Theo…? Would he even have a choice of clothing in the future or would he be wearing a neon-orange suit, compliments of the federal government?

I hurried down to the fourth floor, pulling out the big guns by heading for the shoe department and reminding myself that I was a wage earner again. But it was hopeless. The beautiful nude shoes with the delicate fur straps didn't make me swoon. I just wondered where in the world I'd wear such a thing. A fabulous holiday party was not in my immediate future, especially after the debacle that was our last party.

And so I went back downstairs and called my dad. I knew he wanted more contact with Charlie and me, but he just didn't know how to obtain that. So I thought I'd be gracious. And maybe someone who had spent his whole life away from his family, watching his life from afar, could give me some pointers about how to handle what was going on in my life now.

When he answered, I sat on the stone rim of the Macy's fountain, and instead of beating around the issue, I simply told him, "I'm sad, Dad. Really sad. And confused. And..." I stopped then, realizing we'd had little experience with such conversations and sensing oncoming discomfort from his side.

But I was wrong, as I so often had been with my father. "Where are you?" he asked.

"Macy's. In the Loop."

"I'm not too far. Meet you at the restaurants on the seventh floor?"

"Okay," I said, feeling a little more calm just having something to do next.

"Let's go to Frontera Fresco."

"What's that?"

"Rick Bayless's place."

Rick Bayless is a well-respected Chicago chef who specialized in gourmet Mexican. I would not have expected my father to know that.

"See you in fifteen minutes."

Thirty minutes later, my father was making good work on something called a huarache, a Mexican pizza of sorts made of cornmeal and topped with chorizo and salsa.

"Go on," he said, pointing at the tamales he'd ordered for me when I was stumped on what to choose. The words were kind, spoken in a tone that indicated welcome. Then he nodded at me, and I knew he was telling me to continue our conversation.

So I told him about Eric, how I felt so guilty about the way I'd given him such a hard time in his office, when really I didn't know if the problems at HeadFirst had anything to do with him. I told him how awful Theo felt about hitting him, and both of us wondered if either encounter was what had led to the suicide attempt.

My father listened, and listened. He put his food down at one point, and took off his glasses. He closed his eyes, leaning his head back. When I paused he opened one eye. "Keep going," he said. Then he closed his eyes again.

I kept talking, telling him about how there were a number of initial investors in the company. I told him that Theo had said the Feds likely took (or were given by Eric) documents having to do with the initial formation.

During this, my dad kept his eyes closed, face tilted toward the ceiling, as if he were listening to a symphony.

When my words slowed, his eyes opened. He returned his copper glasses to his face. "Suicide is rough, because when you want to kill yourself, you really just want it done and over with. Your life, I mean. And you simply don't care about anything else."

He sounded like he very much knew what he was talking about.

"If you're smart…" He paused, thought about it. "And by smart I mean aware enough to see outside the pain in your mind, you think about the people who would be hurt by you hurting yourself. And you stop yourself. But really, it's just too much to handle, that's what you think. You think you can't get past it. And it isn't anyone's fault. No one else's."

"But if I hadn't gotten so mad at Eric—if Theo hadn't—maybe he wouldn't have felt so bleak about himself, maybe—"

"No." My dad shook his head. "Doesn't work like that. Even if you told him to kill himself, it's not your fault. No one does these things except the person themselves."

"So what do I do now?"

"Help Theo. Help him find out what's going on at HeadFirst. Keep an open mind as best you can. In other words, keep doing what you're already doing."

I sucked in air. I must have been holding it tight since I heard about Eric. Then I thought some more about my dad's words. "Did you ever feel like that? Like you wanted it to be over?" The answer seemed obvious, but I wasn't sure how to talk to him about this.

"I did," he said without hesitation. "Many times. But I always thought about your mother. And you and Charlie. I knew you would be hurt."

"But we already thought you were dead. Well, Charlie and I did." My mother had said once that she *knew* my father wasn't dead, even though they said he was. She'd always known it in her bones.

"I felt…somehow…that you could be hurt. Psychically, I guess. Subconsciously. I didn't want to add to the pain you'd already suffered."

It seemed a strange thing to say and yet one of the kindest things I'd ever heard.

And right at that moment, I felt something toward my dad I hadn't felt in a long, long, *long* time. What was it?

I tried to think it through. Maybe my father would disappear again. Maybe not. Maybe we would be good friends someday. Maybe not. But right then he was one of those people with whom I could let go completely. He had only good in his heart. At least toward me.

I did trust him, I realized, for the first time since I was a kid. I trusted him entirely and completely.

And then I realized there was someone else I felt like that about—that no matter what our history had held, no matter what he had done, I trusted him. Well, I thought I did. But in deciding to trust—or whom to choose to trust—I always felt better making that assessment in person.

"Thanks, Dad," I said. Then I picked up my phone to text him.

37

"Unfortunately, this is not a foreign thing for you," Sam said.

"What's not foreign?" I asked, my elbow on the bar table where we sat.

"Having someone in your life in trouble with the law. Because of me." He looked at me so sympathetically.

How in the heck (meaning how in the hell) *was it that my ex-boyfriend (my ex-fiancé, for frick's sake) was now counseling me? On my relationship?*

Stranger waters my life had never entered, it seemed. But I'd walked willingly into those waters. After my dad and I said our goodbyes, I'd texted Sam again and suggested we meet for coffee or a drink. Preferably a drink, I'd texted.

Theo was still at work, didn't know when he would leave, and I wanted to see Sam suddenly. I wanted to test my internal trust-o-meter.

"So you shouldn't feel bad about your questions," Sam said. "You had questions about me." He stopped then, scratched his dark blond hair above his ear. He seemed to be waiting for a response for the first time since he'd been doling out advice, which I'd been soaking up, eager for someone who understood. And how many people actually understood what it was like for *me* to be me right now— someone whose fiancé had disappeared and who had wondered and worried and feared? Probably two people: Sam and Maggie. And Maggie had been distinctly keeping more and more to herself, clearly worried but not confiding in me about whatever she was worried about. It had left me feeling helpless that I couldn't help her, and a little helpless for myself.

"I did have questions," I said. "A lot of them."

His eyes were eager, too. He needed this, I realized, as much as I did.

I leaned in. "And yes, I did come to believe you after those questions. I do trust you."

Utter relief, like I've never seen it, took over his face. Suddenly, he looked much younger, his martini-olive-green eyes more clear, almost sparkling.

We were at Hubbard Inn, one of those one-stop-shopping kind of places that had a small bar, a bigger bar, a dining area and a number of tucked-away private dining areas.

Sam and I were in the small bar. We were sitting across the table from each other, elbows on the table, talking like he would with his buddies.

"I'm glad to hear that, Iz," Sam said. "Really glad." He paused before turning the conversation back to me and Theo again. And then we both seemed to relax. And we talked. And I let Sam help me.

And for the first time since it happened, since he'd taken off about a year ago (how long a year can be), I felt something unfurl inside me.

I was grateful then, watching Sam give me advice while he chewed on a cocktail straw between the lips I used to kiss, lips that, even stranger, didn't hold much pull anymore.

I looked at my watch. Theo, I hoped, would be getting home soon. "I should..." I said, standing.

"Do you have to take off?" Sam looked at his watch, then looked at me, and right then a wave of love for him washed over me, like some kind of cellular memory locked in my body and released right when he'd said that question, right when he had made me feel, as he so often had when we were together, that he couldn't get enough of me, that I was fascinating and delightful and smart. And loved.

And that, I realized, was something I hadn't been feeling from Theo lately.

Still, I'd never been one to be unfaithful when I was committed, and I didn't want to get sucked into a relationship with Sam where I was even emotionally connected. Because I had a commitment with Theo. Sort of. Anyway, it was something I wasn't willing to destroy blindly and then regret later.

So I pulled my bag from the table. "Yeah," I said. "I have to go, Sam."

38

On Monday afternoon, Brad Jameson sat in the office of the federal prosecutor who had charged his son with embezzlement and money laundering.

He shot a glance at his lawyer—an older guy named Nicholas Grand who he'd heard had negotiated deals with thousands of prosecutors, both state and federal. Grand had told him that it wasn't very common for the prosecutor to offer to meet both the defendant and his counsel to talk about the case. Grand said it could only mean good things, but now Brad wasn't so sure. Was it ever a good thing to be in the office of a federal prosecutor? What was about to happen here? And why couldn't he get a full breath of air in his lungs?

Nicholas Grand looked at Brad, seemed to recognize his questions. Grand held out his manicured hand and pushed down at something imaginary, telling Brad to *relax*.

A young woman came in, not acknowledging them, going through some documents on the prosecutor's desk, moving away his empty chair to open a drawer. Then she sat in a chair at Brad's left and scribbled something on a yellow pad, still failing to acknowledge them. Brad shot a look at his attorney, who seemed unperturbed by the appearance of this woman, apparently a young lawyer or an assistant.

They sat in silence for at least five minutes. Brad was just about to lose control and storm from the office when a thin Indian man came into the room. He strode to Brad and then his lawyer and pumped their hands warmly. "Sorry to keep you waiting. We have a thing before Judge Haden and…" The guy shook his head and laughed at the craziness of Judge Haden's courtroom, making Brad feel oddly jealous that his case, his son's, suddenly didn't seem to require more serious attention and reflection from their lead prosecutor.

The Indian guy greeted the young woman, then sat behind his desk and nodded at Nicholas Grand, as if to say, *Go ahead.*

"Anish, we've sized up the case," Grand said. "And what we've seen so far is that your case is primarily against—" he looked down at the white pad of paper in his lap "—against a Mr. Theodore Jameson." As if Theo wasn't Brad's son! As if Brad wasn't sitting right next to him.

"Of course," Grand continued, "we'd expect that Mr. Jameson's partner, Eric Deringer, would be next on the list of culpability."

The prosecutor, whose full name was Anish Desai, looked at him frankly. Brad returned the gaze, but he felt weak, the arrest of Theo and then

Eric's suicide attempt having taken much from him over the past few days. His gaze shot to his lap. He recovered some strength and raised his head again.

"You know Mr. Deringer attempted to kill himself Friday night," Anish said.

"We're aware," Grand said. As if it were an inconsequential matter.

"I asked you here to discuss your client, not Eric Deringer. As one of the key stockholders in Head-First, we believe Mr. Jameson may have insights into his son's case," Anish said.

"What are you looking for?" Brad's lawyer said.

"Testimony. Against Theo Jameson."

Brad shot to his feet. He couldn't help it. "I will *not* testify against my son!"

He felt an admonishing gaze from his lawyer.

Brad found his seat again and calmed himself. He employed the mental techniques he'd learned over the past few months to control the aggression, fear and anger he experienced whenever he got a phone call from that one overseas number.

There was a time when that phone number conjured up images of sand and sun and palm trees—images representative of the place itself—and he could recall the happy calm he used to get from speaking with the bankers, from hearing that their money was safe, was even multiplying.

How fast things changed.

39

Mayburn, my father, Charlie and I sat around a table in a German restaurant on Lincoln Avenue. I knew my father wanted to spend more time with Charlie and me, and after our talk yesterday at Macy's, I did, too. So when I suggested we get together after work on the Monday before Thanksgiving, he had quickly agreed. Since my dad and Mayburn were working together and I had to talk to both of them on a work level, I'd invited Mayburn, too. Now we made a strange foursome. Theo was, as usual, at the office of HeadFirst, picking through the graves.

It had been good to go back to work today, the bustle of the office soothing to me. Q had called early saying he wanted me to clean up a bunch of old cases around the office. I knew he was giving me a break, and I appreciated it, throwing myself into the work.

At the end of the day, I'd popped my head in Maggie's office. "Anything?" I'd asked. She shook her head. No new information about Theo or Head-

First or why they believed he had stolen money from the company and its customers.

At the German place, things began to feel a little more comfortable after a round of large Belgian beers. Charlie and my father discussed his work at the radio station, how he was beginning to turn his sights on different things in the radio and TV world. Mayburn and I chatted about Lucy. Lucy was what Mayburn always wanted to talk about.

"Don't think I forgot about how you set her up," he said at one point, sitting back in the booth, throwing his chin up in the air.

"What's that?" I said, pointing at his face. "What are you doing there?"

I thought he'd drop the macho pose, but nothing about his face moved. I noticed then that he was even thinner than when I'd seen him at our party a few days ago.

"Dude," I said, "I didn't *set* her up. I didn't go to her with the idea. She asked me to take her out with Theo and some of his young friends, and she met C.R. And I think they went out once or twice. Look, I don't even know if they—"

"Okay, okay," Mayburn said, holding up a hand. "I don't want the details."

"I don't *know* the details. I'm telling you I know little about it and had little to do with it. So stop being angry at me."

"I'm not angry." He picked up his mug, sipped at it, then shifted his gaze out the window. On Lincoln, cars were slowing down. "Holiday traffic," Mayburn said glumly. "It's starting already."

Thankfully, the second round of beers was delivered, and Charlie stood to say hi to a bartender he knew.

"Okay, guys," I said. "I want to talk about you doing some work for Theo's case. Officially."

My dad and Mayburn looked at each other. My dad seemed to drop his gaze for the slightest of seconds before he returned it to me.

I told Mayburn about Eric's suicide attempt, told him about going through his office, but how we really didn't know what to look for, how I still didn't understand really why Theo was arrested and, more important, what in the heck-fire he had to do with the Cortaderos.

"Can you please help?" I asked. "Dad, I know you were checking out the situation. Would you continue? Would you guys take it on together like a real case?"

They just looked at me. Finally, my father adjusted his round copper glasses and spoke up. "We've decided to cease the amount of pro bono work we're doing."

Mayburn said nothing.

"Okay." A beat went by, then I understood. "You consider *me* pro bono work."

"If we're going to make this a business, we need to make everything business," my father said.

"I did the bank visit with Tatum Reynolds for free," I pointed out.

"Yeah," Mayburn said, "but you were still paying me back for a bunch of work I did for you over the summer."

I was about to take issue with that, but when I opened my mouth, I saw Mayburn giving me a wide-eyed stare, trying to tell me something without saying anything. I paused. He shot his eyes to my dad and back. Right then, in his gaze, I read something. *Go with it.* It dawned on me suddenly that my father had probably brought in little in terms of business. Rather, he had been helping Mayburn with his cases. Mayburn, I saw then, might have taken my father on as something of a project, in kindness to me, even though he had done a lot of gratis work for me. As Mayburn glanced at my dad once more, I saw something else there, too. He liked my dad. And he wanted him to get some confidence in his new city. It was more than Charlie and I had been doing for my dad.

I nodded.

My father spoke. "Actually, we could swap services, as long as they're relatively equal assignments. We do need you again with Tatum Reynolds."

"No, we don't," Mayburn said. "He deposited the extra cash that he was supposed to give Izzy that day."

"But not until the weekend. And after he had played a poker game where he could have taken in that kind of money."

"Yeah, but the bank said that we had him. That was enough."

"They sent an email saying they would need more after all," my dad said.

"When?" Mayburn sounded a little irritated. "When did you see an email that said that?"

"About five minutes ago."

Silence.

"I read it on my phone," my dad said.

Mayburn and I looked at each other, then back at my dad. I'd seen no phone since he arrived. But then again, I hadn't been looking at him when I was talking to Mayburn, and even if I had, my father had ways of doing things under the radar.

Mayburn made an impressed face. "Okay, well then, Izzy, we do need you. Are you ready to go to Tru with Tatum Reynolds?" He looked back at my dad. "I assume you set this up already."

A single nod from Christopher McNeil. "Tonight."

40

When I got home, Theo wasn't there. I looked at my watch. Seven o'clock. An hour before I had to meet Tatum Reynolds at Tru.

I looked around for a note from Theo. Nothing. I tried to think about whether he'd said he had any plans that evening. But Theo and I hadn't talked about plans of any kind. Not since he was arrested.

I tried to call him, but no answer. I texted, Hey, where r u @? I heard nothing in reply.

I changed into a charcoal knit dress that had a wide collar. Then I remembered Tatum Reynolds checking out my cleavage, so I pulled the collar lower, and threw my curls over my shoulder. I put on some sparkly silver earrings that hung almost to my shoulder and zipped up my gray high-heel boots.

I still had about fifteen minutes until I had to leave. I went to my home office, thinking I might as well look over the records I'd brought home on Friday. I'd gotten nothing done over the weekend due to the news about Eric.

I stopped completely as I was hit with a wallop of sadness at the thought of Eric Deringer. How was he? Maybe Theo was with him. I hoped so. I hoped Eric would be all right. And, God, if I had anything to do with it, I was so, so sorry.

I got myself moving again, went into the office and sat down, pulling the bag I'd left at the side of the desk toward me, the one I'd carried home from the office last week.

From the bag, I lifted the stack of research. But as I sifted through it, planning to make different piles for the various documents, I realized the coke-in-a-boat file wasn't there, the one that said *Cortadero* on its file folders. I looked in the bag again. Definitely not there.

I scrolled my mind back to when I'd brought the file home. Last Thursday, before we knew about Eric. On Friday, I'd hit on the idea of picking up Theo's spirits by planning a party. I'd spent most of the day cleaning my house, running to Treasure Island grocery for booze and snacks, making phone calls and emails, telling people to come over.

But before all that on Thursday, I'd definitely taken the Cortadero file from my office desk and put it in my bag. It was the first thing I'd put in there. The research on Theo's case had gone in after that. I'd come home, put the bag down and not opened it until now.

Which meant one of three things. Either we'd had another break-in. Or someone from the party took it. Or Theo did.

41

"She's going into Tru."

"You fucking kidding me? She's going to *that* place?" José Ramon was at home, trying to take some time off for Christ's sake.

He strode across the glossy floors of his penthouse apartment. It was in a building he loved, a building that had said *fuck you* to the rest of the Chicago skyline by soaring above it, just like he did.

He reminded himself what a star he was, much more than his brother. Except now his professional jealousy was flaring. Even though the restaurant was a cover, he took whatever he did seriously. And goddamned Tru got way more PR than his place did, and way better reviews and way more little motherfuckers on Yelp who didn't know anything, blah-blah-blahing about how great it was. Goddamned Tru.

"Yeah, so anyway…" The kid was clueless to his emotions. Which was good. He didn't like the people who worked for him to know he had any.

"I don't know how I can follow her in that place. It's too hard to be inconspicuous in the restaurant itself. Maybe what I could do—"

"Don't do anything," José said, "I've got it."

"You've mean 'you've got it,' like you—"

"Don't ask questions." He stopped in front of the huge window that allowed no one to look inside, even if they could get this high. Yet he could see everything. Although it was dark now, he could picture how it was in daylight, when he could see over the Wrigley Building and over the river and over all the hotels and even over the band shell at Millennium Park, right to Lake Michigan. He had everything in his sights right here.

To top it off, Lucia was coming over later. She'd been cat-and-mouse with him. Coy. Knew just when to blow his brains out with a night together and then she disappeared for a while.

"I just think you should—"

"Do not think!" José barked. Now he was annoyed. And it was distracting him from his view.

"Hey, you told me that you appreciated it when I—"

"Shut the fuck up!" He was yelling now, his view blurred by anger at the insubordination. "I'm getting Freddie on this," he said.

He hung up then, because he was afraid of the anger he was directing outward. His father and mother had conducted many a discussion with him about lashing out. It was why Vincente, his brother, got to get his MBA and live in fucking Barrington Hills and buy fucking ponies for his kids.

He had been in control of it for a long time. But sometimes when people were defiant, when people didn't give him the respect he deserved, this was when it flared. The fury came back to him with a taste so familiar, it almost felt a relief to bring it forward into his consciousness.

And now this situation with HeadFirst was almost taken care of. Almost. One kid had tried to kill himself. It was perfect! Now he needed the other one to go away so that no one would testify, no one would name them. But it would be too obvious if the other kid just happened to get caught with a needle in his vein in an alley in Lawndale. Way too obvious. So he would handle it another way.

But still there remained the unrelenting pressure of that anger that he'd let come forward—wanting to be let out even more. He knew he would walk around feeling like a live wire, twitching and waiting for it to bring ruin to someone eventually.

He forced himself to see again, see through the shining lights to the blackness that was Lake Michigan at night. He looked into the depths of that black. Then he lifted his phone again and gave Freddie a little more latitude than he had last time. Last time, a warning was all that was needed, in the form of a break-in.

This time he only had one rule. *No one dies.* They both heard the other side of that admonishment—*Don't kill anyone, but other than that...*

42

I felt guilty. So very guilty. Because Tatum Reynolds looked so very happy.

The staff at Tru were such experts they made Tatum feel like a man of industry, a man of wealth, a man of power. And then I added to that aura for him—flirting by leaning across the table, showing a little cleavage, sharing funny stories, asking him about his family and his friends.

In the spirit of getting him to confess about his client-incentive money hoarding, I'd made some "confessions" of my own. Such as how I had fallen for him right when I walked in his office.

And *boom,* just like that he started talking. He told me about the money he was supposed to give me for the client incentive program; divulged that instead he'd pretended it was money for Tru. "Because I wanted to go with you," he said. "I knew there was something between us when I first saw you, too."

Oh, I felt terrible. I was positively stringing the poor guy along. Not to mention the fact that I had a boyfriend! And even though this was just a job, it didn't feel right acting like this with someone other than Theo. (The thoughts of Theo kept making my mind go around, back to the Cortadero file. That Theo seemed to have taken from my bag. Or someone from the party had lifted.)

The necklace cam I wore was just amping up the situation. The camera wouldn't work unless I stayed still, so whenever I found the right cleavagey angle, I halted, frozen as if caught gazing at Tatum, in love and unawares. And while I was in such poses, sweet Tatum Reynolds described how he had taken the bank rewards that he was supposed to be giving new customers for himself—and then deposited it into his account.

"I was doing it for fun," Tatum said, staring back at me with these big brown eyes from his thin frame, "until I met you."

He'd said it with such earnestness, which he then followed up with a sideways look that I could tell immediately made him feel mysterious. He started telling me then about the issues he had with his mother, who hadn't been around much, with an older brother who "just doesn't get me."

I didn't want to get Tatum Reynolds's hopes up and I didn't want to break the already fragile heart he seemed to be offering up to me.

"So," I said, trying to take a sideways dash out of the conversation, "this wasn't the first time you did something like this? Take some of the money and get a date out of it?"

He looked at me, his eyes pained. "No," he choked out. "I feel so bad now because I know you and I will be together for a long time, and I'll never stop feeling bad that I did that with other women. Because you're the only one that matters."

Now I didn't feel as bad for him. The kid was a bullshitter.

"I bet you say that to all the girls," I said, allowing the nasally voice to come back a little.

He shook his head fast. "No, no. I've *never* said that to anyone. Honestly!" His eyes looked in mine, waiting for a response, and I could see there that he *was* being honest.

"I've never felt like this in my life." He took my hand. "I think you're..." Those earnest eyes kept searching mine. "I think you're the most amazing woman I've ever met."

Oh, Tatum, I thought. *Poor Tatum*. My heart wrenched for him because he was going to get fired and arrested. And he was also about to lose what he seemed to believe to be the love of his life.

I couldn't make it worse for the guy. I had to go to the bathroom to break the spell, then I needed to finish dinner quickly and get out. Luckily, we only had the dessert course left.

I stood. "I'll be right back," I said, slipping his hand from mine.

"I'll be waiting," he said, a happy smile on his face.

On the way to the bathroom, I thought of Mayburn and my father in Mayburn's white van parked at the corner, the one that, lately, was stenciled with the name of a faux construction company on its side. I raised the necklace cam to my face. "Ladies' room," I said. "See you guys later." I reached behind me, felt for the quarter-size panel that operated the camera, which was held with a strip of Velcro inside my dress. When I found it, I pushed the tiny button along its side that turned off the camera.

I wondered what they talked about, sitting in that van. Did they talk at all? My father, I knew, could go days without speaking and without even feeling uncomfortable about it. From the minimal information I knew about his life, it sounded like he had probably gone months without speaking to anyone.

I stepped into the bathroom. I was about to lock the door when it got kicked back open and someone pushed inside.

"Hey!" I said reflexively, but I wasn't scared right away. I thought it was probably the too-eager Tru waitstaff.

But then one of us moved and the mood lighting in the bathroom shifted and I saw him. *Holy shit, that's a big guy. That's not the Tru waiter.*

"Hey!" I said with an accusatory tone, my nerves zinging.

"So how's it going?" he answered, as if we knew each other, as if we'd simply bumped into one another. He was maybe fifty, with a square jaw and towering heft. He seemed the size of two of me. Easily.

And yet with some kind of insane optimism telling me this situation wasn't as alarming as my nerves were telling me, twanging through my body, making me almost shake, I answered him.

"It's going great," I said. "You?"

But then. *But then*—words that, in my mind, always preceded something bad happening.

But then he snatched one of my arms and twisted it behind me. "Pretty," he said, just that one word. He locked the door. Then he repeated the word, drawing it out. *"Pre-e-etty."*

The guy's hands were on both arms now, clamping them to my sides, and he spun me, faced me to the opposite wall and then shoved me against it. A hard *oomph* escaped my gut.

I tried to quickly assess, to decide.

Mayburn and my father were out in the van, ready to give me ten more minutes of blackout time before they thought anything was amiss. Due to what was surely state-of-the-art acoustics at Tru, I could hear nothing outside the bathroom, and I was sure it would be tough to hear me if I screamed. Anyway, I wasn't sure if screaming was the best thing to do with this man, who was big and violent and volatile. You could just tell.

"How's Theo?" he said. Just those two words. He shoved me hard from behind so my ribs were crushed against the wall. Some fearful sound came out of my throat, a sort of moan.

"How's Theo?" the man demanded, louder. Another push, so my lungs felt smashed, deflated. I tried to suck in air, but it was nearly impossible. I was thinking about picking up my high-heeled boot and smashing it down on his instep, just to get him off me for a second, but then he spoke again. "When you go home tonight, I want you to tell him something," he said, with another hard shove against my back, now making it impossible for me to get any room to lift my feet.

"What's that?" I managed to squeak out. I hoped that speaking out loud, in a rather calm way, would make me feel as if the situation weren't desperate, making my mind panic and scream along with it. No such luck.

"Tell him it's not his fault," the guy growled. "We know that. But in business, when you have partners, you gotta accept responsibility." Another shove. "Ya hear that?"

"Yeah."

"You understand that, right? You're a lawyer. Big firm, now a small firm."

Great. The guy knew my bio.

His hands gripped my dress harder. He shoved me again. "You tell Theo to take responsibility and figure out how to pay everyone. Then it's all good. You get it? This doesn't have to happen." He yanked my long hair. I felt tears sting my eyes, whether from pain or fear, I wasn't entirely sure, but it made the wallpaper blur into a streaky portrait of yellow and white.

"This doesn't have to happen." He pulled me

back and dropped me, and I crumpled to the ground.

I sucked in air finally, tried to concentrate on his retreating back as Mayburn yelled in my head, *I don't give a shit if you're in pain. Memorize him. Details! Details!*

But all I got was dark clothing, big height and build. All I got was a hard knot of fearful certainty that this had all gotten way, way, *way* out of control.

43

He handled the downstairs security system like he'd been told—he ripped the goddamned thing off. And it had felt good.

He climbed the stairs, taking them as quietly as possible. He was a little short of breath when he reached the top, and that disappointed him. He wasn't a big guy, but standing for his job for so many years was making him get a little fat. He had to get himself back into the gym. Back to his fighting weight. Or so he liked to call it.

Another security system outside her place, but he tried the door and it was open. Huh. Even more simple than he thought. Maybe he could start doing more side jobs like this. Problem was, he had a code of ethics, he really did, and that code didn't take lightly to beating up women. But he'd been given a cool grand for what should just be a couple of punches, maybe a couple of cracked bones. And then he'd collect another two grand.

Until then, he'd pocket a few things to make it look like a robbery. In the dark apartment now, he clapped his hands together, rubbed them and pulled them apart in a show of ease.

But right then he heard something—a scratch of some kind, maybe a drawer closing? He froze, listened some more but heard nothing. All the lights were out. He took a tentative step inside, then another, heard nothing. Then a minute sound, like someone moving just a little bit. Was the redhead home? If so, why was she in the dark? Maybe she'd gone to bed already and been startled by the door opening? But his contact had said that she lived with her boyfriend, and that the door opening wouldn't startle her anyway because she would think it was him.

Another sound. He took a step toward it, then another, walking slowing through a living room, passing a small kitchen, toward the room he thought the sound had come from. As he approached it, he saw the glow of computer equipment. An office, he thought. And that was the last thought before—*bam*—he was hit on the side of the head with something hard. His head splintered with pain. *Jesus, she wasn't surprised! And she knew how to hit someone.*

"Fuck!" he yelled. The sound of his own voice made him leap into action. His right hand shot out toward his attacker. He felt a swatch of hair and he yanked hard, then grabbed her around the throat. She groaned like an animal caught in a trap, but then she wrangled out of his grasp and threw a punch that hurt like a son-of-a-bitch. The girl was a badass. Why hadn't he been told? Had he been conned into this job so he could take a fall?

Then *wham!* He felt himself get cracked over the head with a book or something heavy.

He lunged at her. In his brain, he called up the MMA skills he'd learned recently by watching a ton of it on his computer. He grabbed her around the neck again, but she drove an elbow into his stomach and it caused him to loosen his grasp momentarily.

He snaked his hand out and snatched her by the waist. She snarled and scratched his face.

"Fuck!" he yelled again, and he tasted blood.

He took a swing, and *phwack,* he connected with her jaw.

She screamed. In the dark, he couldn't see her, but he knew the punch would probably give him a moment while she recovered. He headed toward the door, but she was still right behind him.

Wham! She'd hit him again with something. Then as he turned to her…*arrgggghhhhh!* She cracked him with that thing in the nuts. His rage made it easy to punch his arms out and grab her around the neck.

"Bastard!" he heard her say, then her words left as he knocked her head against the wall. Once, then again and again. Soon, his hands were wet. She was bleeding now, too.

It was that last thought that stopped him. He was just supposed to give her a little hurt! He dropped her fast, and she crumpled to the ground. He froze for a moment, letting himself lean a little toward her body. But no sounds came. She was silent. *Dead* kind of silent.

He thought about what he would leave behind in her condo if he ran. There wouldn't be prints because he was wearing gloves. Some of his blood. Maybe. But the scratches on his face felt nearly dry. There might be nothing. He had to hope for that. He really didn't know anything about forensics or crime scenes and this whole thing was turning his stomach to this kind of work.

He turned to the front door and threw himself through it. When he was on the street, it looked like any other night.

44

In the cab on the way home from Tru, I finally started shaking. Something about my dad's horrified expression had made me play down what had happened in the bathroom and play up the fact that I was fine. And I was—no visible scars or bruises—but I felt a fear that grew more voluminous.

I wanted to run to the van, but I felt bad enough about Tatum to be unable to leave him hanging. I told him I didn't feel well, skipped dessert, dodged a kiss and said goodbye.

When I got in the van, they were in a jocular mood, *jocular* being an adjective I would never, ever have attributed to my father. But there they were, laughing and joking. I must have looked white, because they stopped laughing as soon as they saw me. I quickly told them what happened.

"I can't believe we sent you right into danger," he said.

I was about to point out that Mayburn had never had a problem with that. Then I saw that horror on my dad's face, and I couldn't stand it.

"I'm fine," I said. I held out my arms as if to show them.

My dad could only shake his head. Mayburn went into detective mode, asking me a million questions about the specifics of what had happened, then we debated calling the police.

But I didn't want to make things worse for Theo. If he were telling the truth, and it wasn't him who had stolen money from the company, it wouldn't look good to tell the authorities that some thug had said Theo had to take responsibility.

I texted Theo. Didn't hear back.

We looked at my necklace cam, but I hadn't caught a glance of the guy on film. He must have come behind me as I turned it off.

I brought the conversation around back to Tatum, feeling that the more I talked about the guy, the more real he was becoming and the more confusing the whole situation was becoming.

"I feel so bad for that kid," my dad said then about Tatum. "He's doing the wrong thing for the right reason."

"What's the right reason for stealing money from the bank?" Mayburn asked.

"Love. He's looking for it."

I don't think either Mayburn or I knew what to say to that, but I knew in my mind that was the same reason my father had left us, his family, so many years ago. He loved us. Beyond anything. And therefore, he'd left us to keep us safe.

Mayburn and my dad wanted to take me to

my mom's. If we weren't calling the police, they wanted me to stay the night there, but right then Theo called. He was on his way to our place in a cab, and I convinced them I was fine and to let me get a cab home myself. Theo and I needed to talk. Something needed to give.

"Where were you?" I asked Theo when I was in the cab and had called him again. That's when I started noticing the trembling.

"Working. You knew that."

"Okay, don't snap at me. Yeah, I knew *this morning*. But a lot has happened since then. And I haven't been able to find you!" I hated the shrewish tone of my voice. I was not a whiner, not a complainer. I was *not* one of those women. But I sure felt like one now. The trembling intensified.

"I just got threatened because of you. And...and roughed up!" *Roughed up.* It struck me as an odd phrase.

"What?" He sounded horrified. "Oh, my God, what happened? Where are you? I'm just a few blocks away."

"Me, too." Suddenly, I didn't want to be at my place, alone with Theo. "Meet me at Twin Anchors?" More shaking. What did this mean, these feelings of trepidation? Were they simply related to the guy in the bathroom and all that was happening, or was I getting a greater message from the gods in my universe? If so, it was way too foggy to read.

"Yeah, let's meet there instead of the house."

As soon as I hung up, I concentrated on calming

down. *Breathe, breathe, breathe,* I ordered myself. Then when I caught a few breaths, I took it slower. *Breathe, Iz, breathe. Don't think about anything. Just let your mind relax.*

I must have learned something over the past year. Because I actually started to allow myself not to think about everything, not to analyze. And that's when some words—what were they?—some words I'd heard this past week niggled at my brain, wanting to be recognized.

I tried to replay conversations in my head, but it was difficult. I'd done so much this week, been to so many places. So I backed off again. I just let it go, tried to let everything go. And finally—finally—was struck by the vague familiarity of two words that kept returning to me. Where had I heard them before?

I focused some more. I heard myself say *foreign...trust,* Maggie had said the Cortaderos likely kept money in a foreign trust. *Foreign,* Sam had said. It wasn't a foreign thing for me being involved with someone who was in trouble with the law. And then I told him I trusted him. And Theo—when he'd learned about getting turned down for the mortgage, he'd said something like that. Something about a foreign trust.

I threw a twenty at the cabbie when we reached Sedgwick and Eugenie, crossing the street to where Theo was doing the same.

Inside, it was crowded but we scored two bar stools. There, I told Theo what had happened at

Tru, watching his anguished eyes, watching him fighting tears.

"I don't know what is going on," he said, his voice weary now. "I don't know what's going on with this or the business or where all our funds have disappeared to."

"That's something I wanted to talk to you about. Have you confirmed that your funds have disappeared?"

He nodded. "I've been on the phone with the bankers. Hell, I didn't even know who the bankers were before this, but now I do."

"How did it happen?"

"The accounts that we paid bills from? They were funded by the venture capital money that we got initially. And we had more than enough. *More* than enough for day-to-day operations and for all the expansion we wanted to do. We had no problems paying our bills. But from what I can now tell, money started leaving the account at some point. Small amounts at first, then larger when, I guess, no one noticed. It's been really hard to track where it's gone."

"Any chance it's a foreign trust?"

He looked surprised. "Yeah. Or something like that. I forgot about it. I mean, I heard about it when we formed the company, but I'm not sure I really get it. What exactly is a foreign trust?'"

"It's a vehicle used to protect assets and money by putting them in a country where the laws are different than ours."

"You put money there you want to hide?"

"Not necessarily. You might just want the tax benefits." I thought about it. "Who opened that account?" I asked. "The foreign trust?"

"My dad."

I let a second pass. Then, "Who managed that account?"

He let no time pass before he answered, "My dad."

45

How long did we sit there, the restaurant bustling around us?

I noticed my trembling had started again. Theo did, too, and quickly asked the bartender to bring some water. *You need to eat something,* he said. But that wasn't it. I'd eaten more than enough at Tru.

So I made myself breathe again. Then I finally said it. "Your dad."

"Yeah."

"Did Eric know about the trust?"

"Yeah. But what does that mean?"

"I don't know. I'm just thinking about that guy tonight saying you have to take responsibility when you have partners. I thought he meant Eric, but could he have meant your dad?"

Theo said nothing, seemed to be thinking hard.

"How is Eric?" I asked.

"I saw him today, and he's the same. He's unconscious. They're actually keeping him in a medically induced coma so that certain parts of his brain can regrow. Or something like that…"

Theo seemed to shrink a little, and suddenly I thought of that picture of him in his teens. Theo, before all the confidence and the smarts and the sexiness.

But no matter what state he was in, I had to ask the other question I'd been wondering. "Did you take the Cortadero file from my bag?"

For a second he didn't say anything. And in that second, he scared me. *Was I right that he'd taken the Cortadero file? Why? And why had someone busted into a restaurant bathroom and given me that message?*

"What do you mean?" Theo said, finally speaking. He was looking down though, at the bar top.

Might as well lay it out. "The Cortadero file, about the one case we have left with them at the firm. It was in my bag." I leaned down to look at him. I needed to see his face. "That file was in my bag, in my home office. And now I can't find it."

A sigh. "I didn't mean to take it."

"You didn't *mean* to take it?" My voice rose, but in the loud restaurant no one noticed. Except for Theo.

He looked at me with a nervous expression. "Well, I guess I did. I was looking for something else and I opened your bag."

I held up a hand. "Hold it a second. What were you looking for that you had to go in my bag? Truthfully, I really don't care if you did. Nothing in our place is off-limits, but I'm just curious about what you could be looking for that would require you to go through my bag. A pen? There are pens on the desktop. Some paper? It's in a drawer." I stopped talking suddenly when I realized I was in danger of a rant.

"Okay, I'll just admit it. I *was* looking for this." Theo reached into the bag he'd been carrying. And there was the Cortadero file. "I came back from work and you were gone. I didn't think you would be home for a while, since you had texted that you were out with your brother and Mayburn and your dad. And I wanted to help, to help find out what in the hell the Cortaderos think they have to do with me. Or HeadFirst." He was talking faster and faster. "So I went to Starbucks and read this thing. Studied it. But I didn't find anything. I still have no idea what the Cortaderos have to do with us."

A group entering the restaurant jostled me from behind. They were laughing, happy. I wondered if I would be like that again—carefree. "I want to go home," I said.

Last year, when I was just an average fiancée, just an average lawyer, before I'd moonlighted as a P.I., before…well, before everything that has happened in the past year…back then my senses were not as highly tuned, it might have taken me until we were right in front of my building before my internal alarm went off. To be honest, as exhausted as I was that night, I'm surprised I was able to perceive much of anything.

But when we were a few feet away from my

condo, that internal alarm went off in my brain. *Something is wrong!* the alarm said. *Very wrong.*

I tried to rationalize with myself. *Of course something is wrong. Your boyfriend has been arrested. And now he's admitted to stealing something from you.*

It wouldn't go away—a something-is-off feeling, layered with a sense of being violated.

But I ignored it. My brain was too muddied, trying to keep track of too many things, and decide which of them to believe. *Who* to believe.

And Theo? What was the excuse for him not noticing the keypad by the front door was hanging off? I didn't know. Likely because he was so close behind me, still trying to explain why he'd taken the Cortadero file, still trying to process the new suspicions that were starting to arise about his dad, when he already had so many suspicions about his partner.

But I stopped when I hit the third-floor landing, staring at the slightly ajar door of my condo.

Theo stopped, too. He was saying something about Eric. Then his words stopped.

We froze for a second, processing.

Theo stepped around me before I could tell him to stop. Before I could say *Nooooo,* he had swung the door open.

I don't know what either of us expected. But it was dark. Just like it always was at night in November.

Theo went to switch on the light inside the doorway, but I put my hand on his arm to stop him. "Wait," I whispered.

"Hello?" I called into the condo. If there's anything spookier than hearing your own voice calling into an empty space, I don't know what it is. Still, I took another step inside my door and called again. "Hello? Anyone here?"

Theo switched the light on.

There was someone there.

"Kim?" I said.

She was twisted and slumped on my living room floor.

Theo ran to her, touched her. "She's freezing." He grabbed her wrist, leaned in and turned his head to listen for breath. I remembered then that Theo had told me he'd been a lifeguard during high school, and I got a flash of him, as I did that day watching him with his mom, of a younger Theo, uncomplicated, unperturbed. What was it about Theo Jameson that made me wish he could be an innocent forever?

But that wasn't going to happen. Theo sat back. Looked at me. "She's dead."

46

One week later

His brother began to weep, softly at first, but his distress quickly grew. Soon, Vincente's back was hunched, his shoulders shaking violently up and down.

José Ramon had never heard his brother cry, not since they were young children in Xalapa, Mexico, before his parents had sent them to Chicago to be raised as Americans. And he had certainly never heard him cry like this. In fact, the only time he recalled hearing those types of cries was at the funeral for his grandfather when his grandmother shrieked and sobbed and threw herself upon the casket.

He was glad now for his soundproofed room behind the restaurant, from which his employees could hear nothing. He was grateful for the presence of his parents, sitting across the room, having flown in from Xalapa after José heard about the killing of the girl, after he had called them and told all he knew, refusing to hide his brother's sins anymore. He and his parents had discussed what he knew and they realized the situation in Chicago was veering quickly, quickly away from them. But they still didn't understand it. And they were waiting for an explanation.

Vincente, or Vince as he liked everyone to call him now, had blue-black hair and brown eyes that normally gleamed. He was dressed as he always was—like a handsome, young American businessman. And he didn't just dress the part, he lived it. Vince Cort had a mansion in Barrington Hills, where he and his wife, Carol, kept horses, where his kids were in Montessori schools and where Carol ran the most popular book club in town in addition to being the board president of three very reputable charities. Carol Cort, of course, didn't know the whole story of her husband. She knew, rightly, that he'd grown up in a Mexican neighborhood, that he'd gotten perfect grades all the way up through college and his MBA. She knew he ran a venture capital firm called Barrington Hills Trading that invested in various businesses. The only part she didn't know was where the money he invested came from.

José Ramon often envied lives like Carol's—wealth without knowledge or concern where the money came from.

As Vincente's cries turned to wails, his parents looked at each other. Finally, his father nodded at his mother, a woman who *did* care where her family's money came from. And wasn't afraid to take some responsibility for it. Or make sure others took their own.

His mother stood, crossing to Vincente, her youngest son, sinking to her knees in front of him and wrapping her arms around his neck. He fell upon her, literally fell off the chair and onto her body weight, which had grown heavier over the years as she'd grown more comfortable. She and his father had grown into their retirement, knowing the money they'd made, that their quiet men in Mexico continued to make, was safely being hidden in legitimate businesses in the United States.

Until Vincente started to lose control. And then until the girl died.

She was José's underling. She worked for him. And it was he alone who controlled her fate—or so he had thought. Her murder made them realize they weren't the only dogs in this race, the race they were losing because of Vincente. And so his parents had come to the U.S., something they'd done only once before. It was considered too dangerous for them to travel here, but now, it was too dangerous for them not to, when their world in this country was running away like a wild animal.

From behind his desk, José looked at his father, who was short and fat but always elegant, now wearing a beautifully tailored black suit. His father simply nodded at him. José stood and walked to his mother and brother. He pulled another chair close to where his brother sat.

When they first arrived, he had told his brother to sit, isolated, in the center of the room. He wanted to sit behind his desk, with his parents sitting together, so that Vincente could feel the drift, the soon-to-be severing of his place in the family. His parents had wanted it that way, too, but no one had expected this show of emotion.

José arranged another chair so that his mother could sit next to his brother. She hauled Vincente by the shoulders until he was upright again.

But he couldn't stop sobbing. José looked over his shoulder at his father again.

His father shook his head in disgust. His words, though, sounded kind, as they were intended to. *"Está bien,* Vincente. *Hablaremos mañana."* Tomorrow. Vincente had been granted a reprieve.

47

After Kim was killed, Theo shaved his head.

I couldn't understand. He had the most gorgeous hair. Tawny brown, soft, thick, hanging to his shoulders, framing his face, drawing attention to those lips.

It's not that he didn't look handsome without hair. He did. He couldn't avoid being handsome no matter how hard he tried. But the lack of hair took away whatever curves Theo had, the rounded-out parts of him. He was edgy now, always—edgy in mood, and in other things, too. His music became less restrained, louder, sharper.

Constantly, he picked through his boxes of belongings, the ones he moved into my house only a few weeks before. He rarely put anything away in the same box. At first, I wondered what he was looking for. Eventually I started to wonder if he was trying to say something with all the arranging.

Sometimes, when he wasn't home, I would stand above one of those boxes. I didn't touch anything like I did last time. But I let my eyes travel over everything he had grouped in the boxes now. A framed dollar bill—the first he and Eric made with the company, he'd said. *Before all this.* A silver monogrammed pen holder his mother gave him. Some DVDs, some CDs. Nothing jumped out at me.

Finally, I decided he didn't know what he was saying, either. Rather, he was searching—that's what he was doing. I could tell now. He rarely stopped moving. His eyes didn't linger on me anymore. He was searching for answers. We all were.

48

A week after we found Kim dead, after Thanksgiving weekend, I arrived at the quiet office of Bristol & Associates at 6:30 a.m.

And Maggie was already there.

In fact, she looked like she'd been there for hours in her tornado mode, which is when she shot into hyperspace activity and would pick up steam from anything and anyone around her. I suspected that this particular tornado mode was not due to any particular case or trial, but rather because her best friend had found herself in trouble. Again. And Maggie Bristol wanted to be ready to do anything that was needed.

And yet as I stepped in her office, I sensed there was something else going on, too. That mysteriousness Maggie had been wearing for weeks was still there. But my intuition was off anyway. Clearly. Because I had no intuitive guess about why Kim was in my condo when I wasn't and why someone killed her—punching her, according to the autopsy, scratching her, beating her against the floor or a wall or some other hard surface, and finally throwing her to the floor, causing a brain bleed that brought about death.

Death. Why does it seem to keep seeking me? What does it want?

I stepped farther into Maggie's office. Such thoughts of morbidity and fear were never helpful. I knew that. But they were always near lately. They were downright tenacious.

She waved me to a seat in front of her desk, and we talked like we always did—*What's going on? How's Bernard? How was the holiday?*

"Oh, the holiday," I said. "Odd."

"I'm sure," Maggie said. "After all that happened last week. Was Theo with you for Thanksgiving?"

"No, he always spends it with his mother. That's what we'd decided before...before all this anyway."

Theo had gone to his mom's, had returned pensive, saying he was worried about her health. He always feared her breast cancer could return, and although she said she was fine, she was thin lately, seeming frail, the way she got when she had health issues. She'd promised she would see a doctor.

"I was at Mom and Spence's," I told Maggie. "Charlie was there, of course."

"And your dad?"

"Yep."

I told her about Spence's attempt to have my father partake in a Thanksgiving wine tasting. "Doesn't he know that Dad lived in Italy for decades? He probably knows way more about wine than Spence," Charlie had said while we watched the setup.

I had laughed. "I don't think Spence cares. He's just trying to establish a connection any way he can." Spence had been doing this for a few months now—reaching out to my father and trying to make him a part of our family.

Charlie and I watched as my father's eyes squinted behind his copper glasses and he swished wine around in his mouth. Then he spit it out into an empty glass.

Spence blinked a few times. I'd once heard him say that he'd never understood why people tasted wine like that. *What a waste!* he'd said. *I mean I know technically it's the right way, but it's just pathologically stupid.* My mother, also an avid wine lover, had agreed.

They both watched, their faces slightly pained, as Christopher McNeil picked up the second glass.

Spence held his hand out. "Chris, maybe you should just taste it. You know. Really taste it, swallow it. Because we're trying to figure out what wine we'll pair with dinner."

My dad blinked, looked up at Spence. "You want me to drink it?"

"Right. Drink it. You know, we're trying to see what we like here."

I could tell my father wanted to explain something, probably that the best way not to fatigue your taste buds was to taste wine without swallowing it.

My dad looked at Spence's face and seemed to understand that this *drinking* thing meant a lot to the man. He gave a silent, succinct nod. He sipped the second wine, then the third. He pointed at the second. "I enjoy this one the most."

A massive smile spread over Spence's face. "Me, too! Me, too! Great minds, eh?"

Charlie turned to me. "God, life is weird."

"Amen, brother." I sighed. "I suppose it would be weirder if Theo were here."

"Huh," Charlie said. "That's true."

I stopped talking to Maggie then, when I realized she hadn't said anything during my retelling of Thanksgiving. Instead she was peering at me, as if trying to read something in my face.

"A couple of weeks ago, you said you felt like you were falling in love with Theo," she said.

"I know," I answered quickly.

"And now you look like you have some doubts," Maggie said. "I mean, hey, I don't blame you. You've got reason."

I thought about that. Then I thought about the emotions I'd felt through my time with Theo. From the beginning. And it seemed those emotions had gone through a journey. First, a lifting—a lift of any darkness around my soul, any shadow over my psyche. Back then, I wanted to hug him and kiss him and have sex with him and then hold him and then do it all again. My next emotion was awareness. *So maybe I am still in love.*

But then a questioning came in. At first it was only because I had begun to realize what a massive risk it was to fall in love. Because if I was in love with Theo and I was going to accept that—to continue to take it in, to revel in it the way love was intended (or at least the way I'd always assumed it was intended)—I was going to have to open my arms wide. My eyes wide. I was going to have to trust him. And because everything started happening then, I realized I would have to give myself, entirely and with all of me. I would also have to provide him with trust so that he could confide in me. But how could I do all that now that he'd been arrested, and Kim had been killed and now that I had so many questions?

Maggie must have seen the warring emotions on my face. "Hard to explain?"

"Yeah." I cleared my throat. "I think I need to get my head away from all that. Let's talk work."

"You're sure?"

"Yeah."

She paused for a moment, then said decisively, "Okay. So what's going on with coke-on-a-boat?"

"The U.S. Attorneys let me know that they're ready to go forward with the case. I'm not sure what their rush is, but now they say we'll get the FBI 302s any day."

Maggie clapped. The 302s would provide us documentation about the FBI's investigative reports, interview transcripts, witness statements, bank records and any subpoenas the government had issued. In short, all the evidence they had against the Cortaderos. The 302s in Theo's case, alas, weren't due for a while.

"Great," Mags said. "Let me know what you find. And what else do you have today?"

"Ah, well. In addition to playing catch-up, I have a meeting with Vaughn after work."

"*Detective* Vaughn?" Maggie asked.

"Yeah. I gotta tell you about that."

"I have something to tell you, too. But Vaughn..." She waved a hand at me to continue.

"Well, he was there that night. About thirty minutes after we found Kim and called the police." I paused. Thought. "It was all so surreal."

That night, the bizarre nature of what was unfolding before me—Kim's body, the EMTs, the police, more police—had rendered me shocked. And scared. And my fear increased—went sky-high—when I saw Vaughn cross the threshold of my doorway. But in one look, and a quick shake of his head, as if to say, *It's okay,* I felt strangely better. I suppose that during all of the time I'd spent despising Vaughn, pissed off and bitter at the indignities I'd felt he put me through, I had come into a belief about him—namely, regardless of all his spite and jackassery, he was a good detective. And he always seemed to ferret out the truth, *eventually*—and usually that was the real truth, not just the truth as he saw it.

Sure enough, Vaughn stepped in that doorway, listened for a minute to the update his cops gave him, then began giving a lecture on suspects—"potential suspects," he said—and how it was better to have a number of them. "Keep your fricking minds open," he told the cops.

Since then, nothing had really happened on the case, I told Maggie. But Vaughn had been calling me a few times a day, leaving a message if I wasn't around. *"Hello, this is Detective Vaughn, calling from Area 3. We're going to be talking to the neighbors today. We'll let you know when we find anything significant."*

It almost made me laugh sometimes, Vaughn's professional formality, although we'd had nothing but professional dealings together. And the fact was, that was exactly what I needed from him now—a continued, professional focus on Kim's case. Because if I didn't find out why my neighbor was in my condo and why she was killed there, I was going to have to sell said condo, and soon. Or I was going to go nuts.

"Theo, meanwhile," I said to Maggie. "He doesn't seem quite as concerned about Kim."

"What?" Maggie made a disgusted face.

"No, I mean he feels awful, and he wants to know what's going on, but I don't think he sees it as tied to him or his problems in any way. And I'm not sure it is, either. It just seems like we're both freaked out and concerned but about different stuff. Lately, he's been telling me half stories about his father, Brad."

"What kind of stories?"

"About his involvement in HeadFirst from the beginning. And about this foreign trust that Brad had set up to keep some of the holdings and how more and more of the money seems to have gone there."

"We need all of that," Maggie said. "Every bit of information he's got."

"I know, but every time we talk about it, I mention Kim and then he gets irritated and then we both get sad, and just want to end the pain for a minute. Either Theo hasn't figured anything else out, or he hasn't told me."

We were both silent. Maggie chewed at her bottom lip.

"I figure since it's *our* evidence," I continued, "then technically, if we can get our hands on anything, we can keep it."

"Hell yeah," Maggie said. "We'll keep it and use it." We both looked at each other. I think we both knew that Theo's would not be an easy case. And that thought made me nauseous.

"I thought I'd run it all by Vaughn," I said.

Maggie nodded. "Never hurts to have ten eyes on a case." She paused for a moment. "What does Theo's dad say?" Maggie asked.

"They haven't been able to connect. Theo wants to have the conversation in person."

Q sailed into Maggie's office. "Did I hear someone mention the name of Vaughn from down the hallway?" he said. "Do we like him now?"

"Kinda," I said. "We're meeting after work so I can try and figure out exactly what the cops are doing about Kim's death or if I can help. I can't just sit around and hope for the best anymore. And he actually said something to me about how we should get over our differences."

Q plopped himself in the other visitor's chair. "That's goddamned priceless. *Your* differences. I'm sure he means his. But it would be nice not to have to hate him anymore. Then I can admit that I've always had a little crush on Damon Vaughn."

"What?" Maggie and I yelled.

"Yeah, ever since he came to Baltimore & Brown. Remember that, Iz?"

"Unfortunately." It had been a hellish time— Sam gone, and suddenly two police detectives were in my office.

"His partner was a big guy, remember that?" Q asked.

"Yeah."

"He was yummy, too."

Maggie and I shook our heads.

"Speaking of yummy," Q said. "How's Theo holding up?"

"He cut his hair."

Q's hand flew to his chest. "That man has the best hair in the business. Tell me he just got a trim."

I made the sound of a razor and drew a fist over my head to mimic shaving.

"No!" Q said.

"That's some serious shit," Maggie said.

"It's symbolic," I said.

"Of what?" Q asked. "Temporary insanity? That's like taking a hammer to a stained-glass window. If you ain't Demi Moore, put the clippers down. Damn, girl. Samson done lost his power."

Maggie laughed. "I've got to get some work done, people."

"Okay, sure thing," Q said, looking from Maggie to me and back. When no one said anything, he stood. Then almost immediately he sat down again. "Are we going to talk about the other thing?"

"What other thing?" Maggie asked.

He stared at her, and stared.

"What?" I asked.

"What?" Maggie repeated.

Q shifted in his chair, opened and closed his mouth a few times. "Uh…" He looked at me, then back at Maggie.

"Q, for cripes sake," I said. "What's going on?"

His eyebrows drew lower on his face. "You know how I have no gay-dar?" he said to me.

"Yeah. That's because you were straight for so long. Or forcing yourself to be straight, so your processing got messed up." I was repeating things Q had told me after years in therapy, and he nodded vigorously at my summation.

"Right. And that's why I'm attracted to super-straight guys like Damon Vaughn. But do you remember what I *do* have a good radar for?"

"Um…guys who wax their backs? Didn't you tell me something like that once?"

Q nodded appreciatively. "Yes, that's true. Remember the other radar?"

Maggie untucked her legs, started putting her

feet back in her boots. "Okay, kids, you continue this fun trip down memory lane while I go in search of more caffeine."

Q held up a hand. "You will *not* be drinking caffeine. You're pregnant, Maggie Bristol."

"Oh, Jesus, Q!" I said. "You—"

But Maggie didn't look indignant. She just looked surprised. "How did you know?"

"You're *pregnant?*" I said.

She ignored me. Just kept staring at Q. Then she looked down at her belly. Or the place where her belly would be if she had one. "Am I showing?"

"Oh, God, no," Q said. "You look amazing. Better than ever, actually. I can just *tell.*" He nodded, appearing very proud of himself, while I looked back and forth between the two of them.

"I didn't know you were trying to get pregnant," I said. For some reason, I felt hurt that I didn't know this about my friend. But it did answer the question of why she'd been so distracted and strange.

"I *wasn't* trying to get pregnant."

"Well, then…why?"

She glared. "It wasn't planned."

"Then how did it happen?" Maggie was like a prophet for safe sex. She could pick up on a conversation at the next table at a restaurant and soon be leaning in to give them a helpful lecture about condoms.

She shook her head. "We just weren't… I can't explain it, except that I felt somewhere that if it happened, it would just be meant to happen, but I did *not* expect it to happen."

"Is that why Bernard moved here?"

She nodded. "It was a hard decision. We're going to try to have a family together."

The enormity of it hit me. I started tearing up.

"Oh, Iz." Maggie leaned forward, put her hand on mine.

I let the tears roll. I was crying for so many things—for all that had happened recently, for Q, who was so happy at this job and who didn't know he might soon lose it, for Maggie, who was going to be a mom! A beautiful, wonderful, smart and fantastic mom. And she was promising her heart to a man who would guard it happily and completely. And I was crying because this was the end of Maggie and me as we knew it. The end of an era.

I sniffled. Stopped.

Maggie sat back and looked at Q. "I can't believe you knew."

"Do you want to know what you're going to have?"

"You mean like boy or girl?"

He nodded. "I have a hundred percent accuracy, except when it comes to family members."

"Uh…yeah. No. Yeah." She shook her head again. "*No.* I have to start making decisions with Bernard about this."

"Wow," I said. "Wow."

49

José Ramon's mother glanced at her husband, and they had a conversation with their eyes. *It's time for Vincente to come clean. Yes. He must tell us.*

An orange-white light of midmorning streamed through his penthouse windows, as they sat at the dining room table. His mother, who hadn't prepared her own meals since she was a young girl of ten (before her own father made his money, before she married a man who made even more) had been working for hours to prepare an elaborate Mexican breakfast. The table, now laden with dishes—papaya drizzled with lime juice, corn cakes, chorizo, eggs and tortillas—seemed to be sending the message that a civilized meal (and therefore a civilized conversation) was about to be held. The fact that his mother had not relied on any cooks, had not allowed José to call in his help, either, sent the message that things were also very, very serious and very private.

Now that they were all seated, his father nodded and his mother returned her gaze to Vincente. "You have had a night to sleep, Vincente, to collect your-self. Now, tell us," she said.

She crossed her arms and sat back in her chair. The message was clear—no more crying. *Solamente la verdad*—only the truth.

His brother began talking. Clearly he had told this story to himself in his head or to the mirror this morning. "You all know how it went at the beginning," he said. "We were all consulted on this. At first, it was an investment. I was told about software HeadFirst had created." He glanced at his parents. "You remember, software is something you use on your computer—"

"Yo comprendo!" his father said in a harsh bark. "I know what it is! What I do *not* understand is why..." His father stopped himself short, halting what was sure to be a rage-filled tirade. He seemed to have caught himself, with the last shred of respect he had for his youngest son. He nodded at Vincente. "Continue."

Vincente nodded back, spoke faster. "I was told about the genius of the two developers. The boys from Stanford. I was told about the great influx of cash they had received to develop their product, their staff, their sales and their distribution. I did my due diligence. I did comparables, industry-historical validation, valuation analysis, simulation analysis, everything I learned in school, in business, and from you, Papa."

His father made no response to that. His brother kept talking.

"I made a measured risk. And it was a risk, sure, but that is how things are done in the United States, especially in the technology business. And we all agreed." He looked at his mother, who nodded in understanding, acknowledging that they had all consented to the risk.

"You all saw the returns," Vincente said. "They were small at first, as we'd been told to expect, but then they grew. There was never astronomical growth. Six percent, ten percent, maybe twelve or thirteen percent. Occasionally fifteen, maybe eighteen percent once. And then naturally, there were reports of losses, not much, but it all seemed very appropriate for this type of business. There was never anything to lead me to think it was some kind of Ponzi scheme like so many idiot Americans have fallen for. I still don't believe that was true."

His father opened his mouth, and as the family was highly attuned to his behavior, they all looked at him. But he caught himself this time before a shout erupted from his throat.

"The returns weren't thirty percent or some such!" Vincente said defensively. "We weren't over-promised. Eventually, because it was a good investment, a fourth of our money was in HeadFirst, and I felt good with it there. You all did, too."

Vincente looked pointedly at him, and José couldn't help but nod. He had to admit that his brother had consulted him at one point, wanting to increase the amount of the family's money they were putting into U.S. businesses in order to hide the source of those funds. And he had agreed. But he wasn't the *expert*. That's what Vincente claimed to be. *A venture capitalist,* he called himself. *A manager of wealth.*

Just thinking of Vincente's arrogance made him wish he could take back the nod. He scowled at his brother now.

"And the growth continued," Vincente said. "Just like I'd hoped, like I'd expected. Returns of ten percent, twelve percent, fifteen percent and then sure, like any investment, an occasional loss of two percent or three, but then another fifteen percent gain. All in all, it was the best performing investment we had made. And so eventually we had a third of our money in one company. And then soon one half."

His father spoke for the first time. "Nearly one hundred million, is that right, Vincente? I simply want to make certain I understand completely. I want to make sure that now you are telling me *la verdad.*" His father's voice wasn't raised anymore, but they both knew the tone.

Vincente choked on something, maybe another rising sob. He nodded.

"What happened then?" his mother said.

"Why didn't you tell us?" his father said in the same tone. It was the tone José recognized as the one that preceded some of the worst things Vincente and José had seen when they visited Mexico. Things his father made them see so that they understood that yes, they were his sons, but they could suffer the same fate.

A shiver, like a slick, silver snake, ran through José's body, but he didn't let it show itself. His body always reacted the same way when he thought of the beheadings, of men hung upside down from trees, their necks mere stumps. His father had relished living in sleepy Xalapa and the fact that no one suspected it as part of the drug trade. But the truth was, Xalapa sat right in the middle of drug-smuggling routes that ran north from Guatemala. All his father had to do, decades ago after he married a businessman's daughter, was intercept the traffic and start a small traveler's tax. His business had grown, and he quickly outgrew the colonial reaches of his father-in-law's mind frame. He realized that connections in the U.S., whether legal or financial, were prized. It was why he sent his own children to be raised in the U.S. Yet he always reminded them when they returned that he was the boss, and crossing him meant a certain fate. His sons had learned much in the U.S., had brought the family much legit money by funneling it through regular investments and moving their trade into the U.S., but it allowed them to view ruthless violence somewhat differently than their relatives had, especially Vincente. Since he was the businessman, he left the dirty work to José, who didn't mind it at all. Or who hired someone like Freddie to do it. But demonstrative violence—headless bodies hung out for all to see—wasn't in José's playbook. He didn't have the taste for it the way their father did.

His mother knew that tone of her husband's well.

She feared him also, but not quite as much as her sons did. She shook her head at her husband and nodded for her youngest to continue.

"Once we had half of our money with them, it was the same as when we first invested. But our other investments were not doing as well," Vincente said. "This was the beginning of the economic crash, although no one saw it coming."

His father glared and Vincente glared back. "No one!" Vincente said defiantly. "I shifted more money into the company. Those other investments kept losing. Even though our input into those was relatively small—ten million here, eighteen million there, thirty million in another one—when they began to get hit harder and harder, I looked to HeadFirst to withdraw some of our funds. I wanted to cover the other losses, and reclaim some liquidity."

The room was silent. José knew that despite his father's rage at the situation, he was just as curious to understand how it had all gone wrong.

"Papa," Vincente said, looking at their father, "you told me that no matter what I learned in business school, I had to always remember to keep the family's money—the original money we made on anything—safe."

His father granted him a solemn nod.

"So I asked to withdraw certain funds from HeadFirst. They started paying me, and all was well. But then they missed payments, or could only pay half of them. There were many excuses. Then they said they actually needed some more funding to help launch a new version of their product that they were going to reveal in a few months. I was scared at that point."

His father, who hated fear although he expected it from everyone around him, straightened his spine.

"If I am honest with myself," Vincente continued, his words almost tumbling over one another, "I had an inkling that something was wrong. But I couldn't know for sure, and I was desperate to stay the course, and—"

José's disgust for his brother flamed so high then he couldn't contain himself. "You were desperate to keep your star status as the money manager of the family. You didn't want us to think *badly* of you. So instead of bringing us in, you took us all down without asking."

Vincente looked near tears again, but he collected himself. "Yes. What you say is true. I have been weak. And I have stained the family because of it."

50

When I left the office to meet Vaughn, it was snowing outside. For some reason, the first snowfall in Chicago tends to freak people out, leave them running for cabs. Later, we will all barely notice the snow, so inured to it we become. But that week, on the Monday after Thanksgiving weekend, with one of the first snows dumping hearty, wet flakes, there were no cabs to be had.

Still, I had time to get to the Billy Goat to meet Vaughn. And it was within walking distance.

Twenty minutes later, I was shaking the snow from my curls and walking down the steps under Michigan Avenue into a cavelike bar called the Billy Goat. The place used to be known for newsmen taking a break from the beat. Now it was a lot of tourists and a lot of regulars. Which made me realize Vaughn was probably a regular.

"What can I get you to drink?" the bartender asked.

"Umm…" I glanced at the wine list in my hand, which might as well have read *Wines: White or Red*.

I flipped the menu over then looked on the back at the beer menu, which listed about forty varieties, draft and bottle.

Vaughn slipped onto a bar stool next to me with a "Hey, how are ya?" said mostly under his breath.

As he shed his jacket, I glanced at his waist. Yep, he was carrying a gun. It occurred to me that I'd never had cocktails with an armed person before.

"What are you having?" I asked Vaughn, not exactly sure how this was supposed to go.

Vaughn looked at the bartender. "I'll have soda with bitters and two limes."

I frowned at him. "Does that drink have alcohol in it?"

He shook his head.

"How are we supposed to 'get over our differences' without both of us ingesting alcohol?"

I ordered a can of Old Style, just to give him an implied dig—*I'm more of a man than you are.*

At that, one side of his mouth lifted. And stayed there.

"Do you know," I said to him, "that you're smiling with just the left side of your mouth?"

His lips dropped back to midline. "Sorry," he said. He took a slug of the water already on the bar. "Sorry."

"What are you sorry about?"

"I'm trying not to drink as much. And I'm trying to smile more."

We sat in a pocket of silence. I thought of Q saying he had a crush on Vaughn. I'd laughed when he said it, but now, looking at Vaughn without the usual haze of hatred, I could see what Q meant. He looked to be lightly muscled under his button-down shirt and jacket. And although he was almost always wearing a sullen expression, it sat well on his square-jawed face, made his brown eyes appear brooding.

The bartender came back and delivered our drinks. Vaughn grimaced at his, then lifted it and handed it back to her. "Can you dump half of this and add Grey Goose?" He stayed silent until the bartender returned with the drink.

"Did you know she was Hispanic?" Vaughn said then.

"The bartender?"

"The victim."

"You mean Kim." My heart tanked again at the reminder. "Kim Parkway," I said, as if by stating her name aloud I could somehow bring her back.

"Her name wasn't Parkway. It was Padilla-Rodriguez."

"Really?" I took a sip. Cold beer on a cold day. Really not a bad thing.

"Yeah, she was kinda fair-skinned, but she was Hispanic all right. Grew up in Pilsen and everything. She was a tough kid. Arrested a bunch of times in high school. Twice for battery—she beat the shit out of her boyfriend. Couple of times for PCS."

"Possession of a controlled substance."

"And in her case it was with intent to sell two out of three times."

For some reason, I wanted to defend Kim, who couldn't do it for herself anymore. "But people do dumb things during high school."

"The last PCS was a year and a half ago. She almost landed herself some jail time with that one, but some doctor bailed her out and paid a lot to get her a good lawyer."

"A year and a half ago?" I was stunned. "What kind of drugs?"

"Coke mostly."

"Cocaine? Kim? I didn't see that coming."

"Yeah, well, believe it. I asked around and apparently that girl had a good business going for a while. Turns out she's a big seller on the Northside. You know, for the moms and professionals who want to do drugs sometimes but don't want it to be seedy." Vaughn laughed. Or something approximating that. "They want to deal with someone like them. So Ms. Padilla-Rodriguez has been selling for years and doing well for herself."

I thought about the day I met her. "When people came to her place that day, they were really, really happy to see her. But that doesn't mean anything."

"Yes, it does. They were probably on a tweak mission."

"What does that mean?"

"You're on a tweak mission when you're out and looking to score some coke." Vaughn took a few long sips of his drink.

I told Vaughn about the party—of the different people pulling Kim into different rooms, everyone happy and talkative, Kim coming out of one of those rooms with her eyes very wide.

"Yeah," Vaughn said. "She was chalked up."

"Huh?"

"She was high."

"If that's what was going on, I can't believe I was so clueless."

"Hey, don't beat yourself up. If you're not into drugs, you wouldn't notice things like that."

"Still…" Since I'd started working for Maggie and spending much of my time at 26th and Cal, I considered myself somewhat wise in the ways of the world. Apparently, I had a ways to go. "So who was her source?" At least I knew the right questions to ask now.

"We're trying to figure that out."

I felt a surge of sadness for Kim, then regret. Because I'd liked her. A lot. And no, I wasn't a drug kind of girl. I really didn't get it, to be honest. But clearly a lot of people did *get* the drug thing.

"The fact that she was a dealer—that figures into her murder, doesn't it?" I asked.

"Hell yeah," Vaughn said. "When a regular person is killed, first place you look is at their spouse. But when a dealer dies, we go looking for where they got it. Could be she was behind on payments. Not paying your source is an excellent way to get yourself picked off."

"But that still doesn't explain why she was in

my apartment. Unless maybe she was looking for money."

"Could be. You said nothing was gone, though, right?"

"Maybe she'd just started looking."

"Maybe."

"Or maybe someone came to kill her and she ran to my apartment to get away from them."

"Possible."

I growled with frustration. "Could you say something other than 'could be,' 'maybe' or 'possible'?"

"Hey," he said, his voice irritated, his face snarly. "You defense lawyers are the ones who want me to be this way. You don't want me to pick a theory and stick to it. Nooooooo."

"What are you talking about?"

He drained some more of his drink, then pushed his glass away. "You're always coming after us on the stand, acting like we snatched a suspect out of the air and then tried to stick it to them."

"You guys have been known to do that."

"Hey, maybe some CPD have been known to do that. But *I* don't do that."

"Oh, really?" Now I was irritated. "What about when my fiancé disappeared and you made it very clear you thought I had something to do with it? Or when *Jane* died, and you made me Suspect Number One."

"You were a person of interest. You were never a suspect."

"*Please* spare me a lecture on the difference here."

"Yeah, I'll spare you. I'll spare you altogether."
He got up.

"Well, don't get pissy and stalk off."

"I don't stalk, McNeil."

"You seem kinda stalky."

He laughed, sat back down, then nodded at my beer can. "Want another?"

I thought of going home to an apartment where a woman had died, and to a boyfriend who... God, there were so many questions. "I do."

51

When I finally got home, someone was in my kitchen. I flinched—*who is that?*—before I remembered. *Theo.*

Through the doorway, I could see his shoulder muscles move in his sweater and hear a hard *slice-slice-slice* sound as he cut something.

I closed my front door, but didn't step any farther into the condo, letting my initial surprise die away. But when Theo turned around, he held up something in his hand. And it looked like a handful of flesh—maroon and wet, like blood.

I sucked in a sharp breath of air. *What's going on?* I shot a glance to Theo's face, which although thinner than usual looked calm. Which freaked me out all the more.

"What is that?" I said. Still I didn't go farther into the condo.

He laughed. *Why is he laughing?*

"C'mon," he said, "can't you tell?"

I squinted and looked closer, leaning my torso into the room.

And then I felt a wave of relief. "Blood oranges?" I said.

He nodded.

I walked up to the bar dividing the living room from the kitchen and stood at it, liking somewhat the barrier it put between us. "We haven't had blood oranges since…"

Theo smiled as he cut more oranges. "I know. Since the first night we went out."

"You brought them over to make drinks. It was delicious."

Theo nodded toward the counter across from him where a bottle of vodka sat.

"If I recall correctly," I said, "we never actually made it out that night."

Theo smiled big at me, and I was happy for a moment that he appeared happy, despite all that was going on.

"That's right," he said. "Thought maybe we could do the same tonight."

I sat on one of the high bar stools and put my elbows on the counter, still watching Theo slice oranges and extract the wine-colored flesh. Theo walked around the corner, then used his hands to scoop orange chunks from the cutting block and put them into a pitcher. He washed his hands then at the sink, the bloodlike water dripping away.

"I have to tell you what I just learned from Vaughn," I said.

"You talked to Vaughn?"

"I saw him."

He turned, raised his eyebrows.

I wondered if that would make him jealous, as he had been of Sam, but he only wiped his hands on a towel and crossed his arms.

I told him about Kim being an apparent drug user and dealer.

"What kind of drugs?"

"Cocaine mostly."

I told him about the different theories Vaughn and I ran through as to why Kim was in the condo and why she had been killed here.

It made me stop and shudder just thinking of Kim crumpled on our floor. So wrong. So sad. So unnecessary.

Theo came around the counter and wrapped his arms around me. "It's been stressful and scary. I know. And I'm sorry for that."

After a hug that lasted, quietly, for about a minute, I lifted my head from his chest. "Why are you sorry?"

Theo sighed. "Because my getting arrested has caused such problems."

"But you getting arrested doesn't have anything to do with Kim getting killed, does it?"

"Not that I know of."

I thought of something then. "Remember the morning we found out Eric had tried to kill himself, when we went to the office?"

Theo closed his eyes for a long moment, then opened them and nodded.

"You were telling me about different things as

you came across them, but then you looked at one document in particular, and you kind of stopped. You said it was legal or something like that. And you put it in your pocket. I don't know why I hadn't thought to ask you about it before."

"Because we found someone dead in your apartment soon after."

We both looked, silently, toward the spot where we'd found Kim.

"It was an investor list," Theo said, "like the one I emailed you after we were at the Gage. I still don't understand why the Feds are looking at our initial private offering or what they hope to see in the names of the investors. I just wanted to make sure they were the same as the one I had in my office, the list I'd emailed you. Because, Iz, ever since Eric tried to kill himself, I've had a sense about it."

"What kind of sense? Like that he's guilty of something?"

Theo shook his head. I missed the way his hair used to rustle back and forth when he did that. "When I first realized HeadFirst was in trouble, yeah, I thought Eric was guilty of something. And after I got arrested, I definitely suspected he was, because he'd worked with the Feds. I thought he was throwing me to the wolves. But the more I thought about it, the more I believed he couldn't deal with the guilt that someone else had caused this. Someone he'd worked closely with."

"Your dad."

"He's always been there since the beginning. He

set everything up. He did the venture capital work and dealt with the formation of the company."

"I thought Eric did all that?"

"We always talk about how Eric is the business side, and that's true, but we didn't know how to raise funds like that or how to incorporate us. My dad did that for us."

"Why didn't you tell me this before? That you suspected Eric. And then your dad."

He said nothing, just looked at me. Then, "Should we start talking about dads now?"

I couldn't help it. I laughed. "No, I guess I get it. Fathers can be completely complicated." Mine sure was. The latest I'd heard from him was that after turning Tatum Reynolds over to the bank for what he'd done, my father had pleaded with Mayburn to tell the bank not to prosecute.

He did it for love, my dad kept saying. The fact that my father was still clearly connected to his own life choices touched me. And had possibly spared Tatum Reynolds a criminal record.

I put the drink on the counter. I reached up and drew my hands over his bald scalp, feeling as if I were touching an as-yet undiscovered depth of Theo Jameson.

He dipped his head down and put his face in my neck, breathing in. And even with all that was going on—even with that—I wanted him in that moment.

"Have you gotten ahold of your dad yet?" I asked before I was past the point of rational discussion.

Theo lifted his head, shook it to say no. "LaBree hasn't seen him, either, but she's checking some places they go."

And then I made a mistake. "Does your dad do drugs?"

"What?" His voice was an irritated lash. "No."

"Are you sure? He hangs out in all those clubs. I mean, it wouldn't be too far of a stretch."

Theo put his glass on the counter, pushed it away, liquid lapping over the sides. "What's the next *stretch,* Iz? Huh? That he bought drugs from Kim? That he killed her?"

"I don't know, I just…"

"I'm sorry," he said. "I don't want to take this out on you. This has nothing to do with you."

Theo went into the bedroom. I heard the scrape of keys from the top of the dresser. Then he walked past me through the living room and left.

52

To Brad Jameson, it was so strange, and so god-damned unfair, that something—some*place*—could turn so ugly when it had started out as incredibly unique, so full of wonder and riches.

Their initial falling-in-love with the place didn't just happen because of the palm and the surf and the fact that it was gorgeous, the stuff of a boy's dreams. And not just the ability to hide money. And make more on top of that. Rather, the charm of the place had more to do with the fact that they had found the place together. It was *theirs*.

The manner in which the place had caused such pleasure and yet now was causing so much harm, so much pain, was baffling. There was also the fact that he had worked for this. And so there was much that was *his*—rightfully his, not just his kid's. Now everything was being undone with his own work.

53

"Again," his father demanded. "Again!"

José Ramon watched his brother, Vincente, sag forward. His father had not touched Vincente all day as Vincente told the story—over and over and over—of the money he'd invested, the money that appeared to be gone. That amount of money would cripple their usual operations. And if the Feds kept charging forward, it could kill them all. His father had long ago decided that the U.S. was the future. He had gambled and not only invested his money and his people and his product, but also his sons. So far the gamble had been a boon for everyone. But they had gotten lax. They had placed too much trust in Vincente.

And so now his father wanted to hear the story again. He was poking holes in parts of it, screaming and berating Vincente. And Vincente continued to lose steam, his shoulders hunched forward. At one point during the day, he began to sob, claimed to be having a heart attack, asked for his wife, Carol.

His father ignored his claims, kept pushing.

"Tell us!" his father screamed. "Why did you keep throwing our money away? I want the entire story, Vincente. I want the whole truth."

His mother came into the room. She'd taken a few breaks from the day, unable to watch the abuse, although José knew she supported her husband above all.

Vincente sucked in air, kept going with his story. "I began to put more money in… I believed—"

He cut himself off then. This was part of the story that had brought on their father's rage before.

"I *let* myself believe," he corrected, "in their promises that this would lead to even bigger gains." He held out his hands and looked around at all of them, his fingers still outstretched and straining for something invisible. "Truthfully, if you think of it, I had no reason to doubt them."

José groaned, let his own shoulders and head sag. Vincente was refusing to take complete blame for the situation. Again. And he didn't seem to understand that his father would accept nothing less.

"You had no—" The words exploded from José's mouth, but Vincente stood up and shouted over him.

"Aside from the few months!" Vincente said, panting, forcing himself to take a breath. "Aside from those months where they weren't making payments, they had always been true to their word. For years. And that has been very, very much to our benefit. So yes, I gave them more money. But it didn't help. The payments to us were missed. Not always, though, and—"

"And so you stupidly kept believing," his father said.

No one said anything for a moment, because they had all felt the shift. His father had gone suddenly calm, was now using a patient, placid tone, almost as if he were telling the end of the children's story he used to read to them when they were little. *And then I was home, although I dreamed of my friends in the orchard.*

But Vincente seemed determined to finish his tale—his decidedly sordid and decidedly adult tale. "I felt that they were able to regain control. I felt—"

His father *smacked* the head of his walking stick on the floor, the sound a sharp crack that vibrated through the room. Both José and his brother flinched. They recalled that sound. It always heralded bad things.

"No more," his father said. "And no more discussions of your *feelings.*" He said the word *feelings* with undisguised revulsion. "Tell us what is here. Right now."

His brother straightened his shoulders and looked at his father. "They became unable to make any kind of payments. Then they stopped making excuses. I reported a problem to all of you." He took a massive inhale, as if needing to marshal all possible oxygen before he continued. "We have now lost two hundred million dollars."

There was not a sound in the room. Not a cough

or a scuff or shifting of any of the four bodies that sat facing each other, like actors on a stage, frozen at the end of a scene until the curtain falls.

"I know that you tried to address this…problem," Vincente said, "by pulling support from the other families, by putting all that product on the boat."

"And then that disappeared, too!" José said. "Was that because of you, as well? You have brought down this family!"

"No!" his brother yelled. Then his shoulders rounded, his head hung. "The other families may have been wanting to get back at us. I don't know."

José's eyes dodged to his mother, then his father. They seemed to both be thinking. They looked at each other.

Was this his last chance to say goodbye to his brother?

For surely the punishment would be swift. Vincente had made too many mistakes, had failed to come clean too many times. He was a son, yes, a direct member of the family, but other family members had been killed for lesser offenses.

His mother's brother had been one of the men hanging, minus his head.

54

With Theo gone from the condo, I was antsy, anxious. I needed to do something, anything. But what? I was out of ideas for finding out what was going on with HeadFirst, figuring out who had killed Kim in my condo and why. I double-checked that Theo had locked the front door, then went around the condo inspecting all the window locks—even though someone would have to use a ladder to climb in one. What else? I suddenly felt very alone. And very scared.

I decided to check the new downstairs lock on the front door. I took the three flights of stairs, pausing to look at the second-floor door. The last place Kim had lived. I fought off tears. Who was she really?

Downstairs, I opened and closed the door. I stepped out into the cold, just to see if maybe Theo was standing outside, getting some air. I saw no one. I tried the new keypad, then again. Seemed to be working fine. Tomorrow an alarm company was coming to install an entirely new system that

I was going to pay way, way too much for. And I was very happy to do so.

I was about to go back inside when I glanced across the street and saw a surveillance camera high on the streetlight outside, to the right of our condo. Strange that I'd never really noticed it before. But then Chicago had the most extensive surveillance system in the country. Cameras were everywhere now. The ACLU had even sued, citing privacy issues. And yet, I'd apparently been walking in a blissful ignorance below one every day.

Something occurred to me. Crossing my arms over myself, I stepped into the street and studied it. It was impossible to tell whether the camera's eye included my building. I hoped it didn't, because I didn't like the thought that my day-to-day actions, my coming in and out of my house, were recorded occasionally or not. And yet, what if the cameras had caught whomever had killed Kim?

"We have it," Vaughn said, when I went back to my condo and called him. "It's being analyzed."

"Analyzed meaning…"

"Meaning the evidence techs have it, and it's waiting to be looked at. They got a huge backlog."

I growled with frustration.

"I know," he said. "I wish I could push it, but we got a bunch of high-profile cases that are at the front of the line."

"Can I get a copy of the tape?"

"Let me go see what I can do," he said.

He called back. "Can you come into the station to look at it?"

"Give me twenty."

Vaughn and I sat in an interrogation room. I'd taken one look at the white walls, the surveillance mirror and cameras and said, *Hell no.*

But he told me the station was crowded. There had been a big gang fight. So if I wanted to see the video…

"Fine, fine." I sat at the table, next to a laptop he had set up. I didn't like being in there. Not one bit. Vaughn had interrogated me in a room similar to that in the same station.

"Are you freaking?" he said, looking at me, a slight curl of derisiveness in his words.

"No," I said, employing false bravado. "Take a seat, Tex."

Vaughn chuckled, sat on a stool that he pulled up to the table.

"It could take us a while to see anything we recognize," he said, turning the laptop to face me. "It looks like this thing is at least ten hours long."

"Can you speed it up a little?"

Vaughn made a few adjustments on this laptop and there was my little neighborhood, moving just a little bit too fast, just like my life lately.

"Want anything to drink?" Vaughn asked.

"I'm all right."

He got up, left, came back with a Diet Coke for

himself and one for me. "In case you want something later."

"Thanks." I kept an eye on the screen. "Hey, look!" I said. There was my first-floor neighbor, leaving the morning of Kim's death.

We kept watching.

"Theo!" I said.

Even on the grainy footage, Theo was gorgeous, his hair still long. He had his work bag slung across his body, a silver coffee mug in his hand. He left the building then disappeared.

"Hey, there's you," Vaughn said.

But soon I was gone, too. No sign of Kim.

"She could have been in the apartment building all day," I said.

Since Kim's time of death had been set loosely at 8:00 p.m., we fast-forwarded the video to that evening.

"Is that her?"

Sure enough, there was Kim leaving the house, wearing jeans and a puffy black coat, a flare of a scarf around her neck. She returned shortly with a plastic bag in her hand that looked like it was from a convenience store.

From the timing, we figured that soon after Kim entered the building she must have gone to my apartment, but that didn't give us any clue as to why.

But then I heard Vaughn grunt.

I looked at the screen. There was a guy, not too tall, but heavy around the middle, the kind of guy who carried himself as if he'd once been in shape, arms out away from his body, walking with what looked like hard footsteps to my front door. He took out some kind of instrument, wrenched off the front panel of the keypad, just like that.

And then just like that, he was gone. He was in my building.

55

When I got up the next morning, Theo was sitting on the couch, rubbing a hand over his head, as if trying to remind himself what it was like to have hair, trying to remind himself why and how and when everything had changed.

"I heard you come in around four in the morning," I said.

Last night, after watching the video and driving home in the snow, Theo still wasn't home. I kept thinking of that guy, so easily wrenching off the keypad on the front door and stepping inside. Wanting some kind of comfort, I'd dug out an old T-shirt of Sam's I used to sleep in and liberally helped myself to some Tylenol PM. I'd woken only once when I heard the door open and close. I could tell that the footsteps were Theo's.

Once Theo didn't come into the bedroom, I'd let myself slip back into a fog of sleep.

I told him about the surveillance tape. "I didn't recognize the guy," I said. "I have no idea who he is." I looked at Theo. He had dark half-moon shapes under his eyes. "How was your night?"

"I was looking for my dad," Theo said. "I went to his usual places. Then I got a hold of LaBree and we went to all of them again."

"And you didn't find him," I said, finishing the story for him.

"He's gone." Theo blinked. I noticed that above the dark circles, his eyes were round, like blank canvases. Those eyes had seen many things. Theo was one of those people who had lived different lives in his relatively short number of years, knew much. But now, whatever information he possessed wasn't registering.

"He's gone," he said again.

For a moment, I wondered if he meant someone else. "Do you mean Eric?"

"My father." His eyes changed. All Theo's knowledge, all his know-how about software and business and sex, it all came back. But it was tinged, marred.

"Where?" I asked.

"LaBree says she doesn't know."

"How does LaBree know Brad's gone anywhere?" I asked Theo.

"Brad didn't show up for a few things they had planned. He was texting like he was in town, saying they should meet here or there. But he never showed." I noticed he was calling his father by his first name again. "LaBree called his housekeeper, who comes once a week, and she said she didn't know where he was. But last time she'd seen him he asked her where his passport was. We went to his house and she could tell he hadn't been there in a few days."

"And the passport?"

"Gone."

Just saying that word made his eyes seem more deeply tinged with something dark, fearful. "I wish Eric were here. He knew Brad better than me in a lot of ways."

Theo started rambling about how well Eric had known Brad. Finally I put a hand up to stop him.

"Think," I said. I had decided it was time to take charge. I'd been mostly sitting back, trying to let my presence support Theo, thinking this was one of those times people have to process and figure out by themselves. But Theo wasn't doing it. He couldn't seem to do anything but circle around in his head. The situation had, I realized, shifted into one where he needed help. Badly.

I thought of Q. When he needed my help, he would say something like, *Give me some of your fiery redheaded decisiveness.*

I gave Theo my army-general stare, the one that had served me well in many a deposition where you needed to get people to think, to deliver information, even information they weren't consciously aware they possessed. "Think," I said again. Then I let more words come. "What would Eric say about where your dad is? Instead of wishing Eric were here, put yourself in his head."

Theo nodded, nodded again, took a breath, the vacant tinge in his eyes lessening. "He'd say that Brad has probably gone to wherever the money was."

"But the money is gone. Your company is penniless."

But Theo's eyes were clearing, looking again like someone who knew things, many things.

"Foreign trust?" I said.

"Yeah. And I know where he is." He looked at me. "Will you help me leave town?"

Before I had time to answer, Theo's phone rang. He pulled it quickly from his pocket, looking at the screen, his eyes going even wider than before. "Eric." He looked up at me. "Or what if it's not Eric? What if it's someone calling from his phone."

The second half of that question was clear. *What if someone's calling to tell me he's dead?*

"Answer it," I said. "Face whatever it is."

56

"You sound like a blues singer," Theo told his partner.

As we stood next to Eric's hospital bed, I put my hand on his lower back. Theo was trying to be funny, I knew. Because he didn't want to say the truth, which was, *You sound like an old man. You sound like you're almost dead.*

"Right?" Eric said, his voice barely making out that syllable. "But a blues singer like Clapton? Not like…" He coughed then, hard, and each cough sounded like a pained bark, like knives were incising his throat with every one. The truth was close enough, we had learned from Eric's mom. He'd been intubated, a large tube placed down his trachea to help ventilate his lungs while he was in the induced coma.

In the hallway outside Eric's room, she'd shown us photos of Eric over the past week, white tape over his eyes, that tube taped to his mouth.

"He looks dead," Theo had allowed himself to say then.

Eric's mother closed her eyes at that. "He was," she said. "In a way."

Tears popped into Theo's eyes. "Why did he do that to himself?"

His mom explained that he had never been a guy to take medications easily, but he always stockpiled meds he got from various dental surgeries and flus in case he really needed them.

Theo had allowed himself a small laugh at that. "Sounds like Eric." Theo told Eric's mom then about their fight at our place, the night before he tried to die. "Did *I* drive him to this?"

He looked at me, and it was as if he were challenging me to stay for the answer, no matter what it was. He knew I'd wondered the same thing about him and about myself.

She was silent. "You are boys." She smiled. "Men." The smile left. "And men fight. Don't do that to yourself. No one made him do this. I have to tell myself this all the time, too."

She veered from the topic then, and she told him how removing the tube after Eric woke up had caused a laceration and now an infection. He would have to be on IV antibiotics and remain in the hospital for some time.

She stopped talking and her eyes asked the question she couldn't help asking again. *Why? Why did this happen?*

"I'll ask," Theo said.

And then we'd gone into the room.

"Yeah, Clapton," Theo said now.

Eric hacked. And coughed. It wouldn't stop. His mom came in with a nurse, both looking concerned, but Eric barked out, "I'm fine." And although he didn't sound fine, not at all, they left the room.

After a long minute, Eric's hacking stopped. Then he began trying to operate the bed, apparently to raise it up, but the sound of a motor kept starting and the bed would move minutely then stop. Theo hurried over and looked at the remote for the bed. "It's on lock," he said, pointing this out to Eric. He unlocked the bed, raised it a few inches. "Good?" he asked.

"More," Eric said, a rasp of a word.

When he was finally at a decent incline, Theo sat next to him on the bed.

I made a small gesture to Theo. *Want me to leave?*

He shook his head.

He and Eric looked at each other, eye to eye. Theo asked him. "Why?"

Eric's head fell against the back of the bed. "They scared the shit out of me," Eric croaked.

"The Feds," Theo said.

"Yeah. They said it was simple. HeadFirst owed all the VC people."

"Venture Capital," I said.

He nodded. "All the initial investors in the business. Our money dried up. We couldn't pay our bills."

"You knew all this?" Theo asked. "Before I

moved out of my house and applied for a mortgage?"

That caused Eric to begin hacking again. The answer was clear though—*yes.* "They told me someone was going down for it, and if I didn't help them it would be me. I assumed they meant Brad. It almost killed me when they arrested you." More coughing. "They told me not to talk to you after it got started."

"And so then you almost killed yourself," Theo said.

"I wanted to so bad," Eric said. I wasn't sure if he meant he had wanted badly to talk about things or if he was referring to the statement about killing himself.

"The Cortaderos," Theo said. "What do they have to do with us?" He told him that they had pulled their work from Bristol & Associates as long as the firm represented Theo.

Eric shook his head. "No idea. Really, man. No clue. What does Brad say?"

Those four words—*what does Brad say?*—made Theo stand, and his face filled with a hard look of hatred. "I don't know. But it's time to find him and find some answers."

57

"I feel so terrible about Kim," Maggie said, after I told her about the tape, about the guy entering my condo building.

"I know. Me, too." I reached across the table at Lou Mitchell's and touched Maggie's belly. I couldn't stop thinking, *My best friend is having a baby!* It was the closest I'd ever come to pregnancy, and I was fascinated.

"When you told me about Kim, I got this feeling that we were all going to be friends," Maggie said.

"Me, too," I said again. "At least Eric is awake now. And he's going to be okay."

We both breathed, fell silent.

Maggie looked down. "I know I'm not supposed to be able to feel anything yet, but I swear I felt her move."

"You think it's a her?"

"There are so many hers in my family," Maggie pointed out. "I guess I'm just used to them."

I looked up at her. "You're going to make a great mom, Maggie Bristol."

"Really? You told me that before, and I've been thinking about it. I'm starting to get a little scared."

"You've been taking care of me—"

"And you me…" she said.

"For years." I completed the sentence.

"Oh, Mags," I said, struck again by the enormity of what Maggie was about to do, the act of creation.

I leaned farther forward and gave her a quick hug.

We talked about all things baby then—onesies and car seats and breast pumps and all-terrain strollers versus prams.

I sat back on the upholstered booth, talking more. Around us, the diner was the same as it was in the 1950s—Formica and coatracks abounded.

"Enough about my eggo being preggo," Maggie said. "Tell me about you."

"Well, now that you mention it, I had a couple of favors to ask."

"Shoot," Maggie said. "Wait, hold on." She waved at the waitress, waved her coffee cup at her and said, "Decaf, please," with a defeatist-sounding voice, then added plaintively, "And bacon, *please*." She looked back at me. "I want bacon all the time. I go from the old-style slabs to Oscar Mayer to turkey bacon."

"I'm not a vegetarian, but that's a little ick."

"I know, I know." She nodded at me to continue as the waitress filled her coffee cup.

I took a sip of my green tea. "I need a few days off work."

"Izzy, you've had a lot going on. Until the cops can identify that guy entering your apartment, I say get the hell out of Dodge. If you want a few days or a few weeks, take 'em."

"I'll take work with me. I have two briefs to write, but I've got all the research done."

"You're a professional, Iz. I know you'll do your job. You don't have to ask me."

"You are technically my boss," I reminded her.

"Technically."

"And you are technically the lead attorney on Theo's case. So here's favor number two." I put the tea down. Took a breath. "I need you to get Theo back in front of the judge. I want you to talk them into letting Theo leave the country. To get evidence on his own case."

"They'll never do it."

"Will you ask?"

Maggie's faced pursed. "They'd need him to post a significant bond. Like someone's house. That they own outright. And they have to be willing to lose it if he doesn't return."

I called Theo and told him that. When we were done, I turned back to Maggie. "His mom owns her place outright. He says she'll do anything for him. She'll put it up for collateral."

"Okay, then I'll try," Maggie said. "And, Iz, you understand you have to get ready for that possibility."

"What possibility?"

"That he might not return."

I paused. "I'm going with him."

58

"And so, Your Honor," Maggie said to Judge Diana Sharpe, "we request a change of the conditions of bond."

Theodore Jameson, she'd told the court, had reason to believe that his father had left the country to deal with some business associates. He had reason to believe that he alone could reach his father abroad and he alone could convince his father to tell the truth. In short, Mr. Jameson could, and should, be allowed to collect evidence on his own case. Theodore Jameson vehemently denied all charges in the complaint against him, and in order to be able to prove his defense, he needed to see his father in person and determine the entire situation behind the investors and the money that had been put into the company initially by venture capitalists.

As Maggie summed up her argument, Theo and I stood, unmoving, to Maggie's left, all of us readying ourselves for a knockdown argument.

But then Anish, the Indian prosecutor, spoke. "We would consider, Your Honor."

Maggie and I were both so shocked, neither of us said anything right away.

"We would, of course, require bond."

Maggie jumped to it, produced a quit claim deed for Anna Jameson's home.

"And Mr. Jameson will be required to agree that anything he does and says during said travel abroad can and will be used against him, and that he recognizes that additional charges such as racketeering may be levied against him upon his return."

"Judge, it sounds like counsel is advocating an agreement to a waiver of constitutional rights, which I cannot agree to. But I'd like one moment to confer with my client." She turned to Theo and I, motioned us to lean in. "You guys have any idea why they're giving in so quick?"

Theo and I shook our heads.

"Hmph," Maggie said, thinking. She stood straight again. "Your Honor, my client will consider the agreement counsel refers to, but we'd like an accounting now of the charges the government is suggesting."

"We couldn't possibly be specific, Your Honor. Federal Rule Sixteen is very limited as to what the government is required to provide a defendant. But suffice to say that the charges will be similar. And perhaps other defendants will be named."

Maggie swung her head to look at her opposing counsel. "Other defendants?" She squared her shoulders back to the judge. "This is the first time there has been mention of other defendants. We would argue that this court be apprised of this."

The judge put her hands together, looked at Anish. "I would like to know more, as well. Counsel? What are you referring to?"

Anish backtracked. "Your Honor," he added, "I was hasty in my words. As always, we keep our eyes open for other avenues, should they come to light."

"But they haven't come to light?" Judge Sharpe said. "Is that what you're saying, Counsel?"

"Your Honor," Anish said, "I'd like to point out that a woman was murdered in the apartment of the defendant last week."

That drew a raise of the judge's eyebrows.

"Objection!" Maggie said, although since we weren't in a trial, there was really nothing to which she could technically object. "Mr. Jameson's neighbor died last week, but the police have never indicated Mr. Jameson is involved in any way. I'd be happy to get the superintendent on the stand *right now* to testify to the same."

I raised my eyebrows, deeply impressed and grateful. The newly named superintendent of the Chicago police was a dear friend of Martin Bristol. There had already been talk at the firm about not dialing out his name or getting him involved in the firm business unless it was essential, to avoid any accusations of impropriety. But now Maggie was tossing his name in the ring.

"Your Honor," she continued, "the government is using my client as a pawn. He is not a flight risk, as evidenced by him coming to the court with this request, and the government cannot be allowed to run roughshod over these cases. We've seen them do this before—bringing down regular business people. Once that businessperson's life is dismantled, and the government has collected what they need for someone they consider to be a bigger fish, they move on with no thought to their actions."

The judge nodded, looked stern.

"We've seen people kill themselves," Maggie continued, "because of *them*." It was true. At least that was the word on the street and in the papers. The public and the press were getting louder and louder about the audacious, reckless and expensive prosecutions of someone low on the totem pole in order to get the big dogs, politically or otherwise. They'd been doing it in Chicago forever, but with news of defendant suicides and rampant costs hitting the press, there was some indication that the tide could be turning for the government, that they might not be able to get away with such tactics unscathed.

"Your Honor!" Anish said, indignant and loud.

"That's enough speculation and rumor, Counsel," the judge said, looking at Maggie.

"Thank you, Your Honor," Maggie said, as if she hadn't just been admonished. "At this point, defendant not only moves to remove travel restrictions from Mr. Jameson's bond, we move to dismiss the charges."

"We are not dismissing, your Honor!" Anish went through his argument again but the judge's questions showed she might be leaning toward Maggie's argument, at least about travel.

"Given the government's apparent indecision about prosecuting Mr. Jameson, the travel restrictions on his bond are lifted. Counsel," she said, looking at Anish, "you've got two weeks to decide what you're doing."

Maggie shot Theo and me one of those delighted looks that only Maggie can get from being in the courtroom. "You're out of here," she said to Theo.

59

The airport wasn't like any he'd been in before. And Theo Jameson had been in many. But lately, his experience was with private planes, landing in a small airport, greeted by a smiling employee who put them into a car or dropped them at their beach hut, their ski cabin, whatever.

But here, in Rarotonga, (he was still having trouble pronouncing it—*ra-roh-tong-ga*) there was a man playing a little guitar. Izzy clapped her hands at the sight, then gave him a chagrined glance as if she'd just realized her reaction wasn't appropriate to their situation. He hugged her. Thank God for Izzy.

There were women at the Rarotonga airport, too—smiling women with shiny black hair—advancing toward them, their arms filled with fragrant flowers of white and purple. They were holding, he realized, necklaces of flowers, and they were placing them around the necks of deplaning passengers.

He drew back a little. It seemed like a vacation thing to do. And they weren't on vacation. They were here to find his dad. His deadbeat, god-damned, steal-all-his-money, make-his-friend-try-to-kill-himself-and-disappear dad. But Theo was confused. And maybe because of that confusion, he still loved his dad a little. Wanted more than anything to find out what had happened, what was still happening.

Izzy wore a yellow dress. It looked hot on her, but then everything did, just as wearing nothing looked hot on her, too. Despite the situation, the thought of Izzy naked, red curls hanging down over her smooth, white shoulders, made him erect. He pushed the thought away, watched as a flower woman advanced on Izzy, a necklace of mostly purple outstretched. Izzy didn't seem to care if wearing the thing would make her look like a tourist. She closed her eyes in a—what was the word?—*beatific* kind of way and bowed her head. The woman slipped the flowers around her neck, framing those orange-red coils of hair, and then Izzy raised her face, smiling at the woman, who smiled back silently. The two held the moment. Izzy had that kind of mesmerizing effect on people, he'd noticed. The funny thing was she didn't notice, not really. But he noticed, and the scene in front of him made him love her all the more.

He did. He loved her. Sometimes she wondered

about that, he could tell. She thought maybe he was too young to know about such a thing, to know love.

She wasn't wrong often, but she was wrong about that one.

60

The bellman at our beachfront room on Rarotonga swung open French doors and pointed across the beach. That sand was fine and white and had a bit of sparkle lifted from the sun. Beyond the beach was a calm ring of light blue water. Maybe five hundred feet out, the water darkened at the edges and navy blue waves crashed.

"That is an atoll," the bellman said. He was a big, smiling man. He wore a flower behind his ear, oddly without femininity. "You understand?"

I nodded and I said a silent thank-you to Q, because not only had he booked our travel, but he'd also run to three bookstores to find guides about the Cook Islands so Theo and I could pore over them (and then sleep over them on the fifteen-hour flight). Because of those books, I knew that I was in the Cook Islands, roughly somewhere in between Hawaii and New Zealand on the main island of Rarotonga, which had a natural breakwater around it. More important, I knew the Cook Islands was an international banking hub that saw more business than Switzerland or the Cayman Islands.

"During low tide you may walk out there." The bellman pointed to the waves.

"Is there surfing?" I asked for Theo. I'd allowed myself to occasionally envision taking a vacation with him, and that was always something I imagined him doing. I wasn't much of a water girl, but maybe he'd teach me. It would be a true vacation, unlike the time we'd been to Italy together, which definitely wasn't a pleasure trip. But hell, as Theo and I had discussed, we weren't on vacation now, either.

"Yes," the bellman answered, "but it's not so good." He clapped his hands. "Wait! There is a tour. You get a bus…." He gently grabbed my arm, pulling me through our room, to the main lobby and down the dusty drive to the street.

"You see?" He pointed to a sign in an upstairs apartment across the street that read Scuba Tours & Surf Tours. "See?"

"Yes, I see, thank you."

"You go there for tours."

"Okay, will do." I wished, desperately, that I were just a tourist, flip-flops smacking against my feet as I walked across the road and signed up for a scuba lesson.

Instead, I thanked him, turned and headed back.

When I got to the room, Theo was standing at the threshold between the tiled floors of the villa to a slate patio outside. He was silent, staring at the water.

I put my hands on Theo's waist, just to let him know I was there, both physically and otherwise. The only upside to seeing Theo go through this was that my belief in him had begun to grow again.

He turned and put his hands on either side of my face. "Iz, thank you for being here."

I hugged him, standing on my toes. Over his shoulder, I took in the tall, shading palm trees, thatched hut roofs, orange-and-white cats coolly watching us from low, white stucco walls.

But then, for some reason, the iconic beach images slid to the side. What was that feeling? I'd had it before, many times over the past year. *You're being watched, Iz.* I kept my eyes open, scanning the beach, feeling like something was coming more and more into focus. And that's when I noticed the man.

61

"Whoa," I said. A bristle of fear ran up my body. I suddenly felt like one of the cats that were all over the island, but instead of being slow and lazy, it was as if the cat's back arched and its hairs all stood up.

"What?" Theo said. He turned and I felt him following my gaze to a guy thirty feet away, sitting on a wood-backed beach chair. There were other people on the beach, too, but...

"That guy," I said, my eyes narrowed.

Then I couldn't stop myself. I launched into action and started stomping through the sand toward the guy. I didn't care if the wind lifted my yellow dress or if I looked like a crazed woman with wild orange hair, barreling her way toward a man who was fully dressed—red shorts and a black T-shirt and longish black hair.

He was one of the islanders, you could tell from his brown skin, and as he turned, I saw he had the round, brown eyes a lot of the guys had—eyes that seemed really nice, really kind, but sort of like they'd seen a lot, too.

The man's eyes got a little bigger when he saw me stomping toward him. I heard Theo hurrying after me.

"Kia Orana," I said. That was the way to say hello in the Cook Islands and I had practiced it under my breath on the plane. But the way I said it now was pretty demanding.

The man repeated my words. He sounded nicer, and not surprised that I was in front of him. But his eyes weren't on me, I realized.

Instead, the man's eyes had strayed past me and looked right at Theo.

"Bradley would like to see you," the man said.

He was looking at Theo, not me, but I almost wanted to say, *Ha! I knew it.*

I'd *known* he was looking at us. I'd *known,* somehow, that he was on that beach because of us.

But my triumph at my intuition faded when I saw Theo's face. The face of a sweet, young boy who had been hurt, and now the reminder of that hurt had pained him all over again.

"Where is he?" Theo asked.

"I'll take you."

In a small, old, tan, beat-up car that we would never have entered with a stranger if we were in Chicago, Theo turned to me. We were both in the back, which made me feel out-of-control, but the man had insisted. In a very kind way. He seemed a good guy, like most of the other locals on the island. But what did I know about a scrap of island in the middle of the South Pacific? And what were we doing?

Theo looked at me. I waited for whatever it was he had to say.

"I've never heard him called Bradley," he said.

I looked out the front window, over our driver's shoulder, where the two-lane road made me dizzy because we were driving on the left lane. I patted Theo's leg, feeling the uselessness of the gesture. Through the front window I saw a small, hand-painted sign stuck in the roadside dirt that read Jesus is our God! Not money!

"It's okay," I said, turning back to him. "It's going to be okay."

62

Theo laughed, harshly, when he saw the house, a small shack that couldn't have been more than one room. The outside walls had once been painted a light purple it seemed. It made me think of the color of an Easter egg.

"Faded houses make me sad," Theo said, under his breath.

"Really?" I'd never heard him say anything like that.

"Yeah. It's like somebody once cared, but now they don't at all." Silence. Then I heard him speak, but only barely. "I wondered if that's how my dad feels about me." He looked at the house. "Everything must be gone. All our clients' money, everything."

The driver pulled up the emergency brake and pointed at the house. "One of the nicest on the island."

I squeezed Theo's leg. "Ready?"

He looked as if he was having a hard time swallowing, as if he felt a clog of tears lodge in his throat.

"Go ahead if you need to cry," I whispered.

Theo kept looking at the house. "I'm ready."

I held his hand as we walked across the yard. We were nearly there when a black-and-red rooster climbed onto the single cement front stoop, standing there.

"My dad lives with a rooster," Theo said.

I burst into giggles, and when I immediately tried to stop them, that made him laugh, too. We looked at each other, laughing, me covering my mouth.

"Sorry," I whispered. "Inappropriate laughter."

"I know."

We recovered somewhat. Theo's face lightened a little, and we took another step toward the front door. Then another few steps.

The rooster jutted away. Theo reached for the door, when it opened.

63

He's bigger than he used to be, I thought. *More... menacing.*

Theo, I think, noticed it, too, because I felt a pause, a stillness take over his body. He got that way only two times that I'd noticed—right after sex, when it seemed he wanted to hold the moment inside himself as long as possible, and also when he was scared but he didn't want to admit it.

Brad's face had been bland, but now he smiled, a smile of relief. He looked so happy to see Theo that I forgot for a second how much I'd hated him.

He wore khaki shorts and a black golf-style shirt that read Muri Beach on the left side. He'd grown a belly, where just last week he had been lean. His face was puffy-looking, as if he'd eaten too much salt or drank too much alcohol or maybe both.

He took a step down and started to open his arms, as if to hug us, but Theo drew back, and he dropped his arms.

"I know, Dad," Theo said. "I know you stole the money from HeadFirst."

Brad opened his mouth. "I didn't…" But he seemed to think better of it.

"Please," he said, gesturing to the house.

Inside, the place was much nicer than it looked from the outside. The first part of the large room was a kitchen with decent appliances and a table. The table was beautifully designed, the legs made from tree branches and polished to a high sheen. The table itself was a huge wooden bowl filled with coral and covered with glass.

I looked around the rest of the place—brightly colored art that appeared Polynesian hung on the walls. A thin, vivid rug with intricate patterns of blue and pink and yellow covered the floor.

"So, this is where it all happens," Theo said, sarcastic. When no one said anything, Theo spoke again. "You stole all that money from HeadFirst."

Brad Jameson sighed. "Let's discuss this. I helped you raise money."

"Yes, you helped *us* raise money—me and Eric. You know Eric tried to kill himself?"

His dad nodded, his eyes closing for a long time, as if he could not stand to see what was in front of him.

"He tried to kill himself because of what *you* did!" Theo said. "Do you get that?"

"Look, please sit down," Brad said.

"I don't want to sit down! I am sick of the questions and of you making me doubt myself and my partner, when the only person I needed to doubt was *you*."

"It's complicated," Brad said.

"Well, make it easy!" Before I knew what was happening, Theo lunged at his father.

I pulled Theo back. "Wait, wait, wait!"

He took a step back, panting.

A few years ago, I had taken a seminar on mediation. It was time to put those skills to use. "Gentlemen, sit down," I said, pointing to the couch and chairs at the end of the big room. "Please."

Theo looked at me. I saw a flash of gratitude in that glance, and he nodded. Brad Jameson nodded even faster, looked even more grateful.

When they were seated across from each other, I sat between them and put my hands on the glass coffee table.

I looked at Theo's father. "Brad, I think Theo just wants a few answers."

"What I want—" Theo began to say, his voice loud.

I held up my hand. He went silent. "Let me run through some things so we all get on the same page." I looked at Brad. "Starting from the beginning. You raised money for HeadFirst when Theo and Eric launched the company, right?"

He nodded.

"Venture capital funds."

Another nod.

"But you kept some of those funds for your own use."

A pause, but then he said, "Yes."

"Jesus, Dad!" Theo said, his voice full of accusation and of surprise as if he finally—*finally*—understood. "I cannot believe you did that!"

I gave him a stern stare and he clamped his mouth shut.

"You kept some of those funds in a trust on this island. On Rarotonga."

"Yeah," Brad said.

I crossed my fingers together and sat a little taller. "You did that to avoid taxation and detection of the funds, right?"

"Yes."

I thought about it, pieces falling into place. "So you kept those funds for your own use."

"Money that HeadFirst wasn't using," he pointed out.

"And were you able to pay back investors as planned?"

"For a while."

"Then you got into trouble."

"Well, *I* didn't get into trouble."

Theo scoffed.

"Look," his dad said, seeming to get frustrated for the first time, "I might have been running something on the back end here, but it's not just me that brought this thing down."

"What do you mean?"

"That's what I came here to find out for sure." He exhaled a long breath, and looked down. "Listen, we got so much money when we started the company. You and Eric were doing great," he said, looking at his son. "So I used some of those funds for my own…what would you call it?"

"Your own *greed?*" Theo said.

"Yes," he answered fast. "I was greedy. But it wasn't me that caused the whole thing. At some point, the funds started disappearing." His chest seemed to drop, as if losing muscle tone. "The funds are nearly gone now."

I could tell Theo wanted to yell, to question, to cry. I shot him another glance—*don't.*

"See," Brad said, "a number of trustees were set up on the trust account for different reasons. It's complicated. I'm still trying to understand it. That's one of my biggest regrets, not completely understanding the setup."

"Oh, *that's* your big regret?" Theo barked out a laugh.

"Please," I said, my voice low, "keep going."

"Some of the trustees were the initial investors in our business. Some…"

Theo had his eyes closed. Brad sighed, as if weighing his thoughts.

I wanted him to keep going before Theo exploded again. From my purse, I pulled the contact lists that Theo had sent me from HeadFirst, the ones that the Feds had been interested in seeing. I showed them to Brad. "Are these the people who invested money initially?"

Brad glanced at it. "Yes."

"Are there others who aren't shown there?"

He shook his head, looked at it closer.

I got a clear image of Maggie, and I knew what she'd want me to ask. "Brad, I don't know if this is all connected, but while I have you here, I have to ask you something or my best friend will kill me. Do you know the Cortaderos?"

He said nothing.

"If you do, can you please tell me what they have to do with HeadFirst? I mean, they're not on that list, but we lost business because of them." I explained they wouldn't let Bristol & Associates represent them if we represented Theo.

Brad Jameson sighed deeply. He took the list from my hand, pointed to one business. *Barrington Hills Trading.*

"We did investigations on all these names," I said. "And if I remember correctly, that business was owned by Vince Cort."

He nodded.

I suddenly got it. "Cort," I said. "Short for Cortadero."

64

Maggie stepped into the office of the A.U.S.A.

"I'm glad you could stop by," Anish said with a grin. U.S. prosecutors weren't usually flirty. Whatever was going on, it was a good sign.

"What's up?" She pointed at the chair in front of his desk and he nodded.

Maggie sat, tried to cross her legs, but it felt weird now that she was pregnant. She wasn't even showing. There was nothing yet to show! But she felt something solid there. This pregnancy thing was strange. On that topic, she veered from ambivalent to freaked out and back in a matter of seconds.

"We've been thinking about you," Anish said.

"About *me?* Why?" Did he sense she was pregnant? Was this going to cause people to view her differently as an attorney? She broke into a faint sweat thinking about it. Jesus, all the work she had put into her career. Was *this*—this *baby* (she had to get used to that word) going to sideline it for her?

Anish's black eyes narrowed. "I meant your case."

"Oh."

"The Jameson case."

"Oh," she said again.

"What did you think I meant?"

"Nothing. I'm with you now. You're talking about those other 'avenues' of the case, as you put it?"

"Yes. And we think they're important. So we want your help on those avenues. Let me show you first what we've done." He pushed a written document across the desk at her. It was a plea agreement in the case of the *United States versus Theodore Jameson*. She looked closer. The agreement had been made in the name of Brad Jameson.

She looked back at Anish, asked a few questions. Then she said, "I need to make a phone call."

65

Maggie called a few times. I went outside Brad's house and was finally able to get service on my BlackBerry to call her back.

Her voice rushed, she told me about Brad Jameson's plea agreement.

"I can't believe they would plea-bargain with Brad," I said, "when he's the one who created this."

"He can't have created all of it."

"That's what he's saying right now." I looked through the sliding doors into the house. Brad Jameson leaned forward, elbows on his knees, looking at his son, who was staring at his phone intently, ignoring his father.

"Anish would only say it had to do with family."

"*Family* as in organized crime?"

"I assume so. I don't know why they're so intent on using Theo to get to the Cortaderos."

"I think I know. Brad just told us that someone named Vince Cort was one of the original investors of HeadFirst."

"Vince Cort?" Maggie repeated, like she was

sounding out a puzzle. "Sounds a little like Vincente Cortadero."

"You got it. You know him?"

"Nope, but I know of him. His name appears occasionally here and there, but I've never worked with him. He's like the prince of the Cortadero family. They keep him away from the commoners."

"So any information I get about his investing in HeadFirst…"

"We can *definitely* use. We were never his attorneys. So we can trade that information to get Theo a plea bargain."

"I don't want him to plea-bargain," I said. "He didn't do anything wrong except take the wrong advice from the wrong person."

How good it felt to say that, and for it to feel true! Except that Brad kept saying he hadn't caused all the problems at HeadFirst. *What did he mean?*

I looked back through the glass. Theo wasn't there. My eyes moved to the right. He stood at the kitchen sink, just looking out the window, not moving.

"I hear you," Maggie said, "I hear you." I could tell she was thinking. And hard. "I definitely touched a nerve with my argument about the Feds using the little guy to get to the big dogs. They don't care about Theo or people like him, they just want to take down the bigger players. In this case, I'd guess it's not just the Cortaderos they're concerned with."

"Who else?"

"The Cortaderos are a cartel family. Which means they're one in a group of families from Mexico. That's probably what Anish was talking about. Not only was Vincente an investor in Head-First, but I bet they're hoping it'll lead them to other families. Because usually within one cartel, they all steer their money the same direction."

"So let me see if I get this. They want to bring down all the families in a particular Mexican drug cartel. So they follow Vincente Cortadero and the money trail."

"And then they keep watching until something gets fucked up with the business they put money in," Maggie said. "White-collar crime is so freaking easy to prosecute these days."

"So they can go after the business, but really they're looking for the way the cartels are laundering money."

"Well, I wouldn't use the term *laundering*," Maggie said.

"Allegedly laundering," I said, having learned well from her.

"Exactly. And the judges are attuned to this game of theirs now. I could tell the judge responded well to my argument, and I can tell I have the prosecutors running a little scared."

"Keep working on it?" I said.

"You got it. You guys okay down there?"

I looked back through the window, seeing Theo still standing, motionless, looking out the kitchen window at an empty yard.

"I don't know," I said to Maggie. Because I knew, just by taking in the way his shoulders sagged, his normally straight posture a little hunched forward, that Theo Jameson was broken-hearted.

66

The only good thing about him—the only thing—was that he told her straight out.

"I killed her," he said as soon as he sat down across from her. That was a week ago, a day or two before Thanksgiving. She'd been waiting for him, ashamed. She could barely even believe she had hired Manny, or whatever his name was. But now those words were coming from his mouth!

"You *killed* her?" Her hand flew to her mouth. Hot tears of regret and anguish sprung from her eyes. "You weren't supposed to kill her, just hurt her, sideline her, slow her down."

"I know but she fought. And hard. Like a street fighter, that girl."

"Izzy McNeil?" she said incredulously. "That girl is a lot of things, but there is no way she's a street fighter!" Her voice had shot up in volume, despite herself. She glanced around, saw other patrons at the restaurant frowning at her.

She looked back at Manny, the *idiot*. "What in the hell happened?"

"I went in, like you said. Had to break the thing by the front door to get in, but the door to their apartment was open when I got there."

He'd been hired to find Izzy when she was alone sometime, give her a little hurt. Just a little, that's what she told him. She rather liked Izzy. She didn't want her *dead*.

"Christ," she said, but the word was muffled. Both hands were on her mouth now. She hated it when she watched a movie and the character threw up shortly after receiving horrible news. She always thought it a clichéd way to show the character was upset. But now she understood that the gesture was true. She was very, very close to vomiting.

"The place was dark," Manny continued.

He didn't even look upset. Why didn't he look upset?

She shook her head, hands still on her mouth. *Such* an idiot. And she was an even bigger idiot for hiring him. She knew him because he worked at the Lexus dealership that serviced her car. He always hit on her when she brought her car in, hinting more than once that he had a tough-guy background, telling her he could help her out "with just about anything she needed."

What she needed was to get Izzy out of the way for a while. Just for a while! She was too inquisitive, and so were the people she had working with her—her father and some guy named John Mayburn. And although Theo had been relieved when Izzy's firm got on board to represent him, things had only gotten worse. She knew Theo and Izzy had already had one break-in, so she figured if Manny could stage another break-in and hurt her—just a little!—then the dad and John Mayburn would put their efforts into finding the person who'd done that to her. Take the spotlight away from Theo and HeadFirst and what had happened to the money.

Once in Izzy's place, Manny was supposed to deal with her—*minimally*—then steal a computer and a TV and then trash them somewhere. He said he'd leave no trace of himself, and the police would never be able to connect him to the crime, certainly wouldn't be able to connect her.

She removed a hand from her mouth and stared at Manny, trying to hear what he was saying although she was having a hard time focusing. She seemed to have lost her own words as well as her ability to comprehend others.

"I thought it was going to be an easy job," he was saying. "Just walk in, take a couple of things, wait for her to get home, pop her a few times and get out." His casual tone made her find her words.

"What the fuck happened?" she spat out. She had only said the word *fuck* a handful of times in her life.

"She was there when I walked in. The lights were out. I guess because she'd just got home. I walked into the place and *wham!* She cracked me over the head with a book or something."

She listened as he told her how they fought, how he didn't mean to hurt her or kill her, but *Shit, man, she was a fighter.*

She wished she had never started down this road—one that began long before Izzy came into the picture. Izzy wasn't even *in* the picture. That was the thing. The situation had to do with the love and support she was entitled to. How many therapists had told her that? And finally she had believed. She had really let herself believe about being deserving. And that had been when she started simply taking what she deserved, what had been sitting there all along.

She used the money to pay for things he had said he would help her with. Then she kept draining the money for spite, knowing Brad would eventually take the heat, knowing he deserved it. She had no idea that Theo's business would get so near to destruction. The coward just kept trying to make more, kept losing more. And by the time she realized it—by the time that Theo was arrested—she couldn't put the money back. The bankers had made that clear. That wasn't how the trust worked. She was not the founder of the trust. She couldn't put any money into it. So she let the situation go, thinking it was so absurd that it would have to remedy itself. It would have to go away.

But it hadn't left. In fact, it got worse.

67

When I walked back into the house on the beach, the air conditioning hit me like a blessed breeze, a respite from the rising humidity outside. And yet, although the temperatures were cool, the tempers inside were something else.

Theo was pacing now, talking low to his father, not looking at him. "I cannot believe you, Dad. What kind of person does this to their son?"

Brad was looking angrier and less chagrined.

"Eric looks up to you like a father, you know that?" Theo stopped to see if this registered to Brad, but as soon as his father opened his mouth, he again kept pacing and talking, not letting him answer. "Eric wasn't close with his father. And he was so jealous of me when he first met you. He thought we had the best father-son relationship he'd ever seen." Theo's face became stricken. "And I agreed with him. I thought we had a great relationship, too. But I thought you were someone different. And now you're not that person and I—" Then Theo, who had so much to say, stopped suddenly.

His mouth just hung open, as if looking at a horrible accident.

"I didn't—" Brad said.

"You didn't what?" Theo shouted. "You took drug cartel money—illegal money—to put in my business, right?"

Brad nodded, a firm set to his mouth.

"And you hoarded that money and you used it for your own...whatever. And now it's gone."

"Theo, I don't know how to explain it—"

"Then don't! Is anything I said untrue?"

Silence, then a soft "No" from Brad.

Theo looked at me. "Izzy, I'm sorry you had to see this. Let's get out of here."

I noticed that Theo didn't look back before he stormed from the house, waving at the driver when he got outside.

But something about Brad made me halt and look at him. There was so much anguish on his face that I wanted to embrace him. But my loyalties were to Theo. So I turned, and I left.

68

Theo's eyes were above me, his hips slowly moving, hand snaking its way upward, stroking, over my hips, past my ribs, between my breasts, touching, then a pinch, more stroking…stopping there, then upward until ever so lightly his hand was on my neck.

Outside the French doors of the hotel's bedroom was a dark beach, lit by a few solitary lamps and a lot of stars. No one was on the beach, and with the door just slightly ajar, we could hear the soothing *swoosh, swoosh* of the water lapping the shore.

"Trust me," Theo said, his hand still light on my neck. Then he repeated the words, but he said them in a different way. "Trust me?"

There was definitely a question mark there. We had sat on the beach for hours talking about this very issue. Theo had lost faith in his father—the person he'd most counted on in his life. He no longer trusted him. He no longer knew who to trust. But he trusted me, he'd said.

And now he was asking if I returned the sentiment. Did I trust him? With my love. With my life.

Then there was incremental pressure, his fingers on either side of my neck, the flat of his palm on my throat.

"Trust me," he said.

Trust me, trust me, trust me, trust me.

The words resonated in my brain. No longer did he speak them, but I heard them from somewhere, like church bells in distant hills.

Trust me, trust me, trust me, trust me.

More pressure. His thumb was feather-soft on my jaw, nearly my ear, but his palm pressed. It didn't hurt. It felt…strange.

"Trust me?" Again a question followed by a little more pressure. He moved inside me. Faster. He knew how to get me where he wanted me. He knew how to get me there quickly. My breath came shorter. I moved with him.

Theo's eyes didn't move from mine. The question vibrated around us, entwined with the concept of love. I looked at him. I said yes with my eyes.

He read the answer, moved faster. I raised my hips to meet him. When I was nearly there, I closed my eyes, felt just enough pressure on my neck to freeze the breath in my lungs.

An explosion of silver, convulsions of pleasure, another burst of silver, a firecracker blast of gold, all around, shimmering, shaking, making it right.

69

Twenty-three hours later, after flying overnight from the Cook Islands to Los Angeles, then L.A. to Chicago, our plane touched down in a cloud of white-gray.

Outside, past the passport checks, Theo and I pulled our bags into an already dark afternoon. But the sky seemed to glitter with reflective snowflakes. We both took huge breaths. The cool air tamped down the heat we'd collected in Rarotonga, the heat of Theo learning, face-to-face, of his father's betrayal.

We stood like that, just breathing for a few minutes, then Theo stepped forward and hailed a cab.

We were silent on that taxi ride home. There was really nothing left to say at that point. There was a barrier that we'd broken through when we had sex the previous night, when I let him put his hands on my neck and let them stay there, trusting him, trusting him in so many ways—trusting him to back off at the right time, to never let me feel for a moment it would go too far. It was a big responsibility in a way. He not only took it, but he also stepped up into it. And it was like I'd let him into me. And me into him.

My phone rang. *Detective Damon Vaughn.*

Oddly, the sight of his name, one that used to bring snarling scorn from my mind, felt like some kind of relief now.

"Hey, Vaughn," I said, answering. There was no way I was calling him "Detective." It was the last passive-aggressive bit I was retaining from the days when I hated him.

"Where ya been?"

"How do you know I've been anywhere?"

A pause.

"You're watching my house?" I asked.

"Hell yeah, I'm watching your house," he said in a defensive tone. "You had a break-in there. You had a murder there."

My stomach turned over at the reminders. I felt tears quickly marshal in my eyes.

"I'm a Chicago police detective," Vaughn said.

"I know you are."

"And you have an open case. *Two* of them."

"Got it," I said. "Sorry. It's been a long couple of days. Learned a lot about HeadFirst and the Cortaderos." Then I added, "They're a Mexican drug cartel family."

"I know who they are," he said, still defensive. "Jesus."

"I said I was sorry!" Now my voice wore the defensiveness. A pause. "Anyway. What do you know about them?"

"Something I just found out. The Cortaderos were Kim Parkway's source."

"The Cortaderos were Kim Parkway's source?" I repeated for Theo's benefit.

His eyes went wide.

"So she got her drugs from them?" I asked. "And then she'd sell them?"

"Well, she didn't get anything directly from them, you know? She got them from a guy named Eddie from Ukrainian Village, but if you tracked back a few places where Eddie got *his* stuff, and that guy got his stuff, then yeah, you learn the Cortaderos and their cartel were the source."

The cab got off the highway at North Avenue, which was lit up with store signs and Christmas lights.

"And she didn't just sell for them," Vaughn said.

"What do you mean? There were other sources?"

"No. I mean she didn't just sell for the Cortaderos. She did different jobs, different favors for José Cortadero. He manages Blue Glass, the restaurant. Have you been there?"

"Yes, it's excellent."

"Well, it's a legit restaurant, but for José it's just a front. José lets other people run it while really he's running the Cortadero business. But apparently, he sometimes needed some minor surveillance and Kim Parkway did that."

"Are you kidding?"

I felt a wave of grief, thinking that Kim and I—
despite how different we seemed—could have been
friends. We could have bonded about how strange it
was to be a girl who looked like everyone else, but
who walked around with a secret, who couldn't let
anyone around her know the kind of work she did
sometimes—surveillance, investigations…

But then I stopped the thoughts of Kim. "Surveillance," I said. "She wasn't doing surveillance
on…"

"You and your boyfriend," Vaughn said. "Yeah.
Look, we teamed up with the Feds on this, and—"

"What? You teamed up with the Feds?" It wasn't
usual custom for county police to work with federal
agents or prosecutors.

Next to me, Theo's eyes grew concerned.

"Once we got the info that she was a pet detective—" Vaughn said.

But I cut him off. "A pet detective? What's that?"

"That's what I call private investigators."

Vaughn didn't know that I was a part-time P.I.
myself, but on behalf of my sorta profession, I was
insulted. "You know what I've heard," I said, "from
working in the criminal defense world? I've heard
that most P.I.'s are way better and way more effec-
tive than police officers." I had, in fact, never heard
that.

"Whatever, McNeil, listen to me for a sec. Once
we knew she was a P.I. for the Cortadero's, we figured that's a fed thing. One of my guys remembered

a piece in the *Tribune* that mentioned something about the Feds working on your boy's case."

I wanted to say, *Don't call him my boy,* but I was too interested in the other things he was saying.

"So we went to the Feds," Vaughn said. "And started sharing info. The Feds already have an agent working under Cortadero at the restaurant. They were pretty freaking cool to share the info with us. I guess the guy, the agent, he pretends to be the general manager or some shit. Anyway, yeah, she was watching you guys for the Cortaderos. Guess they had some money in Theo's business."

"You guessed right." I filled him in on what we'd learned from Brad—the Cortadero family's investment in HeadFirst and how that investment had grown into hundreds of millions. And eventually into hundreds of millions of losses. I stopped when I got to the part of the story that Brad had drained the foreign account.

I looked at Theo. And I read his silent request. *Don't tell him. Not yet.*

Luckily Vaughn jumped in for me. "Yep. Makes sense. She was keeping an eye on you to see how much you guys knew about the Cortadero involvement. That break-in was probably their first step—mostly to scare you, but also to see what they could find in your apartment, anything about the Cortaderos being with HeadFirst."

"Which they didn't," I said. "Theo didn't keep any business-related documents at home."

"I know. But that probably just made them more paranoid. They needed to know more, see if you would mention them, get a better look at the apartment."

"So they moved Kim in downstairs."

"Sounds like it. We got some info that she suggested it herself. She was trying to make a name with José so she could rise up through his business. She'd already messed that up once by getting arrested. They don't like when you get arrested, so she owed them. And then she really did get dumped by some doctor and needed a place to live. And it makes sense—the Cortaderos didn't want anyone finding out that they were laundering their drug money through HeadFirst. They'd do anything to protect that information. Especially if other families had contributed some of the money. Or even if they'd just bragged about it to one of the other families."

"So on the day she died, she broke into my condo or something?"

"Yeah, she had tons of time to work on your keypad when you left during the day. She already had the code to downstairs. She was already in the building. So she would just have to go through a bunch of steps to work out the code to your condo door. All she really needed was some time. Three or four hours. Then, once she knew the code, she could go in when she knew you were out, and check out your place."

"What does this mean in terms of Kim's death?" For some reason, I couldn't say the word *murder*.

"Means she probably pissed them off. Those guys will kill at the drop of a hat. They really don't give a shit."

"Oh, great. Thanks for telling me that."

"Hey, here's the good part—they know the Feds are digging into them. Apparently, Mother and Father Cortadero came into town to figure things out, but then they got wind that the Feds were circling and they fled."

"That's interesting. But I'm not sure why it's the *good* part."

He sighed, as if I tired him. "Because you don't have to worry about them messing with you. At least not in the short-term. They know they're being watched, and there is no way they'll fuck with you."

I didn't know what to say to that. My mind was too confused with sadness and exhaustion to form words. And yet, there was a sliver of relief in there. At least now we knew what happened. Now we'd have to see how we could use this info in Theo's case.

The cab turned onto Eugenie and pulled up in front of my condo building. My downstairs neighbor must have been out. No one was in the second-floor unit anymore. Kim wasn't anywhere now. And of course, my place was dark. The building looked somber, shrouded by the steadily falling snow.

"Vaughn, I have to go," I said. "I'll call you tomorrow." I hung up. As we paid the driver and got our bags from the trunk, I told Theo an abbreviated version of everything Vaughn had said.

Tomorrow will be different, I told myself. *Tomorrow will be better.*

We knew now that the Cortaderos likely ordered the first break-in. They were responsible, too, for Kim being in the building, Kim being in my condo that day. And another likelihood—that they had killed her. The Cortaderos had also put money in HeadFirst, a lot of money, a large portion of which Brad put into a foreign trust, and then he siphoned funds from that trust. Brad's bleeding of the company led to HeadFirst being unable to pay bills, which led to Theo getting turned down for a mortgage, and to Eric's suicide attempt. Which led me to think about Kim again.

I had to stop the circle in my head. "It'll be better tomorrow," I said out loud as we began to pull our bags toward the building, the snow a gray slush under our feet.

"Yeah," Theo said softly.

We walked up the three flights of stairs, footsteps thudding one after another. Theo followed, his footsteps even heavier.

"It'll be better tomorrow," I said again, this time under my breath, like a mantra.

But when I hit the third floor, I knew it. I knew something was wrong. But that was already apparent. Lots of things were wrong.

So I opened the door, and it was like a flashback. It was like my world had zoomed back—zoomed to that day we opened the door, and Kim was on the floor. It was the same—the same creak of my front door that used to sound comforting to me, when I came home after a long day at Baltimore & Brown. And then another flashback—there was a woman. A woman crumpled on the floor, like the day we found Kim.

But this time the woman sat up. This time she pointed at Theo.

"Mom?" Theo said.

Then she started crying, and she crumpled on the floor again.

70

"Mom," Theo said, "what are you doing?" Then, as if thinking of a better question, he asked, "You used the code to get in here?"

She sobbed, then sucked in her breath.

"When did you give it to her?" I asked softly.

"After the hearing. She was going to drop off all the documents for her house. The one she put up collateral for my bond."

Anna cried. Her head fell onto her arms.

"Mom, what are you doing on the floor?"

She pushed herself up to her elbows. "I was just going to..." She started crying again.

"Mom!" Theo said, as if trying to jar her.

"I knew you were out of town. I wanted to see things for myself, because I never wanted anyone dead." Her gaze slid to mine now; her eyes were crazed. "You're not dead," she said.

"No."

I said nothing else. I did nothing else. I didn't know what to do. The Anna Jameson in front of me was not the lovely, elegant woman I'd met at lunch, the one I'd seen again after Theo was arrested. Her face was distorted, as if one side of it sat higher. Or maybe it was her eyes that kept veering from a sneer to wide-eyed horror.

"Mom," Theo said, in a sharp tone, "what are you talking about?"

"I just wanted to hurt her."

"What?" Theo screamed the question. He looked on the verge of madness himself.

"No, no, no," Anna said. She pushed herself up farther until she was sitting cross-legged on the floor. She wore jeans and a white blouse. The blouse had yellowed stains under the arms. Neither garment appeared recently laundered. "I'm glad she's not dead," she said, waving an arm toward me. "So glad..."

Theo remained silent.

"*Who* is dead if you aren't? Why was she here?" Anna said. "These are the things that are making me insane." She cackled a laugh. "Among other things!" But the laughter died away. "I never meant for him to kill someone. He was supposed to come in here and hurt her." She looked at me. "Just a little."

"Who is *he?*" Theo shook his head, as if thinking of a better question. "Why would you want to hurt Izzy?"

"I didn't," Anna said plaintively. "Not really. I just thought if she did happen to get hurt, then those men she worked with—"

"What men? Who?"

"Um…" She looked confused. "Mayfield?"

"Mayburn," I corrected.

"And Christopher."

"That's my dad," I said.

"I hired someone from the dealership. He said he could take care of anything! And then he told me that those two men were investigating where the money had gone."

"What money?" Theo said.

She sat up straighter, looking suddenly a lot more sober, more sane. "The money I took from the trust. The one in Rarotonga."

71

In the kitchen, I scrambled to make tea, something I'd suggested just to get myself the hell out of that situation, even for a second.

I heard Theo's mom talking to him about how Brad had dumped her years ago, left her adrift. Then when she got breast cancer, Brad had totally avoided her, made her deal with it on her own, financially and emotionally.

"Mom, we've talked about this a million times," Theo said, his voice heavily laced with confusion and frustration. "You have to get over it."

"Get over it?" Anna shrieked. "How are you supposed to get *over* someone turning their back on you—someone you loved—when you are faced with your own death? When you most need a little help and compassion? My cancer was Stage Four, Theo!"

"I know, Mom. I know."

"I had no money. I had to move in with my cousin and her kids."

"I know, Mom. It's one of the reasons I came home from college."

"Do you know only twenty percent of women with Stage Four breast cancer survive?"

Theo said nothing. I felt bad for deserting him.

I brought mugs of tea to Theo and his mother—mugs I put on the table and which sat there, steaming.

"You have to remember!" his mother was saying, her voice plaintive. Theo had coaxed her onto my sofa, and they sat next to each other like two characters in a fantastically awkward play I'd seen at the Orchid Theatre. "Once I got better," she said, "once you came home, your father resurfaced. And not only did he resurface, but he raised millions of dollars for HeadFirst. It hardly took any effort for him, can you believe that?"

Anna's gaze was far away, as if she were looking into the past. "I had filed for bankruptcy. I was eighty-five pounds. And he couldn't even give me a dime."

She moved her head in lagging arcs, her neck wobbly.

Theo looked at me, his eyes pleading.

I took a breath. "Anna," I said, "I'm so sorry for all you've been through. It sounds like too much for anyone to face. But how does this relate to the money in the Cook Islands?"

Her gaze swung to mine, loosely focused. "You're alive," she said in a whisper.

Theo put his head in his hands.

"Anna," I said, a little louder now. "You said you took the money from the trust. How? Why?"

"I knew Brad was using some of that money for himself rather than the company." She scoffed. "I know him so well, he can't escape. I *know* him. And it just made me so *angry*. For years I watched him live Brad Jameson's high life. The girls, the cars, the trips. I was slowly clawing my way back to health. No thanks to him. And it just made me so fucking *angry*."

"But how did you get the money out of the trust?"

She blinked a few times. "I was a trustee. I remembered that one day, like the answer was there, waiting the whole time. I remembered when Brad was forming that trust, bragging about all the money he was putting in. He thought we were fine. He thought I'd forgiven him." That cackle of laughter again. "He had to name trustees. We always used to put each other's name on legal and estate documents. Even after we got divorced." Another garbled, distraught laugh. "He was the one they would've called if I died of the cancer. Sometimes I wanted to die, just so that something would interrupt his perfect little life."

"But even if you were a trustee," Theo said, "why would you do that to me? Because of you, I lost my business and almost lost my best friend."

Anna Jameson began crying again, softly. "I know. I know. I kept the money. I still have it! And when I saw what it was doing to you and Head-First, I tried to put it back. But I'm not the settler

of the trust, only a trustee! I couldn't put it back."
She started crying harder then. "I was going to tell
you, but then you got arrested. The government had
read the situation wrong and thought it was *you.*"

Theo sat back in the couch. He ran his hand over
his shaved head, his eyes searching for the way
things used to be.

"So, you do still have the money?" I asked,
wanting to make sure I got that part right.

She nodded. "I paid off my medical bills, and
then I split it up in a bunch of accounts."

"Does Brad know you were the one taking out
the funds?"

She raised her head, her crying stopping
abruptly. "He figured it out."

I looked at Theo. "That's why Brad was saying
he wasn't responsible for the whole thing."

Anna sat up straighter, like something had
jolted her spine, like something just occurred to
her. "Who is dead? I have to know! Who died if it
wasn't you? He told me how he came in and you
attacked him."

"It was my neighbor, Kim," I said, feeling heavy
with the uselessness of Kim's death, and the responsibility that the violence had been meant for
me. "She was in here because she was doing surveillance on Theo and me. Your guy must have
come in when she was here."

"Kim," Anna said. "Kim." She shook her head,
looking like she was trying to rid something from
her mind. "Kim is dead. Kim is dead. Kim is dead."

Theo sat forward. "Mom," he said.

"Kim is dead," she kept repeating.

Theo put his hand on his mother's leg. "Mom," he said again.

But it was as if some small piece inside Anna Jameson had broken off, had stuck upon the naming of the person she indirectly killed. "Kim," she said. "Kim, Kim, Kim." A slight pause, then, "Kim is dead. Kim is dead."

Theo looked at me. "Can you call 911?"

I dragged my eyes from Anna Jameson, whose mantra about Kim had turned almost into a song.

"Yeah," I said to Theo. "Do you want to talk to the police?"

"No," he said. "I want an ambulance to take her to the hospital." He looked down, kept his hand on his mother's knee, ignoring her intoning *Kim is dead*. "And then I'll talk to the police."

72

Maggie saw the tirade coming. In response, she composed her face in a serene way.

"Listen, you little…" José's face sneered and twisted as he held back whatever profane word he'd really wanted to call her. "Don't try to fuck with me. Don't try to fuck with my family. The kind of shit we can do to you, the kind of shit we will do to you if you don't step aside, is beyond what you can imagine. So much pain."

Maggie looked at him. The guy had always scared the crap out of her before. When her grandfather first introduced her, she couldn't believe he was their client. Sometimes he made her want to run from the room. None of their other clients— even the alleged killers—had scared her before. Because she was their only potential saving grace. They saw that. And there was no way they were going to harm her. She could always feel that. So no fear. But José Cortadero was different.

To the person outside on the streets, they probably looked like a couple, sitting in the window seats of a diner, having a disagreement. It probably didn't look like Maggie was meeting with a former client, a man who was, despite his residency in Chicago, essentially a Mexican drug lord.

But Maggie must have looked like the calm one in that fight. And she *was* calm. Because she was different now. She let a small smile grow on her small face.

"Do you know," Maggie said to him, "do you know what it's like to be pregnant?" She leaned forward as if she was going to wait for his answer, but just as fast, she sat back. "No, you wouldn't know. You're a dude. There are some things you can't do."

José Cortadero's sneer turned toward confusion.

"You wouldn't believe the power it gives you." Maggie placed a hand on her belly. She let her eyes widen, unblinking. She was excited now, and she knew he could hear it in her voice.

José Cortadero sat back in his chair a little. His gaze now made it clear he thought Maggie looked like a madwoman. He was kinda right.

"So do you want to test-drive me? Huh?" she continued. "Please, God," she looked to the heavens, "give me a chance to take this one on."

The silence from José was ticking now, with a steady hum in the background—a mixture of voices and clanging cups and saucers.

"But listen," Maggie said. She let her intensity soften a little. She took a little breath and put her hand to her chin in an exaggerated show of thought. "I'm thinking of something else. I'm thinking that I

can go in there—" she pointed to the federal building across the street "—and I can resign from representation of Mr. Theodore Jameson, because the
fact of the matter is…" She looked over her shoulder to make sure no one was listening, then she
looked back at José. "The prosecutor, Anish, wants
a plea agreement from Theo. But I'm about to go
over there and talk to him again. And I believe I'm
going to convince him to drop the charges now."
She'd spoken to Izzy last night long enough that she
knew about Anna. She knew enough to get the ball
rolling with the prosecutors in the right way.

She dropped her gaze abruptly to his. "You're
the one they really want."

Cortadero's expression hardened again. "You
little bitch…"

"Ah!" Maggie said, a finger pointed at the sky
now. "Don't go any further, because I was about to
tell you the good news."

Some kind of low sound came out of Cortadero's
mouth, some kind of growl.

"The good news," Maggie said, "is that I no
longer represent Theodore Jameson—" she paused
for effect "—and I know where your money is."

Cortadero's expression cleared. He blinked once
or twice. "You shitting me."

"Absolutely not."

He looked out the window toward the federal
building. Maggie hoped he was thinking about
being on trial there, how he would want the best
possible lawyer, because his ass would be on the

line if the Feds found everything they were looking for.

"And yet you understand the situation," Cortadero said. "You understand what the Feds are
doing with this case, trying to get info on us so
they can shut down the other families, too, can find
out where they have their money."

"Right."

"You're hired."

73

It's Thanksgiving. Again. Now that the case is finally over, Maggie and Bernard are throwing a second Thanksgiving dinner at their South Loop apartment. Maggie really wants to do it, she tells me. She never gets to have a holiday at her house—it's always at her parents' or her grandparents' or one of her married sisters' places—and now that she is having her own family, she wants to practice.

I know that the real reason she has done this is because of me. And Theo. And all of us wanting a little celebration and a lot of normalcy.

Theo helps me take off my coat. As I do so often since we found his mother in our apartment last week, I look at his face, taking in his expression, reading his mood. "You okay?" I ask. I say that a lot now, too.

He gives a silent nod, then a small smile. But that quickly fades.

One week ago, we found out that it was Anna Jameson who was behind the disappearance of HeadFirst's money. Not Brad Jameson. Well, Brad

Jameson had used some of that capital. A lot, in fact. But not enough to bankrupt the company, to have them default on commercial loans. He kept more than enough money in the States for the business and had even more in the trust in Rarotonga.

When he'd founded that trust, he had, as a matter of rote, listed Anna as a trustee. Not only was she his former wife, who he loved like a sister, but she was also the one who would manage things if—God forbid—anything happened to Theo.

After a while, he forgot she was even on the trust. And so when the money started leaving, then continued to bleed, he'd scrambled for an answer. Who was behind it? The bankers became cold to him, wouldn't tell him as much as they had before, because technically even though he was the one they'd done business with—the one who had settled the trust with funds that he brought—their fiduciary duty was to the trustee. And one of those was draining the trust.

It took him forever to even suspect Anna. Theo was listed as a trustee, of course. Eric, too. He thought at first maybe Eric was to blame.

He knew Anna hated him, although she painted a different, prettier picture for outsiders. Really, she despised him for leaving her, for not supporting her during her breast cancer. But shit, he didn't have the money at the time.

Once he realized it was her, he had gone to Rarotonga, Brad had told us, to see if he could plead with the bankers to let him know where she'd transferred the money, but of course they wouldn't tell him.

And then we found Theo's mom in our condo. We've since learned the location of the accounts where she'd deposited the money. And Theo is a wealthy man again, and one without any federal charges against him. Just like that.

As Theo introduces himself to some of Maggie's family, I take my protective gaze from him and instead, watch my best friend as she flits between guests, filling drinks and talking about the baby. I notice that many new things, à la Bernard, that Maggie has allowed to take up residence in her sleek apartment. Stacks of sheet music have appeared on end tables, colorfully painted straw mats hang in frames on the once-white walls. Bernard is in the kitchen making Filipino egg rolls, and Maggie, a hand often on her belly, has never seemed so happy.

"Mags," I said, taking her aside for a second. "About José Cortadero. I'm proud of you for the wheeling and dealing. Especially with Theo. The fact that they dropped the charges is amazing. And I know you wanted the Cortadero business back. But maybe this is the time to not rely on them. You know…"

"What are you trying to say? I should get a different kind of client?"

"Well, yeah, maybe."

She laughs. "Izzy, you have to remember you're

in the criminal defense world now. This *is* the kind of client we want. And don't forget—"

"Everyone deserves due process," I say, because she has coached me well. "Everyone. We can't pick and choose who gets treated fairly by the system and who doesn't."

"Exactly." She smiles. "And I know you still want a job, and so does Q."

"Hell yeah," I say and I turn away fast because I really, really don't need the stress of being out of work again. And I don't want to rely on Theo because I think he needs a little break. From everyone.

As I walk into Maggie's living room, I see Theo talking with Maggie's grandparents. Her sisters and brothers are there, too. Q and Shane have arrived and they are entertaining the nieces and nephews, picking them up and tossing them into the air, so that shrieks of joy punctuate the event.

Eventually, Theo moves to my side. I'm sipping a glass of champagne. Him, a beer.

"Man," Theo says. He says the word with a sigh. He says it heavily, as if just that one syllable alone is making him think.

Mayburn and Lucy are there and they come up to us. My eyes shoot downward, because I notice they are holding hands. A moment later, when Lucy goes in search of one of her kids, I look at Mayburn.

"So," I say, "now that Lucy is out of sight, I'm sure you want to take this opportunity to berate us about setting Lucy up with C.R."

"Hey," Theo says. "We didn't set them up. They were both out and they met."

"That's what I've been telling Mayburn, here, but he doesn't want to listen."

"I listened," Mayburn says. He sips from a bottle of Coors Light, and I notice that he looks better than he has lately—fuller in the face in a good way, and stronger, somehow. "And I actually want to apologize."

"What?" I cough up some champagne.

"Yeah," Mayburn says, ignoring my sputtering, which I've dialed up now in an exaggerated effect. "Lucy says that going out with that kid made her realize she wants the real thing." He points to himself. "A real man." He grins in only the way that someone in love and truly clueless about everyone else can do. Then he registers Theo in front of him again and the smile recedes. "Sorry, dude," he says to Theo. "No offense to you or your buddy. It's just he was young and I'm not and…hey, I don't think age matters, and you're clearly on top of your game…." He looks at me for help, but I just give him a shrug.

Theo, of course, takes it in stride, smacks Mayburn on the shoulder good-naturedly. "I get it, dude. No worries."

Mayburn makes an escape soon after that and when it's clear we're alone for a minute, Theo takes me by the hand and leads me to a couple of chairs in front of a wall of floor-to-ceiling windows. Outside, the sun is setting over the city, giving everything a pink-orange glow.

I stare out at it, sigh a little. I used to notice sunsets in the city all the time.

When I look back at Theo, he is on one knee in front of me. "Whoa," I say, the word out of my mouth before I can think it.

He laughs. "It's not that. I'm not asking you to marry me. Not yet." He laughs again. "It's just… Well, I don't know what this is. My life, I mean. I don't know what will happen now—with the Feds or the company."

He shakes his head. His hair is growing back, but he says he's keeping it short for a while. I will always miss his long hair.

"Iz," he says, "I just wanted you to know that no matter what happens from here, no matter where we go or what we do…" He looks down, then up at me, takes both of my hands in his. "I love you." He looks at me, not like he is waiting for me to speak, but like he's just released something pent-up inside him. "I love you," he says again. "I feel like you are family." He looks down at the ground, and I know he is thinking about his father, who he has only spoken to once since Rarotonga, and about his mother, who knows that when she gets out of Northwestern's psychiatric ward, she is going to be charged with murder-for-hire. Theo has already retained counsel for her, hiring someone based on Maggie and Martin's recommendation. He has to do that for her, he says. And according to her lawyers, Anna has hope. It's possible if it goes to trial that she might get off, since she didn't hire the guy specifically to kill Kim. Or to kill anyone at all. They found the guy from the car dealership in Florida and brought him back to Chicago. He was claiming self-defense, so who knows what will happen with him?

But none of that mattered to Theo right now, I could tell. We'd talked long about this. And sadly, he felt as if he went from being an only child to being an orphan. To him, he was alone in the world now. He might have a relationship with his parents in the future. But he didn't know. And so I was family for him.

I didn't have to look hard for a response. "I love you, too."

Epilogue

Two months later, I receive a postcard from Theo. The front shows a beach in Thailand. He writes that the surfing is amazing. He does not mention when he will return, because I have told him many times I understand his need to escape for a while. To regroup. To regain himself.

That you were there, that's what matters. Not what happened before or where we are now, but that you were there for all this. And because of that I am better. I am okay, Iz.

I love you, the postcard says at the end. *Remember, no matter what. I love you.*

* * * * *

Acknowledgments

Thank you to Amy Moore-Benson and Miranda Indrigo for shepherding the book. Thanks also to everyone at MIRA Books, especially Michelle Venditti, Valerie Gray, Donna Hayes, Dianne Moggy, Loriana Sacilotto, Craig Swinwood, Pete McMahon, Stacy Widdrington, Andi Richman, Andrew Wright, Katherine Orr, Alex Osuszek, Erin Craig, Margie Miller, Adam Wilson, Don Lucey, Gordy Goihl, Dave Carley, Ken Foy, Erica Mohr, Darren Lizotte, Reka Rubin, Margie Mullin, Sam Smith, Kathy Lodge, Carolyn Flear, Michelle Renaud, Kate Studer, Stephen Miles, Jennifer Watters, Amy Jones, Malle Vallik, Tracey Langmuir, Anne Fontanesi, Scott Ingram, Marianna Ricciuto, John Jordan and Brent Lewis.

A massive thanks to Loyola University Chicago School of Law—a vibrant, creative and generous place to work. And especially to Father Michael Garanzini, Dean David Yellen, James Faught, Michael Kaufman, Jean Gaspardo, Alice Perlin, Michael Patena, Alan Rafael and Joyce Marvel.

Much gratitude to my experts—criminal defense lawyer Catharine O'Daniel, former federal prosecutor Professor Mary Ramirez and my Cook Islands insider, Margaret Caldwell. Thanks also to Carol Miller and Liza Jaine.

NEW YORK TIMES AND USA TODAY BESTSELLING AUTHOR

SHARON SALA

Witness to a major mob hit, Beth Venable is placed in protective custody until the trial. But after her third safe house is riddled with bullets, she goes off-grid to save herself. What the FBI can't do, her kinfolk will.

The beautiful Appalachian Mountains welcome Beth back. But her homecoming—even her blissful reunion with strong, silent Ryal Walker—is tainted by the fight she's brought to the clan's doorstep. Hidden in a remote cabin with the man she's always wanted, Beth dreams of a new life. But after so long, and with such dangers stalking her? Impossible.

But love can distill life down to its essence: an elixir of pure hope, nerve—and the will to survive.

NEXT OF KIN

Available wherever books are sold.

MIRA | HARLEQUIN®
www.Harlequin.com

MSS1312

NEW YORK TIMES BESTSELLING AUTHOR
KAT MARTIN

She has the face of an angel and the body of…well, isn't that what he'd expect from an exotic dancer? But there's something about this girl that Johnnie Riggs can't shake. The former army ranger is hot on the trail of an elusive drug lord—and suddenly very hot under the collar, as well.

Amy has her own agenda: her sister is missing and Amy seems to be the only one who cares. She'll enlist Johnnie's help and do her best to ignore her growing attraction to finally get some answers. But as they begin to uncover something even more sinister than they imagined, their mutual desire is the least of their problems. They'll bring the truth to light…or die trying.

AGAINST THE NIGHT

AVAILABLE WHEREVER BOOKS ARE SOLD.

PRESENTING...

More Than Words

STORIES OF THE HEART

Three bestselling authors
Three real-life heroines

Even as you read these words, there are women just like you stepping up and making a difference in their communities, making our world a better place to live. Three such exceptional women have been selected as recipients of Harlequin's More Than Words award. To celebrate their accomplishments, three bestselling authors have written short stories inspired by these real-life heroines.

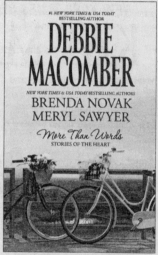

Proceeds from the sale of this book will be reinvested into the Harlequin More Than Words program to support causes that are of concern to women.

Visit

www.HarlequinMoreThanWords.com

to nominate a real-life heroine from your community.

REQUEST YOUR FREE BOOKS!

2 FREE NOVELS
FROM THE SUSPENSE COLLECTION
PLUS 2 FREE GIFTS!

SUS11

leslie TENTLER

Crime reporter Mia Hale is discovered on a Jacksonville beach—bloodied and disoriented, but alive. She remembers nothing, but her wounds bear the signature of a sadistic serial killer. After years lying dormant, The Collector has resumed his grim hobby: abducting women and taking gruesome souvenirs before dumping their bodies. But none of his victims has ever escaped—and he wants Mia back, more than he ever wanted any of the others.

FBI agent Eric MacFarlane has pursued The Collector for a long time. The case runs deep in his veins, bordering on obsession...and Mia holds the key. Eric swears to protect this fierce, fragile survivor, but The Collector will not be denied.

EDGE OF *midnight*

Available wherever books are sold.

LAURA CALDWELL

32932	CLAIM OF INNOCENCE	___ $7.99 U.S.	___ $9.99 CAN.
32666	RED, WHITE & DEAD	___ $7.99 U.S.	___ $8.99 CAN.
32658	RED BLOODED MURDER	___ $7.99 U.S.	___ $8.99 CAN.
32501	THE GOOD LIAR	___ $6.99 U.S.	___ $8.50 CAN.
32183	LOOK CLOSELY	___ $6.99 U.S.	___ $8.50 CAN.
31321	QUESTION OF TRUST	___ $7.99 U.S.	___ $9.99 CAN.

(limited quantities available)

TOTAL AMOUNT	$ _____
POSTAGE & HANDLING	$ _____
($1.00 for 1 book, 50¢ for each additional)	
APPLICABLE TAXES*	$ _____
TOTAL PAYABLE	$ _____

(check or money order—please do not send cash)

To order, complete this form and send it, along with a check or money order for the total above, payable to MIRA Books, to: **In the U.S.:** 3010 Walden Avenue, P.O. Box 9077, Buffalo, NY 14269-9077; **In Canada:** P.O. Box 636, Fort Erie, Ontario, L2A 5X3.

Name: _____
Address: _____ City: _____
State/Prov.: _____ Zip/Postal Code: _____
Account Number (if applicable): _____

075 CSAS

*New York residents remit applicable sales taxes.
*Canadian residents remit applicable GST and provincial taxes.

MLC0312BL